Liddy-Jean
Marketing Queen
and the
Matchmaking Scheme

Mari SanGiovanni

Bywater
BOOKS

2024

For Luca

Author's Note

When I asked my friend Molly Myers to read *Liddy-Jean Marketing Queen*, she didn't hesitate, and I am so grateful for her firsthand understanding of and insight about young adults with IDD (Intellectual and Developmental Disabilities) and Down syndrome. Molly taught me so much more than I *thought* I already knew.

As a young adult, I volunteered time at a center for people of all ages who were diagnosed with Down syndrome and IDD, although IDD wasn't the term used back then. Because of my limited experience as a volunteer and auntie to my sweet and hilarious nephew Luca SanGiovanni, who was born with Costello syndrome, I felt I was enlightened enough to write this story, but I soon learned there would have been many missteps without Molly's guidance and insight.

Molly taught me so much about the vast range of abilities, challenges, hardships, and great joys that people in the IDD and Down syndrome community experience. With great patience she guided me through any unintentional blunders, and like a champ she embraced all the warmth and humor I was pushing for. I especially want to thank Molly for sharing with me all that she has learned from her amazing and beautiful daughter, Riley.

If this story inspires you to learn more or to volunteer, please reach out to the IDD or Down syndrome community center nearest you.

Mari SanGiovanni
Coventry, Rhode Island

PART 1
WORK

One-Legged Grasshoppers
and Ice Cream Cones

When Mom told me that I got a job I cried because I was very sure I did not want one. Whenever my mom says, "Liddy-Jean, we need to have a talk," and sits on my bed in the daytime, I tell her, "This is not going to be a good day, especially for me." Mom usually laughs, but today, she did not.

I am twenty-one, and the problem with that is, the number changes over and over again. As soon as I am remembering my number, I will have a new number to remember the day I get a yellow birthday cake with extra globs of vanilla frosting. And when there is frosting involved, I do not remember much. Mom and Dad tell me not to worry about remembering my age number because they say: "Not much gets past you, Liddy-Jean." Not sure what that means, but I think it is because I am a good writer that I notice everything.

One thing that did not get past me: I noticed a long time ago that Daytime Bed Talks always end badly for me.

Other Daytime Bed Talks:

1. The Daytime Bed Talk after I turned my bicycle upside down to make a taffy-pulling machine

just like the one I saw in Cape Cod with Auntie Theresa. (We had to throw the bike away after a lot of hard scrubbing, which I warned Mom would do absolutely no bit of good.)

2. The Daytime Bed Talk after I used Dad's saw to see if our black kitchen chairs were made out of real wood. (They were.)

3. The Daytime Bed Talk after I taught my baby sister Dawn to draw pictures for the refrigerator door, and I forgot to tell her the refrigerator was only for hanging the drawings. Drawing on the door was not allowed, after I did it the first time.

4. The Talk after I took my grandma's cardboard box of four brand-new baby kittens and hid them because I was afraid she was going to mail them. It turned out Grandma was not going to mail the kittens, Grandma just loves to recycle. (Grandma also loves kittens, which ruined her plan to let her best four friends keep them, and Mom says that makes her a crazy cat lady.)

While Mom sat on my bed, I tried to guess which thing I had done wrong that she could have found out about, but there were just too many to choose from. I used to tell on myself whenever I did anything bad, because I learned in Sunday school that I would burn in H-E-Double-Hockey-Sticks if you didn't.

The problem was, I did not always know which things I did were wrong until much too late. Because of this, I had to check with my mom all the time to see if there was a problem, but this started to drive her crazy.

Mom finally "cut me a deal" and said that unless I had sneaked around to do the thing, I did not have to tell her. This seemed to work out pretty well and stopped me from asking things like: was it O-K to put a pencil on the T-V (it is) . . . is spilling a cup of water O-K if you are outside (it is), but then Mom had to tell me to stop doing it on purpose no matter how much fun it was, and that it was never O-K to spill water on my sister, whether she was outside or inside, unless she agreed and she had a bathing suit on.

So much to remember!

Because of this new rule of not having to tell Mom everything, and because Mom is very busy with her two jobs, there were plenty of times I did things that seemed fine to do, since I was not sneaking around, but it turned out I was wrong. So, I sat on my bed today, trying to think what I had done that was so bad it made Mom stop cooking Dad and Uncle William's ravioli dinner with Auntie Theresa.

The worst part was the sun was coming in the window shades and making bright stripes on her green shirt, just like a jail costume. It made me wonder if the thing I did was so bad that I might wind up in jail. Mom took my hand and rubbed my fingers with just one thumb like she always does.

Uh oh.

"Liddy, the folks at The Center have recommended you for a job, and your dad and I visited the job when you stayed over at Grandma's house last week. We both liked the people there, and Dad and I think you will love working there."

It looked like Mom was trying to sound much more excited than she actually was, and this meant bad news. I started to cry. Mainly because the sun stripes on her shirt were getting bigger and brighter, and I was sure this was a terrible sign.

"Why on earth are you crying, Liddy-Jean?" Mom asked. Even though she asked in her most gentle voice, I thought it might be best if I could cry harder. My Auntie Theresa believed in signs and so I did too, and because now the stripes were brighter than ever, I just knew this job thing was very, very bad news.

"I don't want to," I said, which sometimes works when I say it sounding grown up and not whiny, but Mom's face told me it did not work this time.

"Why don't you want to?" Mom asked. "You go to The Center all by yourself now, and you even know how to ride the bus all by yourself."

I answered, "You and Dad talk about your jobs at dinnertime and they sound awful . . . so why do I have to get one?"

Mom looked at me then, and touched my hair until it was out of my eyes. My tears made my hair all wet at the ends just like the ends of all the Q-tips when I dropped the entire box in the tub to see if they would float. (They did.) Since I liked when Mom touched my hair, I cried harder to make more tears, but I knew Mom would figure out what I was doing, because even though I am a good actress, I was not so great with the fake crying.

"Liddy-Jean, stop that now."

This was not her gentle voice, so I stopped the crying quick as a frog, or, as Mom says, I needed to stop Prom-Toad.

"Your dad and I talk about the bad things at work, because . . . well, it's what grown-ups do. And maybe that's stupid of us. There are so many good things about work, too, like Mrs. Sullivan. You like her, right?"

"She gave me a gingerbread house once," I said, and my mouth watered like I was eating it right now. I remembered how I pretended like an actress to like the spicy cookie house, but I secretly liked only the candy parts and the crunchy frosting that Mom said was "Stale on Arrival." I never found out what that means, only that I should not have said that to Mrs. Sullivan next time she came over.

Mom said, "I can't believe you remember that gingerbread house. That was such a long time ago. You were only four years old."

"It was a big house."

"It was. Now, do you remember how I know Mrs. Sullivan?"

"She is your friend."

I knew this was not the answer she wanted, so I went back

6

to talking about the house. "It had pretty gumdrops around the windows and a honey graham cracker backyard porch with coconut snow all over it…I hate coconut, so I swept that part off with your dustpan broom." Mom made a gross face, and I remembered I was not supposed to tell her that part.

Luckily, I am an expert at changing the subject.

"It turned out the gumdrops were the spicy ones, just like the gingerbread, and I got a stomachache after I ate the entire backyard fence."

Later, I wrote in one of my notebooks: Do Not Eat Fence, but later I had to ask Mom what I meant and she reminded me and we laughed so hard it shook the same bed we were sitting on now.

I always wondered if Mrs. Sullivan was a pretty gumdrop on the outside and a bad spicy one on the inside, but I didn't tell Mom. I also never told Mom that whenever she wasn't looking, Mrs. Sullivan stares at me like I am a grasshopper with only one leg. (I actually have two legs, but my sister and I played with a grasshopper once and one leg accidentally fell off…and when I showed Mom, she made the same face Mrs. Sullivan does when she looks at me.)

"But where do you know Mrs. Sullivan from? Come on Liddy, you know."

"From your work," I whispered, hoping Mom would not hear me.

"That's right, from my work. I met my friend at work and I bet you'll meet many new friends too. Maybe even a best friend."

"Bobby is already my best friend," I said.

The truth is, on some days when he acts weirder than usual, I do not like Bobby, but I learned a long time ago that you don't bring up a subject if it is the opposite of what you are trying to say. Like the time I asked for an extra Nutter Butter cookie and then said my dentist said I eat too many sweets. (Who told him that?) I learned the hard way that saying that about the dentist is not the best way to get an extra cookie, and I wrote that in my notebook so I would not forget.

Mom kept rubbing my fingers with her thumb, only not as softly now, and she says this helps me pay attention. "Auntie Theresa has a job she loves, too," Mom said. "Remember she told you about the welcome back party they had for her at work when her broken ankle was all better?"

I reminded Mom, "Auntie Theresa said it had white frosting, which is not as good as chocolate, and I already have too many friends at The Center."

"Liddy-Jean, the people at The Center are your only friends because that's where you spend all your time since you graduated from high school. Remember when you were in high school, and you didn't want to graduate? Then finally we got off the long waiting list and you got to go to The Center, and you loved it even more than your school. You can't decide there aren't more friends in the world if you haven't been out there yet."

Mom patted my hand and said, "You'll see."

That was when I knew it was final. *You'll see* always means a decision has been made. *You'll see* means I have to see how it turns out, because I do not get a vote.

Right then, the sun was setting behind the big tree in the front yard and the light from the window was not as bright. Now Mom's shirt looked like normal one-color green, and I hoped this was a sign that the job thing might be O-K.

Mom had that green shirt for as long as I could remember because Auntie Theresa says Mom never buys new clothes for herself, only for me, my sister, and Dad. I wondered if Mom needed money to buy herself some clothes, and maybe that was why I needed to go to work . . . and if that was the reason, I liked the idea of helping Mom and Dad. When I remembered what happened with the ice cream last week, I told Mom I would go to my first job.

Just last week, Mom took me for a special treat to get some ice cream and she got hers in a cone and I got mine in a Safety Dish. She told the ice cream man to stick a cone on top of it like a clown's hat because she knew I loved the cone part but hated to play the ice-cream-balance-game because I always lost. Mom had her ice cream balanced on the cone like most grown-ups do, with no Safety Dish at all, and when she tried to help me hold my Safety Dish so I could climb onto a bench, the top of her ice cream plopped right into the sand, covering it with dirt sprinkles.

I said she could share mine, but Mom said not to worry, that she would buy another one. While I watched her walk toward the truck, I ate fast like I always do. I saw her try to dig out more money from her pocketbook. She stopped walking and began to turn around, but when she saw me watching she just took her empty hand out of her pocketbook and waved and walked back to the truck again and disappeared to the other side.

I raced to finish my ice cream before it would melt, since I hated ice cream soup. I had an ice cream headache and an empty Safety Dish by the time Mom came back with just some extra napkins.

"Where's your new ice cream?"

"I already ate it," she said.

Since Mom eats ice cream very slowly, I knew she did not have enough money to buy another one. And since I had eaten all of mine like a big pig, there was nothing left to share with her, so I had to concentrate not to cry knowing how much Mom loved ice cream.

I can sometimes save my crying for later when I am alone in my room, if I try extra hard to remember what made me sad during the day, but I usually cannot remember if I do not write it down in my notebook. That night, alone in my room, I had no trouble remembering Mom's ice cream plopping in the sand. That same night was when I first wrote in my secret notebook (the red one I keep under my mattress) that I would do something so great it would be worth a lot of money so I could take out my whole family for ice cream, maybe even once a week, as long as it was not snowing (Mom's rule).

Mom says that when it is cold on the outside it is bad to have cold on the inside. In the very cold weather, once a month, after Dad got paid, Mom would make Dad's favorite blueberry pie instead of getting ice cream at the store. Auntie Theresa always brought over the blueberries for my mom. (She always said they were from her garden,

9

but I saw the grocery store green tubs she left in the backseat of her car, even though she comes inside with the blueberries poured into a Ziploc baggie, pretending she picked them.)

I would have to figure out what that something great would be to make enough money to buy ice cream once a week, but whatever it was, the day Mom dropped her ice cream was the day I decided I would have to do something great. I fell asleep dreaming about someday being able to give Mom anything she wanted . . . maybe even blueberry ice cream, and when I woke up the next day, I thought this job thing might be the best answer.

Bad Breath = Bad Boss

When my first day of work came, I was scared, and I had to do the trick the counselors taught me at The Center to do whenever I am afraid. I pretended I was excited to go to work. I kept thinking I was starting a job where I would do so good that not only would I have a bunch of new friends, but then maybe I would do so good at my job that it would make me famous, maybe even on TV.

Both Mom and Dad went with me on my first day, which made me wonder if this job might be worse than I thought. But I kept pretending not to be scared and used the other trick the counselors taught me when they found out about my favorite TV show. (A show that my Auntie Theresa lets me watch.)

The counselors told me to watch how Xena the Warrior Princess would always keep her head up to look at people's faces when she was meeting somebody new, even if her eyes got wide because it was a scary monster. They also taught me that if you do not act afraid, pretty soon you will not be afraid, so I always acted like Xena whenever I walked into a scary place, like the first day of work, or the dentist office. Also, the big shoe store with the cold metal measuring things that clamp on to your foot like a giant cold pincher machine. Mom still has to remind me every time that the shoe measure thing does not actually hurt.

Pretending I was Xena worked so well for most things that I convinced my Auntie Theresa to let me also watch the parts where Xena fights. I told her this would make me even more brave. Mom said "No, absolutely not," and she reminded Auntie how I accidentally clobbered myself doing my best Xena moves with a sword that I made from an orange snow shovel.

When I was younger, and afraid of a lot of things, I used to bury my head against Mom's arm and the counselors at The Center always remind me that adults do not do this, and people would treat me like a baby if I acted that way. I knew that meant people would treat me like a baby, like the way babies have to go to bed early … not in the way babies got treats, like teething biscuits which were for my sister when she was a baby and I was not allowed to eat them. Mom said I was too old to cling onto her, but when the counselors at The Center told me the exact same thing, I believed it.

Mom warned me my job would be in the Marketing Department of a giant building and on my first day of work I was worried about that big building until I met Rose. I knew we would become best friends in the first minute I met her because Rose has long dark hair and pretty blue eyes just like Xena the Warrior Princess, and so I had to stare at one of her ears instead of her eyes, which was a trick I taught myself to do when I noticed someone that was too pretty to look at, so I can remember what they say to me. The problem was that most ears are usually ugly, but even Rose's ears were pretty, so that trick wasn't going to work.

The first thing I ever said to Rose was, "Do you have extra paper and pens?"

Rose answered, "You bet we do. I'll make sure that's the first thing I show you."

"No, thank you," I said, holding up my bag knowing Mom would like that "thank you" business. "Mom said first thing you have to show me is where to put my lunch."

"Okay, Liddy-Jean, let's take care of your lunch first."

Rose talked right to me, not just to my parents. So many times, people talked to my parents when they could be asking me instead, and my mom or Auntie Theresa would have to remind them. Like when I was in the grocery store and a lady saw me half-pushing the cart and riding the back of it like a skateboard. She turned around to ask Mom how old I was, but I knew the answer to that question.

When someone does this, my Auntie Theresa says that it is the one time I have permission to be a little fresh, so I can say my age and also say that I can hear just fine, just like Auntie taught me to do. The first time I did that, Auntie Theresa peed her pants laughing, which was the best day ever.

That first day on my job, Mom and Dad both kept one hand on each of my shoulders, but after I met Rose, I did not want them to do that anymore and I moved my shoulders away from my parents' hands.

"I guess she's ready to start her day without us," Mom said, and then I wanted to say she could put her hand back on my shoulder again, but I knew I would look like a big crybaby. So, instead, I pretended I was Xena again and put my both hands on my hips at the same time. (This is not easy with an extra-full lunch bag.)

When I dropped the bag, Rose said, "So, what did you bring for lunch, Liddy-Jean?"

I was very happy to answer since Mom decided that I should start my first day at my new job with a Grown-up Work Lunch.

"Salami and cheese . . . not peanut butter and fluff," I said. "This needs a refrigerator, now, please."

"Oh, that's an executive's lunch," Rose said, and I had no idea what an Executive Lunch was, except I guessed it was a very good thing that I did not have peanut butter and fluff. I also decided I should use the word "executive" a lot, since it was a grown-up word I never heard at home.

"I'll show you where the refrigerator is," Rose said, and when I didn't move, she put her hand on my shoulder so gently and whispered to only me, "there's lots of healthy treats in there."

"I hear the word TREAT, and off I go," I said, and Rose and I went across the room to the office kitchen. I looked back to see if my parents were still standing there and Rose said, "Trust me, O-K?" But I was already thinking, we will definitely be best friends.

"Okey dokey," I said, because I did trust her, and because saying that always makes adults laugh when they first meet me.

The first day everybody wanted to meet me, so I already decided I liked my job very much, even though I knew everyone could not possibly be as nice as Rose. I was right about that.

One of the last people I met on my first day was Rose's boss, Gina, who was the opposite of Rose. She crouched down to shake my hand, even though I was almost the same height as her, and she did that thing that people sometimes do, talking very loud like I cannot hear, but luckily, I knew better than to say something fresh at work.

Boss Gina whispered to Rose, "How old is she?" and I closed my lips together very tight so I would not be fresh. Mom would have been proud of me, but Auntie Theresa would have given me a little poke in the back to tell her you-know-what.

Later, I found out Boss Gina always acts extra busy for someone who only goes to meetings all day, so she was gone from the room right after meeting me, before I even had a chance to say one word, and she did not come back until much later. When she came back, she smelled different than the other Marketing Girls, like how Mom and Dad do after Aunt Theresa and Uncle William drink red wine with them on Friday nights. I noticed this smelled so much worse in the daytime, and Boss Gina was nowhere near as happy as Mom, Dad, Auntie and Uncle were when they smelled like that after a grown-up dinner out.

When she came over, she bent down to me again. I could see a thin white stripe at the top of her head where her hair parted and noticed there was also a stripe of light brown color, which turned into a dark brown color for the rest of her hair. I wondered why she had so many colors in her hair since if she just had one, it would have looked much better. I decided to tell her that because I like to be helpful, but when I did, she looked around to see if anyone else heard me before she walked away, without even saying thank you. I was glad I did not ask her about her breath.

One of the Marketing Girls everyone called Lisa P. must have noticed I was making a bad breath face behind Boss Gina's back because she said when Boss Gina's breath smells bad, this was not a good sign for the day. I nodded yes to Lisa P. like I agreed, but I hoped she was wrong about Boss Gina, just like I was about Mom's striped shirt, since I loved my job already.

The next time I saw Boss Gina she did not come over but asked loudly across the room so everyone could hear, "How was your first day, Linda?"

I was not sure if I should tell her that many people made mistakes with my name, but instead I said, "Okey dokey," and she stared at me like I was being a fresh-mouth grasshopper with the one leg that fell off.

"Gina, her name is Liddy, not Linda," Rose said from behind me, and this was the first time I knew for sure that Rose was my best friend.

"Oh, I'm so sorry, Liddy!" Gina said even louder, and she walked over to grab both my arms with her hands like she was afraid I would cry like a baby, just because she got my name wrong. "What a unique name you have!" she said in a voice so loud she was hurting my ears.

"I never cry when people say my name wrong," I told her.

"Of course you don't, sweetheart!" she said, and I heard her laugh a little when she turned her head back to the girls like she did not believe me. I did not like her cold pinchy fingers so tight on my arms, and when she finally let them go, I rubbed both my arms so she would get the message.

Rose walked up right next to me and said, "Liddy-Jean did fantastic on her first day. She helped us staple a big pile of three-page booklets."

"So you said, earlier," Gina said to Rose, but she was still looking at me rubbing my arms like my arms belonged to her and not me. Gina made her eyes extra big and said, "Wow . . . you got to use a stapler on your first day?"

I could tell by the way she said it that staplers were no big deal around here, but before I had a chance to say that, Rose said, "Liddy-Jean even learned how to file papers."

I wanted to agree with everything Rose said but I didn't use a file on any papers. Mom did not like me to use her nail files at home, and Dad told me I could only use his big metal file on the woodpile near the garage. (This rule happened after I tried to smooth a corner of the living-room coffee table after bumping my knee on it.)

I just nodded my head so I wouldn't have to actually lie, but I would have lied for Rose because she was holding my hand again, and it felt warm and soft, just like Mom's.

"Good for you, Liddy!" Gina said, but she was walking away from us when she said it, and that was a good thing because my ears were tired of her.

Rose said, "Gina, we still need to meet today on—"

"Not now," Gina said without turning around, which Mom would have said I was rude if I did that. I was just happy I did not have to see Boss Gina's face again because her eyebrows scared me.

On my first afternoon coffee break at work, I sat close enough with the Marketing Girls and Steve to hear their conversations, but I pretended to read a magazine while I had a Diet Coke with two chocolate chip cookies that Rose gave me. I got to hear some very interesting stories.

Here are three things I learned:

1. The man that used to own the company liked all the women who worked for him a little too much, and if they were traveling together, at the end of the night he would shake their hand and press his hotel key into the lady's hand.

2. Employee Appreciation Day was always followed by the worst day of the year, because the bosses would be extra hard on their workers since a whole afternoon of work had been missed when everybody stopped work to eat the employee appreciation cake in the lunchroom.

3. The Marketing Girl, Lisa P., said that drinking wine is not allowed at work even though a certain person in the company did it all the time.

That is when I butted in to say, "Carlo Rossi."

Lisa P. looked surprised and turned around to ask, "Who?"

Rose answered, "I think Liddy-Jean means the wine," and then she winked at me with a big smile. Lisa P. laughed and smiled at me as she said, "Oh, we like you so much already, Liddy-Jean! You are going to fit in here just great!" I looked at Rose to see if that was true, and when Rose winked at me again, I knew it was.

I learned Gina did not like me on my first day, but, the worse thing was, I knew she did not like Rose even more. I knew this because I watched Rose rush to help me pick up some papers I dropped before Gina could see.

My favorite bedtime stories end with good people winning, so, it was on my very first day that I decided I wanted to write a book about this thing called work, and this room they called The Marketing Department. And I would make Rose win.

(Mom says I am good at writing even though she always thinks what I write is funny, when it is not.)

When Mom picked me up after my very first day at work, I told her I wanted to write a story in my notebook and it would have mostly good characters and just one bad, like a wolf with scary eyebrows. When Mom slowed down the car and pulled over, I realized I should not have told her that part. Because that is when the questions started.

"Liddy-Jean, was *everyone* nice to you at work today?"

"Yes, everybody," I said, turning fast to look out my window.

"You sure?" Mom asked, taking my chin to turn my face back to her.

"Yes. I love my job." This was true and Mom was happy enough to drive again.

All I wanted was to go back tomorrow to see Rose, and if I wrote my book good enough, maybe I could create the best happy ending for my new best friend, and an even better ending for Bad Boss Gina.

Tomato Tit Freckles
and the Duel-Die Noses

My real name is Lindsay-Jean Carpenter, but no one, not even my parents, call me anything but Liddy-Jean or Liddy. Once at a cookout, I heard Uncle William say that Mom and Dad should not have given me a name I could not say myself. This made me feel stupid (even though Lindsay is a stupid name with two extra letters that does not do anybody any good, especially me.)

Since my Uncle William does not look at me very much, I'm always secretly happy he has never noticed that Auntie Theresa gets Tomato Tit Freckles whenever she cooks with Mom. Only happy people should get to see Tomato Tit Freckles, and Uncle William is not happy.

Mom says I watch Auntie Theresa like a hawk whenever she comes over to cook with Mom. Every Sunday they stand next to each other at the stove, happy-arguing over a big pot of spaghetti sauce and meatballs. Sometimes I give up watching *Barney Miller* on TV just to get closer to the smell. Nobody knows I watch *Barney Miller* because the old man named Fish has great eyebrows. They are thick and fluffy, like a Muppet, and nothing like Boss Gina's, whose eyebrows look like my bad drawings.

19

It was hard for me not to stare at Auntie Theresa's boobs, especially when they were covered with her apron, which just made them look like they were going to burst out at any minute and start singing, and we better all keep an eye on them. I sure did. Auntie Theresa would be very pretty even if she didn't have giant boobs. But with them, she looks like a movie star—Mom says an old-time movie star, back when it was O-K to weigh more than a thirteen-year-old and still be in the movies.

Auntie Theresa's boobs always ended up speckled with flying tomato sauce freckles since she and Mom always were talking and laughing too much to notice when the sauce got what Mom calls a Hard Boil. I would wait for Mom to say to her, "Fix your tomato tit freckles!" and then Auntie Theresa would dip her finger down to the top of her boobs, then lick it off the tip of her finger, and I watched until she had erased every single sauce-speckle with her spit eraser.

If I had been married to Auntie Theresa instead of Uncle William, I would have made sure she left her tit freckles there until I came home from work to see her do that. Uncle William wasn't Italian, and I heard Mom tell Auntie Theresa it was because she married an English man instead of an Italian man that she doesn't get enough S-E-X.

I try not to lie or make things up. Mom says this is on my Plus Side. But she says I sometimes M-Bellish my stories a little, which means that I add bits to them from my imagination, but I don't think this is a bad thing. My Auntie Theresa says writers do it all the time. Since my first day at work when I had decided to become a famous writer, I argued with Mom that my genius at making things up should be counted on my Plus Side too.

I am not very smart for a twenty-one-year-old, and I have been told this again and again from lots of people, but never my mom and dad or Auntie Theresa and Rose. My mom has told me many times that I am not the "R" word and that she never wants to hear me use that word. Ever. But we both know I have been called the "R" word so many times when I went to school, because I am just not as fast to learn as most people. I might be wrong, but that sure sounds to me like I am the "R" word. It seems very important to Mom that I do not believe that, so I do not argue with her about it. I worry she will be sad if she found out I really was the "R" word, but there is nothing I can do about it.

Once, when I was ten, Mom and Dad took me to a doctor and they told me I could draw some pictures in his office and I told him he didn't have any of the right crayons. I was polite, and I tried the best I could, but I had to tell him the drawings would be much better if the doctor's mom went shopping for more colors like my mom does. Mom smiled at me like she does when I am extra-clever, but the doctor was not smiling. When I was finished, Mom and Dad said I could go play with the toys in the next room.

I was happy to get out of there, but there was something in the way the doctor stared at me when I did my drawings with the bad colors that made me know he wanted me out of there for a Just Adults Talk. I left, but I wanted to hear if the doctor told Mom and Dad about how I was a great artist, so, I pretended I was going into the room which had a big sign on the door with extra big letters: TOY ROOM, such big letters I wondered if it was some sort of a trap, like in a Bugs Bunny cartoon.

Just before I reached the Toy Room, I ducked behind the big couch near the doctor's door, before the lady at the front desk came back. I know how to do an expert Xena Warrior Princess soft landing and practiced this so many times with my sister behind our beds.

That is when I heard *everything*.

I had a small notebook in my pocket like I always do and did my trick of writing down what I could spell. I didn't show anyone but I still remember the three most important things I heard that day:

1. Liddy-Jean has a lot of D-Lays.
   This made me think of potato chips, which I am only allowed to eat at a table. Since there was no table anywhere, I knew that doctor was lying about

21

giving me a lot of potato chips.

2. Liddy-Jean will have the intelligence of a seven-
   year-old.
   He was not a smart doctor. Everyone knew my
   sister Dawn was the seven-year-old, and she is
   very smart for a little sister. Just in case the doctor
   was right, I decided I would never eat D-Lays
   potato chips again.

3. Liddy-Jean may never read or write.

Mom got so mad at that one and yelled, "This is f-ing ridiculous!" Mom was right, it was f-ing ridiculous since I was writing from my hiding place when the doctor said this! (My spelling was much worse back then, and when I try to read my old notebooks, sometimes I have no idea what they mean, and I wonder if the doctor was right that day.)

Dad said, "Maggie, just hear him out. He doesn't know Liddy-Jean like we do, but that doesn't mean we can't learn something that may help her."

I wanted to yell out that I did not need any help, except I was really stuck behind that couch since the lady came back in the room and was sitting at her desk. I made sure I closed my mouth so I could breathe only out of my quiet nose. Mom was quiet now, and that made me squirm. It is not good when my mom is quiet, and my knees hurt from the pinchy carpet, and my arms were trapped against my chest so tight I looked like I had boobs, but much smaller than Auntie Theresa's. When I peeked down the front of my shirt, I could see a tiny, kind of pretty butt crack between them, the same that Auntie Theresa has, only hers were big enough to trap Jesus' feet from her necklace and mine could not even trap a cookie crumb.

Next, I heard the doctor say: "I hope you both understand how lucky it is that Liddy-Jean does not have behavior problems."

I wanted to laugh at that one because I had bad behavior problems all the time, and I was still angry about his stupid crayons. What kind of doctor has three kinds of blue colors, but no red or orange? But then I thought about how Mom taught me tricks to control my temper. The best trick was thinking about being put to bed early before Auntie Theresa came over, or missing *Scooby-Doo*. That always straightened me out. Next best trick was to take deep breaths as I counted. I did this now as I listened to the doctor talk about my drawings.

"Notice how large she draws her own head and how tiny she draws the hands and arms dangling at her sides." He said this meant I had a very strong image of myself and I thought I was as smart as anyone else, but that the tiny arms dangling down at my sides meant I sometimes feel weak. I covered my mouth behind the couch so I would not laugh. He said I might be feeling this way because I knew I could not do the things that other kids my age could do. That was when my mom went crazy.

I heard a chair scrape across the floor and my mother said: "I've heard enough from this stupid, f-ing ... *doctor!*"

"Maggie!" Dad said, and my hand fell off my mouth as I giggled. I love hearing swear words.

Mom stormed out of his office and walked right past where I was hiding and went into the TOY ROOM and said, "Liddy-Jean?"

I popped out and ran fast to her so she would not see where I was hiding. Mom looked at me with her worried face.

"You were supposed to be waiting in here," she said.

"I wanted to hear if my drawings were good or bad," I said, which was mostly true. I could hear Dad still in the doctor's office apologizing for mom's bad word, which I hoped she would say again before we left.

Mom took my hand and said, "Your drawings are perfect. Especially since that doctor had shitty colors." I covered my mouth again but I knew Mom wanted me to laugh, so I did.

23

"He sure did have S-H-I-T colors," I said. Then Mom did something that day she had not done since I was very little. She scooped me up off the floor and twirled me around and kissed the top of my head. Then she asked me to put on my coat and button it all the way up all by myself which I can do without any help.

Mom and I left the office, and we waited in the car for a long time for Dad to come out. On the ride home, Dad took Mom's hand and I could see Mom was happy he was not mad. I pretended to be looking at one of my books and heard Mom whisper to Dad: "What an *idiot!*" I never heard Mom use that bad word before but she was mad because Mom knew I drew faces so big because I loved drawing eyelashes, which is not easy to do with S-H-I-T crayons, and the only reason I draw tiny arms and hands was because I hated drawing fingers, and still do even as an adult!

I have heard the "R" word or *slow* whispered around me so many times it doesn't bother me like it bothers Mom, but it would be better for Mom if people didn't find all sorts of ways to remind her she has a Slow or D-Lays daughter (which is not true if Mom sets an alarm on my watch). I do not like the way people act surprised when I do something so simple, like button my coat or remember to use a napkin to wipe my face. The best is when they see me write. Then, they look at me like I am a magician!

Some people, like Boss Gina, think being slow affects my hearing, but I have great hearing because if someone tells me something, I remember because I write things down, just like a reporter. I tell Mom it is so I can read how different my brain used to think, even one day before.

I actually have very good hearing. Sometimes, I wonder if I have bionic hearing, like *The Bionic Woman.* Mom lets me watch that show and *The Six Million Dollar Man.* I keep telling her they should not show old TV shows because Dad says six million dollars is not a lot of money anymore, so it seems stupid that people would chase Steve Austin for what Dad calls *Chump Change.* Dad says the army spends six million dollars on a "Goddamned Toilet Seat." I think Dad was M-bellishing because he hates the government. When adults *M-bellish*, Mom says it is so they can "make a point," which to me, sounds an awful lot like what I do, only when I do it, they call it "making things up."

Since my hearing is great, that is how I planned to become "Liddy-Jean, Marketing Queen." When you can hear good, and people think you can't because you're not as smart as everyone else, you can learn secrets, even without hiding behind a couch. The secret is: stop staring at people when they tell an interesting story to someone else, and you are not supposed to hear. This sounds easy, but it is very hard to do!

My friend Bobby was the one who told me about my bad habit of listening to other people's conversations while staring with my mouth wide open, like I'm trying to catch all the words. I'm glad he told me this now, but that day I hit him across his bum, and he cried like a baby and I got in *huge* trouble.

That was a long time ago and I do not have that behavior problem because I do not hit anymore. Not because people do not deserve it, but because the punishment was *really* bad. I was not allowed to go to The Center for a week, and I learned sometimes something has to be taken away before you realize how much you love it.

On the Spot

I always learn things when I spy on Mom and Auntie Theresa. When they cook Mom tells stories about the old days when all the boys were so crazy for her sister that Grandpa had to plant poison ivy on one side of their house to stop the boys from coming to her window. I guessed that Italian grandpas liked to use poison ivy instead of policemen to protect their daughters from S-E-X.

I hear mom say that men are still crazy for Auntie Theresa (even though she is old and forty-five) but then Auntie Theresa says, "All the men except my husband" and Mom puts her arm around her and they are quiet for a while before they both forget about Uncle William and have fun again.

Auntie Theresa grunted as she does when she leans over the stove for the pepper mill. I was mad that because I was spying from the living room, I could not see the Jesus Ballet. That is when Auntie Theresa's gold crucifix necklace gets trapped between her boobs when she leans over the stove. When she stands up straight again, the cross spins because Jesus' feet are stuck between her boobs. That was the best. Once I told Mom about the Jesus Ballet and she laughed very hard.

I know they are talking about me when Mom says I was Auntie Theresa's Little Star from the moment I was born.

Auntie Theresa says, "Mag, we always knew she would be our Little Star."

Mom says, "You were the only one that knew all my tears were from pure joy." (Mom cries happy tears a lot and this makes no sense to me.)

"Remember when Dawn was born, and they told you she would not be *afflicted* like Liddy-Jean?"

"Yes," Mom said, "and Stan hugged me as if we had finally gotten it *right*, and it took me a year to forgive him for that f-ing victory hug. But you understood that day."

Auntie Theresa said, "Yeah, I pushed Stan aside and said, 'Don't worry, we'll still love this new one.'"

While Mom sliced up another batch of fresh tomatoes for the sauce, she said, "Remember how Liddy-Jean's first day at The Center almost didn't happen?"

"Oh, I remember," was all Auntie Theresa said.

Mom liked to bring this up because sisters like to remind each other when they were wrong, just like I do with my sister.

Mom said, "I asked you to go since Stan couldn't, or wouldn't, and you offered to gradually take money to pay for it, so William wouldn't know."

"Yeah," Auntie Theresa said, "aside from sex, the only thing the bastard hates to give me more of, is money."

I had to be careful not to laugh out loud at that one!

"Tre, remember the young kid who gave us the tour?"

"He looked like he escaped from a Norman Rockwell painting," Auntie Theresa said. "So clean-cut and innocent . . . I think he was over eighteen, and, looking back, I should have defiled him." They both laughed, and I could hear more chopping on the wood block. Onions. I took a deep smell because even though I don't like to eat onions, I like to smell them because it reminds me of McDonald's.

"They certainly didn't spruce up the place to impress the tourists," Auntie Theresa said, "broken toys and bare floors, for the most part."

Mom said, "No money for extras, The Center has not changed

much. Remember they were getting ready to play that game when we came in? They were gathering the more challenging cases into wheelchairs and rolling them toward the middle of the room near that plastic rolled-up mat."

I loved hearing Mom and Auntie Theresa talk about old stories from The Center.

Auntie Theresa laughed and said, "We had no idea what we were in for! I thought there was something familiar about that white vinyl they were rolling out, so I kept staring at it while our guide kept talking."

Mom said, "I had hoped in a place like that Liddy-Jean might get the chance to help others. So many young people in wheelchairs. Remember the two boys?"

Auntie Theresa remembered, and I remembered too.

Mom said, "When the pair of young girl counselors rolled them closer together, you could tell just by the way their bodies and mouths moved that they liked being near each other. I had hoped you noticed too, but your face looked like you had witnessed a car accident."

I knew Mom and Auntie were talking about Andy and Brian, who scared me at first with all their weird faces and sounds, but then I found out this is how they smile and talk. Andy and Brian are best friends and hate to have their wheelchairs parked too far from each other.

Mom said, "Remember the games they played?"

Auntie Theresa laughed. "I remember Twister!" and they both started giggling.

I knew it was because of how all the clients got so excited at the colored spots and would scream when they rolled the mat on the floor. I copied them and screamed too, which was one of my favorite parts. Some needed help to crawl over to the mat and I would help them get near their favorite color spots by dragging them across the floor like a mop and they laughed. I was the only one who remembered everyone's favorite colors, and sometimes the counselors had to ask me.

I loved the Twister game. It always started when one of the counselors yelled: "Okay, ready . . . set . . . GO!" and there would be lots of squirming around on the mat, and I knew some of the clients didn't know why, but they squirmed anyway while the counselors cheered them on from around the mat, like gym teachers at school.

Mom said to Auntie, "I always think of your face . . . when they explained the object of the game was to drool on a color spot."

Theresa was snorting when she whispered, "Pretty sure I said, 'What the fuck?'"

Even though I heard them tell this story a hundred times, I still had to hold my mouth so I would not make a laughing noise.

Mom said, "Our guide was so patient with us, explaining this was all some of them could do and they loved it, and it took him years to come up with a game that everyone could play."

My favorite part was watching the counselors adjust Andy's head on the floor so he could hit his favorite blue spot, and he would get so happy and kick fast like he was riding a bicycle.

I heard Auntie Theresa slop the extra sauce from the pan into the serving bowl, probably speckling her chest at the front of her V-neck with Tomato Tit Freckles. She said, "So, Maggie, how badly do you need me to tell you I was wrong, and you were right about sending her there?"

"Not necessary," Mom said, and I heard Auntie Theresa snort laughing, just like Mom says I do.

Wearing Roller Skates Does Not Mean You Will Move Fast

Scary-Eyebrows-Stinky-Breath-Boss-Gina is very interested in getting people to call her "Ginny," or "Gin" but hardly anyone does, except behind her back. I am not sure why this is a good joke, but whenever any of the Marketing Girls say Gina should not tell people to call her Gin, everyone laughs, and so I laugh too. But I never laugh around Boss Gina, even though nobody told me not to.

I was lining up all my pens and pencils today, careful to make sure they all started at the very edge of my desk without hanging over. I kept moving them until I saw Gina watching me from across the room. I knew by the way she was staring at me that I had to stop moving them, so I walked over to my favorite copy machine right outside Rose's office so I would not be tempted to keep doing it. I remembered to take a piece of paper with me, so, like, Auntie Theresa says, I would look Legit.

I heard something hit the floor and when I turned around, Boss Gina was walking away from my desk, swinging a file folder, and all of my pens were on the floor. I stood perfectly still until Rose came out of her office.

"You okay, Liddy-Jean?" she asked me.

I nodded, trying not to look over at all the pens Rose gave me spilled on the floor. If she saw them there, she would think I did not take care of the gifts she gave me.

Gina was coming back across the room, and she looked down at the pens. "Rose, can you please deal with this mess?" She looked right at me like I had done it. Gina said to Rose, "I told you this would just be more work for you."

When Gina was far enough away, Rose whispered to me, "Don't worry, Liddy-Jean, accidents happen," and she rushed over to my desk and picked up all the pens, even reaching for my favorite red one that rolled under my desk and placed them back in my favorite spot near my notebook, not so close to the edge of my desk.

"I did not spill them," I said.

"It's okay, Liddy, I drop things all the time!" Her smile was so pretty that I did not need to say more.

The next day, Rose got me my own Pen Cup, red, to match my favorite pen! I was happy to have the cup, but she did not need to get me that because this would be the last time I was ever going to put my pens near the edge of my desk when Boss Gina was around.

I learned that people at work try to copy the people who are having success so they can have success too. This made me wonder if Boss Gina is copying me by trying to get a nickname like I have, since I am already having great success at my new job. It is not easy being an assistant in the Marketing Department of a very big company.

Marketing is just another word for commercials, like on TV, which I like very much. The Marketing Girls always say, "Marketing is not advertising," but I know they are wrong. When you go to the supermarket, you go to buy things you see on commercials, so Marketing is very important. This is why a grocery store is called a Market. When I told the Marketing Girls this, they all laughed and said this was why they loved me. Rose and Lisa P. told me I have Unlimited Potential, and Rose told me later that it means someday I could be their boss.

♡ ♡ ♡

When I first heard about my job, I was not the only one that did not want me to go to work. Dad didn't want me to go either, but I heard Mom say to him in the kitchen that I needed it for my Self-Steam and to learn to be a Responsible Adult, which sounded like terrible times ahead to me.

But I was wrong, like I am sometimes when I am afraid. Being wrong once in a while is O-K, as long as you are not like our boss, Gina, who Lisa P. says is: "Frequently wrong, and never in doubt."

Someday I will be the boss of a marketing department as soon as people stop worrying about the little things I do wrong, like stapling things upside down, or forgetting my smelly lunch bag in the refrigerator because Rose took me to McDonald's for lunch so she could celebrate me for a job well done.

One of the best things about being not as smart as everyone else (and there are many good things) is that I don't worry about the same things other girls do. If I think people might like me because they are afraid someday I might be their boss, I don't worry about it. If the Marketing Girls could do that, they would not be wasting time talking about what people said and what they really meant. Someday, when I'm the boss, I will put a stop to this, but I will do it in my most gentle voice (like I sometimes have to do with my sister). I will be a better boss than Gina.

Gina is the Executive Vice President of the Marketing Department, and it says so on her door on a fancy wood sign with carved-in white letters. While she acts nice to me, it is hard work for her. I have also seen her be mean to many of my friends when she thinks I am too stupid to hear, so I will never call her "Ginny" or "Gin" like she wants us to.

Since boys are very simple to understand compared to girls, the girls in my office are the most interesting. Lisa P. does all our computer website stuff, and she is very nice although she is not my favorite. Lisa P. is the only girl in the office with kids except for Gina, whose kids are old. I think because she is a nice mom, Lisa P. is good at being nice and patient when things go wrong, like the time I spilled a green Pixie Stick all over a stack of booklets and tried to clean it by licking my fingers to sweep it off. I got to eat a lot of what I spilled, but this did not work out good for the booklets. How was I supposed to know if I got five staples into a Pixie Stick all the lime powder would leak out? And how was I to know that lime powder plus spit equals green booklets? Rose said I learned that one the *Hard Way*, but I told her it was very easy.

Lisa P.'s office is right next to where I work, which is in my very own Cube. Even though I want to, I decide to wait to tell everyone how great it is working in a cube, since I only hear people complaining about it. People at work are wrong about so many things. In a cube there is no door to slam, no roof to accidentally toss a pencil in to see if it will stick, and I get three walls to hang up pictures! I had a lot of advice about cubes and how they could make workers happy and since that advice was starting to pile up, I added this and other things I learned into my notebook so I could help other people learn too.

Jackie is the Traffic Coordinator, which I found out has nothing to do with cars or highways. Bad news, because I was hoping it meant there might be little cars or motorcycles or scooters in the hallway. I learned Jackie the Traffic Coordinator is in charge of when all the work needs to get done. I thought she was very lucky since her only job was to tell people what to do, but Jackie has to work very closely with Gina and for this reason, she has to sometimes be a little mean to keep her job, but I still like her. She teaches me new things, and for a while I thought she would be the first one I would tell my book idea to.

Kim is the Copywriter and most like my mom, except that my mom would never spend so much family money on different clothes. The other girls say Kim dresses very Fashion Forward. (Fashion Forward is a marketing word, which means you are pretty, and you never wear jeans, sweatpants, or pajama bottoms to work. Not ever.)

Kim is always worried I am hearing too much grown-up talk. When the girls are telling their stories she sometimes sings out in her pretty voice: "Innocent Eeeeears!" This is her secret code for the girls to watch what they say in front of me. I told her the code is not a secret, since my mom used to say "Little Eeeeears!" whenever Auntie Theresa talked about Uncle William's boring S-E-X.

My favorite person at work is Rose.

Because I am at work, I'm not supposed to say I love Rose, but I do. Mom has explained before that although girls do not usually love other girls in That Way, sometimes they do. Mom also says she loves me no matter what, but girls who love girls instead of boys makes you more different than most people, and with all the challenges I have ahead of me I might not need that one, too. This seems silly to me, since I love girls and boys, and since adults can be wrong about so many things, I think Mom might be wrong on this one, too.

I told Rose that I loved her the first day of my job, because I'm lucky enough to know very fast when I love someone. Lisa P. explained that I might want to stop telling her that, not because I am a girl, but for a worse reason. Rose has a boyfriend named Gary. Even though Lisa P. always tells Jackie that Gary is a big loser, this made sense to me that I should not tell her that I love her anymore and I only tell her if it slips out on accident, like the time a toot accidentally came out very loud at church. (Here is what I learned about that: tooting would have been O-K, if I had been smart enough to say "Excuse me" instead of laughing my head off, making all the people at my cousin's wedding laugh, too. Mom made me apologize to Mom's cousin because she was wearing a wedding dress and saying "I do" when the excited fart slipped out.)

Instead of saying I love you to Rose out loud, I just write, *Liddy-Jean loves Rose* on my very own pad of Post-its and stick them under my desk so I can feel them tickle my legs whenever I move my chair. The only problem with my Post-it secret is that soon they curl up and fall off and stick to my pants without me noticing. Steve saved me once by running across the room to take a Post-it off my leg, before I went into Rose's office. Since then, Steve has been my secret hero, and I tell him this all the time.

Rose looks as pretty as a flower and I guess this was why she was named after one. She looks exactly like the cartoon drawing of Snow White with the shiny black hair and rosy cheeks. Not like the actress Snow White who dresses up in a costume on TV commercials for Disney World, but the real cartoon Snow White. Sometimes I wonder if everyone except Gina is in love with Rose just like I am. Not that I haven't loved boys, because I have, and I probably will love one again, since I like really big muscles.

I am lucky that I can love both boys and girls, and this may be another good thing about being not as smart as other people. I have seen other girls who look like they might love Rose too, but they don't say so, because they are supposed to love only boys. I am lucky because I don't have to pretend, but Mom says I should practice not saying everything I think out loud, especially at work.

Rose is ten years older than me, but she is my best friend, and I can't wait to see her every day. When she takes days off, Lisa P. says she knows it is very hard on me, but it is not fair for me to ask Rose to not take days off, so I don't do that anymore. She says everyone wants a break from work, but I think it is Boss Gina the Marketing Girls need a break from.

When Rose gets back from taking a vacation, I cannot stay away from her even for a minute. I heard Lisa P. explain this to Rose when they thought I was not listening. I knew it was me they were talking about, even though they did not use my name. Lisa P. did me a big favor explaining how sad I am when Rose is not there because now Rose is careful to take "delicate care of L.J.'s heart." Because of this Rose made me a deal.

On the first day back when Rose has a day off, I am allowed to work right inside her office whenever I want, and these are my best days. On that day she hangs a paper sign outside the door that says "Liddy-Jean & Rose's Office." I have kept this part secret: on those days, I pretend we are married, and the office is our house. Once I returned from lunch and accidentally said out loud "Hi, honey, I'm home!" just like Dad does to Mom, but luckily, Rose just laughed like I had made the best joke, so I laughed too.

Rose says her office is small and this is one of the reasons I can only share her office with her once in a while. Also, it is because when I read something, it always has to be out loud, and this can be distracting (to everyone except me, since I get distracted if I do NOT read out loud). Rose says we are such good friends that we would have too much fun and not get as much work done, which is definitely true.

Rose's office always smells like her perfume, and when I hear people talk about what it is like to be drunk, this is how I think it feels when I smell her perfume in a small office. I get a little dizzy, but it is a good dizzy, not like when I had the flu and threw up green string beans on Mom's shoes. Our office will have to be very big so I will not get dizzy from her perfume all day or it will be bad for business.

There is one other guy who works with us, too, but he does not know how to talk to me so I never learned his name. This happens sometimes. Steve is great at talking to me. Steve is very tall and quiet, and he is so handsome that if I did not love Rose, I might love him instead. Then Mom would not have to worry that I was going to have a difficult life. I decided that being around Steve and Rose is like watching *Xena, the Warrior Princess*. Rose is pretty like Xena, but Steve has muscles like Ares, the God of War, and when I see his muscles, I get confused on who I love the most that day.

Steve wears tight shirts and lots of boy perfume. He keeps a mirror by his desk, and he looks in it out of the corner of his eye all the time. This makes him happy. The girls all love him but they make fun of him saying he likes the way he looks too much. If I were Steve, I would look into that mirror all the time too, because Steve is very handsome, even better than Steve Austin on *The Six Million Dollar Man*, who has the same name and muscles.

I heard the girls talking one day that Steve probably has his car rearview mirror pointed at him when he drives. I have never been in his car, so I do not know if this is true . . . plus, everyone laughed, so it might be a joke.

I don't get happy when I look in mirrors. I am not as small as all the other girls in my office, and I still have the haircut they give us for cheap at The Center. I also wear thick glasses and have almost no boobs, unless I squish them together like I learned from hiding behind the couch at the doctor's office. I have the $6.00 Standard Haircut. Someday I hope to get the $8.00 Feathered Haircut when I am more successful, but I don't want to ask Mom to pay extra since she and Dad talk loudly about money in their bedroom, and then sometimes after that, Dad sleeps on the couch, which must cost less money than sleeping on their bed.

Today was not going to be the best day at work because when Gina came into the office, she acted angry with everyone even though she was the one that was late. Since I was in my cube and the first person she saw, I was the first person she talked to.

"Linda—Liddy-Jean, honey, I am going to need you to put your roller skates on today, okay?"

I don't have roller skates at work, but Rose told me before this meant Gina wanted me to work extra fast. I wondered if she acted nice and said "honey" because there was a law about not telling slow people they have to work fast. (I would ask Mom about that one later.) The roller skates was another dumb idea, since I am very slow on roller skates and once I fell and bit my own lip till it made blood go all down my chin and even dribbled onto my favorite butterfly sweatshirt. Luckily, Mom said the stain looked like an extra spot on its wing so I could keep wearing it.

Gina was looking at my clothes when she said, "We have some very important people coming in today and we'll need booklets made by three today. You're going to work with Jackie to get this done for us, lickety-split, okay Liddy?"

Gina always asks, "Okay Liddy?" after almost every sentence. Of all the people who talk to me like I have bad hearing, she is the worst.

Sometimes I wait to answer just to see how many times I can get her to say, "Okay Liddy?" but Jackie figured out I was doing this, and even though Jackie said it was funny, she told me I should try to stop.

"Okay, Gina," I said smiling since there was no Ginny nickname for her today.

Rose called out from her office. "Don't worry, Liddy-Jean, I'll help you too."

This was now turning out to be a good day, even with the roller-skating business. But then Gina showed up in Rose's doorway exactly the way criminals do in the movies. Her voice got low as she leaned inside the office door. I only heard her say "I shouldn't have agreed to this . . . you have your own work to do," and I could tell from Rose's face that Boss Gina was being mean to her again.

Later after lunch the booklets were finally given to us to be put together, which didn't give us much time. This happens a lot in Marketing. The Idea People use up a lot of time to think up things because it is early when they are doing their part of the job, and then the workers (the other girls in the office, and, especially, me) get the job at the very end and so we get asked to put roller skates on.

Gina and the other Vice Presidents never are in the Marketing Department when fast work needs to happen. This actually is a good thing because the department is a lot more fun when Gina is away in other meetings. People talk to each other more, and I get to learn all sorts of things that someday I might need to know. I made a list of things I heard at work today:

1. Money is very important when choosing a boyfriend. (Later, when I asked how much one costs, the girls just laughed.)

2. Gina drinks like a fish. (I guess that is a lot, since my fish tank always needs water.)

3. Sex is something women do when they want to

reward their boyfriends and husbands. (From what I know about it, I would rather get a dessert for cleaning my room.)

4. Jackie likes sex a lot, while Rose and Lisa P. thought it was mostly a waste of time and would rather get facials. (I was too afraid to ask what a facial was because my mom says I know a dirty thing when I hear it.)

5. Girls talk about people behind their backs, even if they like them.

6. Boys don't talk to each other hardly at all, unless it is about girls, the gym, football, movies, or video games. (Unless they are Showroom Decorator Boys, who dress Fashion Forward, and talk like the Marketing Girls.)

7. Jackie says people who talk about working too hard are the ones that do not.

8. Friendships happen at work especially when you have a bad boss.

9. Most Vice Presidents are Idea People and will never, ever help you make booklets no matter how short the deadline is.

10. Steve says people who say "Honestly . . ." are usually liars. (Gina says honestly a lot.)

I wanted to share what I learned with everyone while we made our booklets, but I could tell by the way Rose was doing most of the work for me, that I should not talk much until after the job was done. Rose would leave the table when Gina came out of her office and helped only when Gina was gone again.

When I got home after work, Dad was talking about something bad called a Layoff at Dad's work, and Mom looked worried as she scooped the tiniest bit of food onto her own plate compared to mine and Dad's, which were piled high. Later, I felt bad about the carrot I stole from Mom's plate when I saw her take the pot of stew off the stove to put in the refrigerator, which meant it was tomorrow's dinner, too.

"I get paid on Friday," I said.

Mom said, "I know, Liddy-Jean, Dad and I are both so proud of you."

"I don't need any money," I said, still chewing the carrot. I had wanted to spit it out, but it tasted too good. "You and Daddy can have my money except for the two dollars I need each week."

Mom stopped washing the dishes but would not turn around, and she left to go to the bathroom. I sat with Dad who looked sad even though he smiled at me, putting his fork down before he was even done with his last few bites. "You have nothing to worry about."

I may not have worried if he had not kissed me on top of my head.

When I first started my job, Mom warned me that some people don't keep their jobs because they become a distraction to other people at work. I knew she had not meant Dad, since he was never a distraction to anyone. He was not like me, or Dawn, or Auntie Theresa, or even Mom. He never said a single word whenever he worked on a repair project at his homemade work bench in the garage. It is just big enough for our two stools and he always lets me watch and hand him things, and when I ask a lot of questions, Dad just stays quiet and works and works, and not talking makes me extra enjoy the sounds of his metal oil can (*do-tee, do-tee, do-tee*) and Dad's whistling over the rumble of metal and wood handles when he reaches for something in

40

his rusty green toolbox.

Dad could fix anything, and I wanted to fix things too.

That night, while we all waited for Mom to come back to the supper table, I decided I would make it my number one job to listen more than I talk at work, and to write down anything I learned in my notebook so it would be a real book someday. If I wrote a real book, I would be a bigger success than I was at work already, and then I could worry less about Mom's small dinner and Dad's work layoff, and Rose's bad Boss Gina.

I wondered if I kept quiet, and listened and learned, and worked extra hard, if I could fix everything just like my dad does. Not by using his toolbox (Mom says I have disasters with tools) but maybe I could do something I was already good at. Maybe I could write a real book, one that would make more money than my job, one that could make me famous. Then I could fix everything... at home and at work.

I now had a Secret Scheme, which Mom says is a fancy plan: I would become *Liddy-Jean, Marketing Queen!*

Jesus Never Had It So Good

Today I was stuffed under my favorite chair closest to the kitchen, with a book and a flashlight spying on Mom and Auntie Theresa. I had my flashlight on pretending to read a book, just in case I get caught.

I peeked around the corner just in time to see Auntie Theresa pluck Jesus' feet out of her pretty boob crack with her long nails, just like the way Mom plucks onion weeds out of the garden. Only this Jesus weed looked like it was stuck between two giant pumpkins. Once she freed Jesus, she gave the cross a pat and said, "Jesus never had it so good." (From all the sad stories Grandma read me from the Bible, Auntie Theresa was right.)

"You pay too much attention to your tits," Mom said, and I had to cover my mouth, laughing. Mom never says "tits" unless Auntie Theresa is visiting, and she thinks I am not around.

"Well, someone has to, my husband sure doesn't. Do they, girls?" she said, and I watched as she patted the top of her boobs again. If I had boobs as big as hers, I would pat them all the time.

Mom said, "You have a problem, you know that, right?"

Auntie Theresa giggled and snorted. "Yeah," she answered, "I married a man who prefers to chase golf balls instead of me."

I knew from Mom's sigh that she was going to talk to Auntie Theresa like she does when Dad has a bad day at work. "Remember how nervous I was for Liddy-Jean on her first day? More nervous than she was."

"Of course, you were," Auntie said.

"For the first time she was going to be in a place where nobody who knew her or was like her. Tre, can I tell you something?"

"Sure."

"I'm embarrassed at how relieved I was that Liddy-Jean would finally be in . . . a normal environment."

"Got news for you, sweetie, workplaces are anything but normal."

"Hmm," Mom said.

I could see from under my chair that Auntie Theresa was covering the bottom of the olive-oiled pan with the pepperoni slices, tossing them just like a casino dealer on TV, and I knew from watching so many times that the ends of each slice overlapped perfectly as they made a path into the center of the pan, like Dorothy's Road to Oz. Mom always stopped to watch her do this too, waiting for the last toss of pepperoni slice that covered the last speck of the bottom of the pan. Mom says Auntie learned this from Grandma.

Mom looked serious. "It was so easy for me to accept Liddy-Jean had Itellectual and Developmental Disabilities. So why was I so happy to get her a job in the real world, away from The Center?"

Auntie Theresa's pan sizzled as Mom snapped fingers at her again and she passed her two long pieces of red pepper. She put them at the middle of the pan in what Grandma called a God's Cross.

"It's natural. You feel guilty about the others at The Center. Most will never be able to do what our Liddy-Jean can do." Mom stirred in the remaining peppers and handed a wooden spoon to Auntie Theresa before she asked for it.

The kitchen was filled with the smell of sizzling pepperoni. Auntie Theresa carefully poured the homemade crushed tomatoes on top of the pepperoni, which she says is the *only* way to start a spaghetti sauce. I closed my eyes to hear better and waited to hear the bubbling, one of my favorite sounds. Soon the top of her boobs would be decorated with Tomato Tit Freckles, and I was sad to miss it from spying under the chair.

Mom lowered her voice, "Remember all the questions I had in the beginning about IDD? Would she ever learn to say more than a few words? Would she learn to walk, or run? Would she learn to feed herself? Then, later, after she mastered those: Would she ever go to a regular school? Would she ever read or write her name? Would she ever ride a bus alone, or have a real job?"

Auntie Theresa said, "She has all those things."

Mom wiped a tear from her eye before Auntie could see and said, "Stan always says he wants nothing except for his children to be happy, but I know he just lacks the balls to wish for bigger dreams for her."

"You are so proud of her—"

Mom gives Auntie a little shove as she says, "No. I don't take credit for the sun, just because it shines on my face. I don't feel proud, I feel lucky."

I hear the slap of the wood spoon as Auntie smacks it too hard when she passes it to Mom and she yells at her, laughing. It was like watching my favorite TV show over and over.

"Shut that lid! Liddy-Jean would say you'll have Tomato Tit Freckles!"

When I went back to my room, I looked at the three-letter word I wrote in my small spying notebook: IDD.

Professional Authors Don't Use
Brown and Yellow Crayons

"Liddy-Jean, Marketing Queen,
does the finest marketing ever seen
her pants are too short,
but her hands are clean."

This was a poem I wrote and only showed Rose because she likes pretty things to read. I knew this because she collected twenty-six dollars' worth of Hallmark cards and pinned them to her corkboard (I added the prices on the back of each one on Lisa P.'s adding machine when Rose was on a day off. I added the dollars only, not the cents, just like Rose taught me, to keep math easy.) She lets people think her boyfriend gave the cards to her, but the Marketing Girls say that her boyfriend would never do anything that nice for Rose, because he spends his money on *you know what*. (I do not know what.)

Rose said she liked my poem very much and would take down a couple of her cards to make a special spot for it on her corkboard. She also told me that she thought my pants were just the perfect length, but I know she was telling a Nice Lie because the other girls' pants all touched the top of their shoes perfectly, and it is impossible for that many Marketing Girls to be wrong about fashion.

Mom said she would hold my paychecks in the bank for me, but she made sure I got a few dollars to do something fun with each week. Since fashion is something that all the Marketing Girls knew about, I started saving the dollars to buy fashion magazines. It was either for that, or ice cream, and I thought *Vogue* might help me to be less big and soft, but I stopped after just buying one issue. Problem was, *Vogue* didn't answer any of my fashion questions at all. In the first issue I saw two models together in the same photo and one model was wearing pants that were much too short, and another was wearing pants that were much too long, so I realized this would not be helpful, not one bit.

Mom tells Dad that things like this send me Mixed Messages, and those are bad for me. Fashion is filled with Mixed Messages. Like the way fashion is supposed to make you feel good, but mostly makes you feel bad because you can't buy the expensive clothes, and even if you did, they probably would not fit. I did learn one thing: I was a little bit like a model. It does not matter if a model wears crazy clothes, and, thankfully, it must not matter what I do either, since Rose tells me I look nice, and every day I wear whatever I want.

Yesterday in the Marketing Department, I heard Lisa P. and Kim laughing like they do when they are telling stories, so I moved my sticker project over to the table closest to where they were. I heard some of these stories before, but they were still laughing as if they were all brand new. I would have laughed with them, except I was doing my secret listening and I had to keep my head pointed at the stickers.

The Marketing Girls were telling the story about a business dinner, where Boss Gina fell asleep sitting up in a chair, and no one noticed until they thought they heard the sound of someone peeing, but it was just wine pouring from Gina's glass onto the carpet. Another time, Lisa P. came in to work extra early one morning to find Gina sleeping with her head on her desk, drooling!

Then, Lisa P. pointed to Gina's office and said to Kim, "She did it to Rose again."

Kim said, "Oh no."

"Yup," Lisa P. said. "A report was due to the CEO yesterday, but Rose says Gina never asked her for it." She pointed to Gina's closed door again. "She is giving her shit about it right now, trying to cover her own ass." I saw all the girls look over at Gina's closed door, like they wanted to get Rose the heck out of there.

What would Xena do? She would get Rose out of there, that's what she would do.

I kept my head down over my sticker project. My job was to put one sticker on the front cover of each of the shiny booklets. Rose told me these were very important and expensive booklets so I was not allowed to throw any away, even if a sticker label was put on wrong, Rose said she would help me fix it, and that is when I got a brilliant idea. I am lucky because I get ten or eleven brilliant ideas every day.

I tried to forget the counselor at The Center who told me making mistakes on purpose was Seeking Negative Attention and I knew Negative Attention is bad to get, especially at work, but I slowly reached for a sticker. I looked at Gina's closed door...they had been in there a long time. I peeled the back off and slowly turned the sticker like a doorknob, until it was upside down, and held it over the book cover trying to decide if I was as brave as Xena. Then I heard Gina's voice which sounded like yelling far away, and I could not hear Rose talking at all, so I jammed the sticker upside down and pushed it hard with all the tips of my fingers onto the booklet, before I could change my mind. Staring at it, my heart pounded like Christmas morning but in a bad way, and I picked up the booklet, shoved it under my arm, just like Rose does, and marched over to Gina's office.

"Liddy-Jean, where are you going?" Kim asked, but I pretended not to hear her and Lisa P. calling my name. Just like Xena, I put my hand on my hip as I heard Kim and Lisa P. getting closer, but they scattered when I reached Gina's door and knocked on it. Loudly.

Nobody *ever* knocked on Gina's door when it was closed, but I knew Xena would kick it down, so knocking loud did not seem so bad.

Gina yelled from behind the door, "How many times have I said when my door is closed—"

It was too late for me to run. Then the door flew open, and a very angry Gina was standing in the doorway. She wanted to yell at me, I could tell, but instead, she did what I hoped she would do since I learned most people won't yell at someone like me. I know because my sister Dawn gets yelled at way more than me, when Mom tells her she should know better.

Gina took a deep breath, just like Mom does when I spill something bad on something good. Behind Gina, I could see Rose sitting in a chair behind her, her eyes widened at me in surprise, since she was the one that told me about the Gina and the never-ever-closed-door rule.

"Is there something you need, Liddy-Jean?" Gina asked as she sighed heavily, like Darth Vader, breathing her Saturday night breath on me. I wondered if the real Darth smelled that bad under his helmet?

"I need Rose," I said. Then I held up the expensive booklet with the upside-down sticker. "I made a bad mistake." I knew Gina thought the bad mistake was me knocking at her door, so I made my lower lip go up and down like I see on cartoons when somebody is about to cry.

It worked, because Gina backed away from the door as if I was the one with smelly breath, turned to Rose and said, "We're done here Rose, go take care of her mess."

Rose left Gina's office and put her arm around my shoulder so I would follow her to her office while all the Marketing Girls peeked at us. When we were inside her office she said, "Liddy-Jean, you know you broke a rule, right? But I don't want you to be upset about the booklet. My boss tells me I make mistakes all the time." She smiled just like Mom does whenever she thinks I might cry.

"I am not upset," I said, smiling right back at her.

Rose looked confused.

"Sorry about the upside-down sticker," I said leaving it on her desk before going back to my work table. I went back to my sticker job, carefully putting another one on a booklet, but when I reached for the next one, I saw Rose at her desk, carefully peeling off the upside-down sticker where she saw my perfect one was under it.

When she looked up at me, I winked at her, even though when I wink, both eyes close. Rose gave me another huge smile as she shook her head at me, and it made me so happy I had to copy her. Then I looked over and saw all the Marketing Girls smiling at me too, and Lisa P. gave me a thumbs-up for how brave I was.

This was the moment I knew *exactly* what my book had to be about. I knew right then that I needed a special notebook to write all the work things I would see and hear, so I could tell what it is like for people like Rose to work for a bad boss, like Gina. Maybe some executives did not know it was wrong to talk mean to people, and to walk away instead of listening, and to slam doors like my little sister does, and I could tell them in my book.

Later, when I told Rose that Gina gets angry at her door because she hates her life, just like when Mom makes Dad clean the garage and Dad makes lots of noise and kicks boxes around until it drives Mom crazy, until she finally tells him the garage is clean enough. I explained that Dad doesn't really hate boxes just like Gina does not hate doors, they just hate what they are doing.

Rose laughed and said, "I am just beginning to realize how clever you are."

Later, I added that story to my notebook and I started noticing as much as I could, so I could write it all down in between sticker or stapling projects. This is called Taking Notes and great writers always do this.

I wondered if I sold a lot of books, then maybe I could give Rose some money so she would not have to work for Gina anymore, and maybe she could get away from her boyfriend, too. I might even be able to afford to buy some Fashion Forward Clothes, since I guessed this was one of the things stopping me from running the whole Marketing Department. If I sold a lot of books, I could help the Marketing Girls, and help Mom and Dad so maybe then they would always be as nice to each other as they are to me, and Mom would not stare out the window with her worried face when she has her checkbook on the kitchen table.

You might think I would be afraid to write a book all on my own, but actually, this would be my second book. I finished my first book when I was much younger, Mom said the things I wrote in it were not the sort of things you share with the world. She said a Bathroom Book about my "private doings," along with colorful drawings, was not appropriate reading for anyone, except maybe my doctor, and only if I was sick. (I was very surprised to hear this, since I would find it very interesting to read about what other people did in the bathroom.)

I also wish she told me this before I wasted the real leather notebook I got that Christmas, filling it with details of every bathroom trip. I never missed one. Mom said it was very thorough, and that the pictures really helped explain some chapters, even though she made funny faces when she looked at them.

Luckily, Business Books are not very personal, and I wouldn't need to use so many brown and yellow crayons, since I ran out of those two colors in all my crayon boxes. Business Books teach people, and that was another thing I like to do since I have already taught some of the other people at The Center so many things I have learned at my job.

Last Saturday at The Center, I made a pretend copy machine out of an upside-down cardboard box and taught Rachel and Natalie how to use it. Everything was going well until I got in trouble when tattletale Debbie Riley told the counselors I had made her stay inside the box for a really long time to collect all the milk money that came through the hole when they used the copy machine I made. I tried to explain she was not in there just for money collecting (which made me sound greedy), but because the copy paper needed to be pushed out of the machine.

Even though I was right about this, I got in trouble anyway and the counselors made me give back all the money even though I was going to use the money to buy things for The Center.

Since Debbie Riley loves Negative Attention, she also lied and said she cut her thumb on a staple inside the box, but she forgot she already showed me her stupid thumb cut on the bus that morning! When I am a famous author, I will never sign a free copy of my Business Book for Debbie Riley. She will have to buy one like everyone else, since this will help me make Mom and Dad rich and they will never have quiet discussions after bedtime about the money it costs to send me to The Center. I never knew that it costs a lot of money to send me to there, but I should have guessed by the way I was not allowed to take home the brown and yellow crayons.

A few nights ago, after I was in bed, I heard my mother's voice, and it sounded like she was crying. I went to the hallway and heard Mom saying how much I needed to be able go to The Center, and my dad said he would find a way to get more money once he started his new job. The next day, I saw Mom write a note and put it in his lunch bag, so I snuck over to read it while she was getting dressed and Dad was taking his usual long bathroom break before work.

The note said:

Hi Honey. Please don't worry about anything. We always make it work! Besides, who needs money when we have so much love? Xoxo Maggie

I loved going to The Center because the counselors taught us how to fix problems ourselves and sometimes, they even fixed things for us. One time, when I was much younger, when I said I was afraid of the dark during naptime. Instead of laughing at me like some kids did at my school, many of my Center friends said they were afraid, too.

The counselors found a way to fix this. Every day before nap time they would hang up a new glow-in-the-dark Halloween decoration somewhere in the nap time room, and our entire class would lie on the floor at nap time and try to find the one new decoration. Ever since then I am not scared of the dark because my mom bought me my own glow-in-the-dark decorations to hang over my bed. I was thinking how this was a smart way of training, and I now had some ideas to add to my Business Book, like this:

Companies should let their workers go into the fancy boardrooms to eat lunch once in a while. This way, if you have to make a marketing speech, it would be much easier if you have already been in that room to eat a peanut butter sandwich with extra-crunchy potato chips. Instead of feeling scared, it might feel as good as seeing happy Halloween decorations, smiling at you in the dark.

I had so many responsibilities now that I had a job and when I am at work, just like at The Center, I feel smarter than a lot of people. Mostly because so many people needed my help . . . and some did not even know it yet.

Secrets and Plans

I must really want to be an author since I was thinking of it even as Rose was going through the drive-thru to get me my favorite Egg McMuffin as a special treat. Mom gave Rose special permission and warned her that I usually cannot think of two things at once when an Egg McMuffin is around. Mom is usually right about that but today I was thinking about two things at once. I tugged at Rose's sleeve even though I know I should not do this when the arm is driving.

"Rose."

"Liddy-Jean," Rose said, and I laughed because she is good at copying me.

"Will you help me type some things? It takes me too long to type, and plus Mom says my spelling is Downright Dread-filled."

"I'll help you type anything you need," Rose said, but I knew she would say yes before I asked.

I tugged at her sleeve one more time and her bra strap showed. Then I pointed to it, and tried to cover my mouth before a giggle came out, but I wasn't fast enough.

"It's lucky I can spell good since the doctor told Mom and Dad I would never be able to write, and Mom swore at him." I whispered that last part, since Mom does not like it when I tell people she swears (or farts).

"Do you need me to type another sign for your cube?"

The last sign she typed for me said: "Liddy-Jean, Marketing Queen," but I was too shy to hang it up, so I just keep it in my desk.

I told Rose, "I am writing a business book to teach how to make companies better so the workers will be happy."

Rose looked surprised, and did not say anything right away, so I kept "Selling It" as Mom says I do, whenever I want something.

"I started on it my very first day at work but didn't know it would be a business book back then. I thought I was just keeping a bathroom journal that was outside the bathroom."

Rose slowed the car before we had reached the McDonald's drive-thru speaker.

"Rose. You have to pull up more, or you will have to yell too loud to order my McMuffin, and that would be rude."

"A business book?" Rose asked me, and I almost forgot we had been talking about that, since now I could smell the McDonalds *loud and clear*.

"Yes," I answered, "I am writing a book about all the ways our company could be better, but it has to be a secret from Mom and Dad since my last book did not turn out very well. Can you move the car up more? Please and thank you," I said, which always works with Rose. She moved the car up more.

"I'd love to help you with your book, if we can do it after work," she said, and I guessed she would say that and not just because of Boss Gina. All the Marketing Girls say Rose hates going home.

Rose ordered an Egg McMuffin for me, and a coffee for her and soon the order was shoved though the window. I was so hungry. I reached across to help Rose with the bag, but at the last second, my hand decided to dive right in there to grab my McMuffin. Rose tried to ask me more about the book, but I couldn't really hear her with an Egg McMuffin in my hand, so finally she stopped asking so I could hum to myself my favorite Egg McMuffin song between bites.

I was a little worried because my pants were already too tight before I started eating. Once I heard the Marketing Girls say when Rose was younger, she said she was chubby. The Marketing Girls whisper to each other that Rose still thought of herself that way, and this was why she was with disgusting Gary. They also said she could have anyone she wanted, even someone as handsome as Steve, who loved Rose from his first day at work, just like me.

The Marketing Girls say Gary teases Rose by calling her "Fattie" even though she is not, and that is why Rose has no idea how pretty she is because she has been with that jerk too long.

Once, I snuck over to hear a private conversation between Lisa P. and Kim who call each other on the phone pretending it is a business call, so they can tell stories in secret about people at work. I thought this was a brilliant plan and I wanted to do this with Rose but was not lucky enough to have a phone on my desk. I figured out their trick because Lisa P. would pick up her phone and dial and, a second later, across the room, I would see Kim answer her phone and start laughing. Kim always says, "Whaddya got now?" and then they gossip, just like Mom tells me not to. This is when I stand very close to Lisa P.'s office door and make sure a file cabinet blocks me so Kim cannot see me spying. I have heard great stories this way, stories they would never talk about near the table where I do my projects. Mostly they were stories about their husbands or boyfriends.

Lisa P. says, "She told me she gives him drinks so he'll fall asleep and leave her alone. I know . . . I know . . . it's no way for her to live."

I knew they were talking about Rose and Gary.

Kim was talking now, but I couldn't hear her from across the room. Then Lisa P. said, "He has bigger problems than drinking. He's got her convinced she has to stay with him because he'll hurt himself if she breaks it off. The loser has not bothered to work in a year, and he doesn't want to give up his meal ticket."

I walked away with my stomach hurting. I was starting to think Rose needed my help more than Mom and Dad, so later I told Rose some advice that she should not give out any meal tickets to anybody. Unless it involves McMuffins . . . and me.

"Sure thing, my friend," Rose said back to me. But I could tell by the way she smiled she did not know me and the Marketing Girls worry about her. Rose was in big trouble at home and at work, and I needed to figure out a Secret Scheme to save her.

ROSE

I was scared today for the usual reasons . . . but not as scared. I tell myself, Rose, maybe you're getting numb to this insane way of living. Or . . . maybe I'm finally seeing the light, and will come up with a way out, before something (more) terrible happens. Distractions are good, and I've got plenty at work, but at some point, I know I need to land on a plan. Liddy would have had a plan already!

I'm careful not to speak to LJ as if she is younger than her years, and today I wondered if this would be the last time I would have to try. Even though I sensed how intuitive she was the first day I met her, I'm still underestimating her. She surprised me today when I took her out for her Egg McMuffin. She tugged at my sleeve, like she always does, and asked for my help typing.

I figured she needed me to type another sign for her cube, and then she hits me with: she wants to write a business book! The moment she said it, I knew she was going to do just that, with or without my help. That is the thing about LJ—sadly, I have more confidence in her than I do in myself. I knew before she gave me any details that her unique way of seeing the world would be a book I would love to read . . . a look into LJ's incredible mind was a only a book away, and I could help her. The world needs to know how she thinks.

If I am being truly honest, I need to help her, just like I need to keep writing this journal . . . temporary distractions save me time and time again…but I wonder when my luck will run out.

LJ is so brave—busting into Gina's office like that, and me underestimating her again, that she didn't know exactly what she had done. She knew. She wanted me out of there. I wanted me out of there, too.

Writing this journal has helped me so much—I wonder what writing a book could do for LJ? What could it do for so many people to know her, and what a corporate job looks like from her perspective? I see glimpses that make me laugh and sometimes want to cry, and now I want to see exactly what she sees, know what she knows. I want to help her capture that in a way that could be shared so people will know how capable she is. How brilliant she is, in her own way.

And it could help her in other ways too . . . the way writing helps me. A place to remind you when what you see is wrong, or twisted, and in my case, dangerous. I see the way the girls look at me at work—they are worried. I'm way past worried but I don't want to stay numb to this life I am in.

If I had thought to write a book like LJ has, I'd have killed the idea instantly with a million reasons why my idea would never work. This is one of LJ's greatest gifts—she never has the merciless doubt that accompanies a new idea. I always doubted that writing was worth my time—I doubt that I'm worthy of having freedom from where I am, that I'm worthy of having someone wonderful in my life . . . someday.

Any idea I have gets hammered at the fledgling stage, before it ever has a chance. LJ would never do that! She believes anything she wants is possible, and what I wouldn't give for a tiny speck of her confidence.

I love to help her, and selfishly I am thrilled for any diversion to justify me spending more time away from home . . . away from my house that I love, that no longer feels as if it is mine. This is the only room in the house where I can't smell him.

I want a change so bad I can easily ignore my worry if the book contains critical views of the company—I have to push away thoughts of who might see it. If it was seen, was a success, it would get me fired.

It could be the push I need to get out of there.

Caught between two toxic environments . . . how did I get to this place?

This makes me smile like a fool, and I think about what I look like right now, sitting on a fuzzy bath mat, writing behind the only locked door in my house that won't raise suspicion. Funny that LJ wrote her first book in a bathroom . . . and now I am stifling a laugh. I love LJ's simple yet magnificent way of seeing the world around her—betting on her is immeasurably easier than betting on myself.

This just in . . . incoming doubt: would working on this project further amplify LJ's crush? When she came to the company and instantly fixated on me, I knew it had nothing to do with my charm. LJ seems to have no distinction between the sexes when it comes to affection (she swoons when S walks by). But for some reason, I am her favorite, and in fact, she is mine. To her that probably means love. Actually . . . shouldn't it?

She gets to love whomever she wishes. God knows I've suppressed my share of inappropriate attractions over the years; when I was a kid it was female teachers. As an adult I managed to keep my attention/ attractions from drifting where they didn't belong, and I'm jealous how LJ simply follows her heart.

If I had listened to my heart, I wouldn't be here, hiding in a bathroom writing to my only true friend, a friggin' journal. I have written countless confessions . . . how many times I attempted running away from my father when I was twelve . . . I realize as I write this how much my father was like G—the alcohol, the explosive moods, the unsafe feeling that fills whatever room he is in. It is no wonder my body seems broken and unable to feel anything for a man. Not that I desire women instead, but I certainly admire them more—in more ways than I dare to write.

Maybe in another life.

How many times have I written that? What if this life is all we get, and I am spending it writing in journals I keep buried under bath towels—closeted? Not exactly a foolproof plan, more like fool-filled. Staying in a bathroom waiting for G to pass out may not be the best plan, but it is the best way to avoid sex.

When I was younger, I had sex for so many different reasons: It was prom night . . . I had dated a guy for more than six months . . . I liked the guy's family better than my own . . . I craved the release of sex (though not specifically for anyone I was with)—sometimes I agreed to sex to punish myself. I have stopped doing that. But never have I once said yes to sex because my heart compelled me to.

Not once.

Even with kind and attractive men (like S) it seemed inevitable that if our friendship turned sexual, I would eventually turn off to him like all the others . . . so I won't go there. I also don't want a nice guy to get mixed up in this.

The plus side of being with an addict is that I rarely have to dread sex. It was only in the beginning, the hiding from him just became a habit. I always have in the back of my mind that if I started over with someone else, the cycle might begin again: The nights of romantic excitement until we were just about to be together, then the inner fight or flight dialogue in my head, or, almost as bad—wait, is "intense disinterest" an oxymoron? At least with G, even if he did sense my growing distaste for intimacy back in the early days, I wasn't hurting a *good* man.

I wanted to ask LJ more about her book, but I couldn't compete with an Egg McMuffin, so she ate while I drove, listening to her smack her lips and hum to herself in between bites. She is adorable. As a young person, I struggled with my weight, and I never felt adorable, I'm happy to think with her confidence that LJ does feel adorable.

I have long since shed the protective fat of my childhood years, yet I still feel it clinging to me. I start each day by searching for it, starting with my belly, feeling it still there, even knowing that it isn't. From the day I confessed that to G, he took pleasure in convincing me that it was true. When I walked past, he would pinch me, not sweetly, and say I should change my dress to something less clingy, so nobody has to look at all that, for Christ's sake."

Of course, I knew it was his way of keeping me down, his toxic insecurity lashing out at me—but still, it worked. I finally know that now.

I kept the secret of my obsession pretty well, since I didn't want to be one of "those" women, obsessed with a weight problem that was not obvious to anyone. My inner Fat Girl started and ended days the same way: jump on the scale, hundreds of sit-ups, even if I was sick with a cold and my head pounded from doing the first twenty. Regardless of what the scale said, it was still a Fat Girl who climbed into bed at night and woke up each morning.

I threw away my scale weeks ago, and G never noticed.

Early in our relationship, Gary would say "Come here chubby," indicating he was thinking about sex. Back then, I was so messed up that I felt grateful he wanted me despite my size (which was, and is, normal)—although I never wanted him.

He still wants me, I would think, fat and all, as he rolled me onto my stomach. I had come to prefer his habit of rolling me over so I would not have to face him, though I hated this when we were first together. It felt anonymous, just as the dog name implied, but had the benefit of him not seeing my imperfect belly, and I could keep my eyes firmly closed, not having to fake any expression as he made his way closer to me.

As his drinking got worse and he had difficulties with sex, he would get furious—and say this only happened with me. At first, I believed it was me, until I learned he had demons of his own and had started drinking first thing in the morning to stop his tremors. When I couldn't convince him to stop, just like my mother couldn't convince my father, it ended up being me who served him his fifth and sixth drink in the hope he would be too wasted to come near me. Or was it I feared his anger?

Can I get you another drink?

I was guilty of assisting him. It was always in the back of my

61

mind—if he got better, the sex would come back—and so I wouldn't refuse when he asked for another whiskey. When I started journaling, that is when I saw things from a bit of a distance, learned the way things really were, not his telling of his story.

I have served him a lot of drinks in our time together. Later, when he turned to stronger drugs, I pretended not to notice, grateful that I didn't have to serve him anything anymore.

I need to help LJ with her project. She is an exceptional person, and I feel grateful she asked. I can't afford to turn away a distraction wherever it's offered—I alienated all of my friends by not leaving him, only left with the girls at work who I know feel sorry for me. Would they choose to be my friend if not for work? I'm not sure if I would—too much baggage. Who wants to be around a weak woman who has not taken control of her own life?

I wondered, what would LJ do?

Aside from the great energy LJ has brought to work, why is my gut telling me something good is heading my way? I hope I am right—and, I hope I will recognize it.

Throwing Up from Boobs

"What do the other departments do at work?" I asked Lisa P.

"You don't have to worry about that," she said.

"My mom says that is not an answer," I said. And then I waited, with my notebook ready and my pen already on the paper, but she only said, "You're right, Liddy-Jean," before she answered her phone.

This made me wonder if nobody knew what the other departments did either, and what if there was a whole department who spent the day lying on the floor playing with Tonka trucks, and nobody knew about it? If that was true, I thought someone better find out.

The only time I ever go to visit other departments is when I had to bring mail that was delivered accidentally to the Marketing Department. Since this didn't happen very often, I thought for the good of the entire company I had better pull off *The Great Mail Caper Scheme*. (I don't know what a *Caper* is, but Mom read it to me from an old Nancy Drew book, and Nancy is definitely smarter than me, and her last name means she is a good artist too.) *The Great Mail Caper Scheme* is when I borrow a few envelopes of mail off the cart when the delivery person isn't looking. This way, I could deliver mail that I borrowed to the other departments and find out what they do.

The first thing I learned:

A lot of pretending goes on in a big company, and nobody works hard all day, like Rose and me do. People watch things on their computers that have nothing to do with work, and they switch it back *quick-quick-quick* when anyone comes by. I know this from seeing the flash of light change on their faces from the screen, just like when Dad watches TV at night with no lights on in the living room, even though Mom says it will ruin his eyes. (Dad says: Turning forty-three ruined my eyes!)

The first department I had extra mail for was the Customer Service Department. This was an easy department to find out about since they talk the most about what they do, especially in the bathrooms. So, I started taking my smallest notebook into my favorite bathroom stall on each floor and this is how I learned so much about customer service that I didn't have to ask them many questions or borrow their mail anymore. The first time I heard them talking, I was lucky enough to have a pen with me, but I had to use toilet paper to write my notes down.

There were two things wrong with that idea:

The first is that the ink goes right through the paper and makes an exact copy onto my hand, because I used my hand like a tiny desk. This was bad because when I went back to the Marketing Department, Lisa P. noticed right away, and I had to tell a Small Lie that I was using my hand to write my life story. The good part was, the next day, Lisa P. and Rose brought over to my desk a set of four notebooks that I did not have to choose from—they were every one, all mine! The first thing I thought of was I would never tell my sister that I had four new notebooks, or she would want one and Mom might make me share. This was another great thing about work. I had a secret grown-up life away from home!

Rose stacked the set of notebooks from big at the bottom to small at the top, so I wouldn't have to, and she winked at me and said: "For writing your life story!" I had to stop myself from happiness-crying because I do not want to do that at work.

My favorite notepad was the tiniest one, and this was the one I carry right now in my pocket. Right after she gave it to me, I wrote

Rose's name in tiny letters in the middle of the notebook. This was so someday I would be surprised when I find it while I was writing, and it would make me happy like Rose's name always does. I learned this from my favorite teacher when I was still in school, who had written me a secret note on one of the middle pages of my school notebook and I was so happy to find it after I was Graduationed!

The second bad thing about writing notes on toilet paper was that it is easy to forget they are your notes when you are hurrying to pee and wipe. This has happened to me once and I only noticed it after I flushed, because I *always* look. This left me with only one copy of my notes, and that was the one on my hand. By the end of the day, I had smudged words on my forehead, and arms and pants and only the words on the side of my hand were still there. Now I never go into the bathroom without my mini notebook to get information on the Customer Service Department. (It's lucky the Customer Service ladies drink lots of coffee, which means they go to the bathroom a lot, like my Auntie Theresa.)

Some things I learned:

There are almost all women in the Customer Service Department, and the women say it is not because girls are better at solving problems than boys are, but because it is a department that pays C-R-A-P. (If I spell a bad word, I do not get in trouble for it, so I learned to spell three of the best ones, thanks to Auntie Theresa. I put a big star next to that bad word, because that needed to be fixed for sure.

Even though Mom and Dad say there is nothing women cannot do, I have learned that (except for the Marketing Department) if there is only one boy in a department of girls, he is usually the boss. I have made many notes on how the company should change that rule, since the smartest people I know are girls. And there are too many white people in every single department, and almost none that look like my two favorite counselors at The Center, Nichole and Michael.

Once when I was in the bathroom, I had to take extra fast notes, which was very bad timing since I was also in there to go to the bathroom. One of the Customer Service Girls said she had a good story to tell, but then the other girl got worried someone could be listening. I got scared that they knew I was listening and writing notes, so I accidentally dropped my favorite pen in the toilet. Thankfully, this sounded just like I had pooped, so I made the "uh" sound right after it, and they giggled and kept right on talking. (By the way, if you use Mom's five-second rule and dry it on your pants, a pen that went swimming in the toilet writes perfectly.)

Next place I had mail for was the Product Development Department, and Rose told me this was where all the designers worked. When I first walked in, I saw a cartoon stuck up on the wall of a big boss telling the little designer that the other bosses just had a meeting at work and have a great plan for the success of the company! The great plan was that the designers need to invent something great that will sell a lot and make the company rich. Then the boss says: How long will the designer's part take?

I got that joke right away because I see a lot of bosses do this. Bosses forget that it takes much longer to do what they ask than it does for them to ask for the work, and I underlined this important idea twice.

I checked the envelope again and asked the first man I saw for someone named Stephanie. He pointed to the third office, and I went to the door. After seeing Stephanie, I knew I would have to keep my visit short since Stephanie had the biggest boobs I had ever seen, except on TV.

I got stupid and forgot why I was there because of those boobs, but I was smart not to tell her. I looked down and saw the envelope in my hand, *"Your mail!"* I said loudly, happy I remembered. Stephanie told me to come on in by waving at me, which made her boobs move so I put my eyes on the little toys on her desk and the stickers and cartoons on the walls.

"Thank you," Stephanie said, as she reached for the mail. "What's your name?"

"Liddy-Jean Carpenter," I said, not looking at her. "Why do you have toys on your desk?"

I think Stephanie smiled, but I wasn't looking at the toys anymore. The boobs had gotten me into a trance, just like Dracula. Because I am a writer, I noticed how her long blonde hair sleeps on top of them, and maybe I should put that in my book . . . that hair looked mighty comfortable.

Stephanie said, "Designers get to break the rules and hang things up that other departments would never be allowed to," she said.

"Oh," I said. I was thinking maybe I should be a designer, after I finish my book.

Stephanie said, "A long time ago, you had to cut off your ear to be considered a crazy artist, but now, you just hang weird things up on your wall and collect toys that you paint yourself."

"A toy is better than cutting off your ear," I said. "I heard all about that guy. He is named after a moving truck."

"Van Gogh," Stephanie said, and this time she smiled at me.

I asked, "Do you play with Tonka trucks?"

"No," she said, but I was not sure about that, so I looked around just in case. She even moved her feet when I checked under her desk.

Stephanie said, "No trucks, but one of the other designers has a toy motorcycle on his desk. And it even makes noise."

She seemed as excited about this as I was, so I said, "We can be friends."

"Sure thing Liddy-Jean."

"Is it his job to play with the motorcycle?" I asked, looking for my notebook in my pocket.

"No," Stephanie said, but she did not sound sure.

I asked, "Why do you hang up all your work on the walls?"

"I want people to remember what projects I designed?" She didn't sound sure of this, but then I realized she always sounded like she had a question. "Around here, people can take credit for your work if you don't?"

"Excuse me, I have to write this down," I said, before sitting in a chair and pulling out my notebook, and having trouble getting my hand out of my sitting down pocket.

"Sure . . . I guess? What are you writing down?" she asked.

That was definitely a question.

It was much easier not looking at her boobs when I was writing, so it came out of my mouth before I could stop it, "I'm writing a book, and only Rose knows about it."

"Can I read it when you're done?" Stephanie asked, and when I looked up I was happy to see she was smiling at me like I was a four-year-old. I did not have to worry she would tell my secret, since a four-year-old cannot write a book.

"You can read it, but you have to buy one," I said. "My Auntie Theresa says, No Mooches . . . and Snitches Get Stitches." Stephanie laughed and said she would buy one. I would have been more excited, if she believed me.

She told me more about the Product Development Department, like the way it's never the designer who gets to show the new designs to the executives. It's the designer's boss that gets to show all the work the designers do. She explained that the designer gives ideas to their boss, and then if the company agrees this is something they should do, the company thanks the boss for the idea! This can get the designers angry, because Stephanie says they are treated like Worker Bees.

I decided that if I was ever running a company that invents things, I would make sure the designer will get more money for her work. I would not give the Vice Presidents any raises because Stephanie told me they already make too much money compared with the Worker Bees.

"I have to go now," I said, taking one last peek of her you-know-whats.

"You can come back any time," she said smiling, and then she waved before tossing her hair off one of her boobs, like a movie star.

"Maybe," I said, trying so hard not to look again, and before I left, I remembered what Mom would say about my manners. "Please and thank you," I and said with a little bow before I left.

I practiced tossing my hair as I walked down the hallway. I was worried if Stephanie became good friends and she ever hugged me against those big boobs, I might get dizzy and throw up. If crying was bad at work, then throwing up would be really bad, especially if it was from boobs instead of the flu . . .

I knew if I wanted to make all the people in the company think of me as Liddy-Jean, Marketing Queen, I would have to spend time with all the departments, even the Sales Department. The Marketing Girls always say: "Sales make the most, talk the most, and dress the worst," so, I was not looking forward to meeting them.

The first thing I learned is that sales people really do talk the most and they talk really loud, even if they have nothing to say. They also seem to have a few things in common with some of the clients at The Center because sometimes the people not as clever as me at The Center don't know what they are talking about but keep talking anyway. The Marketing Girls say that salesmen see what other companies are doing to make money, and they want to do exactly the same thing, which makes the designers and the lawyers very mad.

The best thing about sales people is they helped me invent the perfect title for my book. I started to think of sales people and bosses like Disney Fairy Godmothers that just wave a wand to get things done, while the tiny mice had to make the whole dress for Cinderella.

Boss Gina might be that way. I started to think of myself and the Marketing Girls as Worker Bees and the bosses as Wand-Wavers and this was how I decided the name of my Business Book: *Wand-Wavers and Worker Bees*.

The second I thought of this, I had to tell Rose.

"I am going to be a famous book writer," I said. I figured it was not bragging, if it was the truth. I had proof: I already sold one copy to Stephanie from Product Development.

Rose said, "I'm so proud of you. Nobody should write your life story, except you, Liddy-Jean."

"Nope. Not my life story. It's a Business Book. I want to write how companies and bosses can make the jobs better, and how workers can be better at their jobs. Just like how I teach other people at The

Center all about what I learn at work."

Rose stopped typing at her computer, and even though it was close to five o'clock and she was rushing to finish something Gina asked her for too late in the day, she still turned her chair like a merry-go-round to look at me.

"Tell me more about this book," she said, folding her hands just like my old teacher used to do when I said something smart.

"I learned a lot about working at a big company and I think if other people like me could read my book, then all the things that took me so long to learn could help them, too."

Rose smiled, making my heart hurt in a good way, and she said, "This is so wonderful that you want to teach others what you learned!"

I said, "Not everybody knows what the bosses do and what the workers do, so I am going to call the book *Wand-Wavers and Worker Bees.*"

Rose raised her eyebrows at this, and her surprised look stayed frozen, so I got worried if it was a bad idea to write a book about the bosses. Especially Gina. When I get nervous, I talk like the guys in the Sales Department and forget to breathe. "*Wand-Wavers and Worker Bees* will not have the word *and* . . . instead, I am going to use the pretty music symbol on the keyboard that sits on top of the number seven—and—"

"Liddy-Jean, that's such a great title!" Rose said, and because I knew she meant it, I finally remembered to breathe. If it had been anyone else except Rose, I would worry they were telling me that to make me feel good. But Rose never says things to me just to make me feel good.

She asked me lots of questions about the book and seemed very surprised that I had answers for every one. I even showed her the notebooks I started filling up with stories about other departments in the company. She stared at them for a long time, flipping the pages and shaking her head slowly the whole time, until I started to worry again.

Finally, she said, "Will you let me help you with this?"

"Yes," I said, knowing that I badly needed a typing expert for the book. Typing one sentence can take me a very long time and I know this because I played with Rose's computer once when she was on vacation, and I timed myself: three sentences in one hour. "Because I don't want to be my old mother's age when I am finally done typing."

Rose laughed at this, and I got splashed with that happy feeling in my heart again. Next, she tapped her fingers on the cover of one of the notebooks she held on her lap. She does this when she is thinking. "The first thing we have to do is work out a schedule," she said. "Any important project needs a work schedule in order to get it done."

"Like what Traffic Coordinator Jackie does!" I said.

"Exactly! How about we meet after work for an extra hour two or three days a week? Do you think that would be okay with your parents?"

I hopped up and down, not believing my great luck. "*Yes!* I will ask them tonight!" I yelled, forgetting I should not give people hugs at work, especially when I am yelling.

"Okay, Liddy-Jean. Ask your Mom and Dad and they can call me about which days."

I had a date with Rose, three times a week! (But what Rose did not know was that I had no plan on telling my parents.)

People with Antennas Know Things

Today was not going to be a good day at work, since all the Marketing Girls and Steve had to go to a training so that would leave me alone with Boss Gina. Rose seemed worried as she set me up on my desk with a giant bunch of envelopes to stuff before she left.

I wanted to surprise Rose by getting them all done by the time she got back, so I tried not to look, but Boss Gina kept her door open all day and I knew she was watching me even before she yelled in a fake happy voice, "How are you doing out there without Rose?"

"Fine," I said, but I wanted to go shut her door since now she was staring at me like I was stealing something. "Do not worry," I said, and I yelled back, "Thou Shalt Not Steal!" I thought I sounded like the old guy from Harry Potter or maybe God but yelling turned out to be a bad idea. Gina walked over to my desk and sat on the edge of it, so I could not reach even one envelope. I tried once to reach past her, and she bent until she blocked my arm. When I tried the other side, she went that way, too, so I folded my hands in my lap to look patient, just like in school.

I was not patient. I still had a little bit to go before I could surprise Rose by finishing them all, and I had never worked so fast. "I have more to do."

"I know," she said. "Me too." She smiled down at me and from my seat I thought I saw two pointy teeth that looked like fangs.

"Do you have real teeth or fangs?" I asked.

She looked around, then whispered, "All the better to bite you with." Then she laughed so loud as if she had told the best joke. But my skin had goosebumps like it was the truth. She put her coffee cup down on my desk and I watched how close it was to my envelope stacks.

Rose came back right then, and I was so happy, I ran over to her. Gina said, "No running Liddy-Jean, that is how accidents happen. Remember the pens?"

I remembered.

I whispered to Rose, "I am so glad you are back."

"I am too," she said, and we both watched Gina walking away to her office.

"I had a surprise, but I cannot give it to you," I said.

"Okay, let me finish up in my office and I will come help you finish." I could feel my eyes burning, so I went back to my desk.

A little while later Rose came over to see me standing still next to my chair. There was a spilled cup of coffee on my desk and so many stuffed envelopes had sucked most of it under like a sponge.

"Oh! It's okay, Liddy-Jean!" she said. "Don't worry!"

"I never drink coffee," I said, as Rose disappeared to grab some paper towels. Rose called back that accidents happen, we just cannot have drinks at our desks anymore.

I had made enough spills in my life to know two things: Many of the envelopes were ruined . . . and I had not made this mistake.

While Rose cleaned up my mess, I watched Gina still staring at me. She was smiling.

The next day, after I borrowed a large envelope from the mail cart and told a small lie that it fell on the floor, I was allowed to walk all the way down the hall to the M-I-S Department. The first person I decided to talk to was a guy named Norman Winchell, because he has thick glasses just like me. He also smelled like the floor of dad's closet, so I liked him. Norman Winchell's head had one straight piece of hair sticking up on top, just like a radio antenna, and I liked him for that, too. I think the reason it looks like an antenna and not just a piece of stuck hair (I get those all the time and they never look like an antenna) is that he always has his arms bent in front of him typing on his keyboard like a praying mantis, only his arms are black, not green.

When I stood at Norman Winchell's door, he jerked his head up and looked very surprised and maybe even a little scared. The first time he did this, I turned around really quick because I thought there must be a giant spider behind me, since only something horrible could make someone have a surprised face like that. It turned out he had made that face just from seeing me.

I wanted to be brave, so I pretended I was Xena when I handed him his mail, and he just stared at me while I waited for him to say thank you. I had to wait a while. "Thank you," he finally said, before throwing the envelope in his trash can without even opening it.

"I am not allowed to throw away mail," I said. "Not since the electricity got shut off at my house."

"It's just people trying to sell me things," he said, and went back to his typing.

I whispered, "I do not like salesmen either," and I thought he smiled, but Norman Winchell stared back to his computer as if I had already left, but I saw him sneak a look from the corner of his eye, just like I do when I am spying. "I am still here," I said.

"Oh," he said, still not looking. I was starting to get sleepy listening to the wonderful sound of his keyboard. "Are those keys cherry browns, or reds?" but I wished I had not asked, since that made him stop typing.

"How do you know about cherry brown keys?"

"Everybody has YouTube," I answered, and his antenna nodded yes.

"I brought in this keyboard from home, it's retro," he said. I was not sure what that was, but before I could ask, he said, "Do you watch videos for tech information or just for the ASMR?

I got excited because I knew what A-S-M-R was. My Auntie Theresa told Mom it would help me relax if I watched videos of people doing things that make nice sounds, like typing or whispering, and she was right . . . but I am not allowed to watch the eating videos because Mom said it makes me beg for snacks.

I whispered, "A-S-M-R," and he got the geeky joke, just like I knew he would.

He nodded at me. "I only watch for the tech information, and I nodded back at him, wishing I had an antenna, too. I knew he may not have been telling the truth about that, since some boys liked to pretend they were too cool for A-S-M-R, and everybody knows watching tech video sounds way more cool than saying you listen to videos to get sleepy.

It was my turn to ask him a question, "Why is your department named Miss if there are no girls in here?"

"It's not pronounced Miss, its *M-I-S*. You say the letters."

"Like when I say swear words."

His antennae nodded again, and Norman looked around as if he had not noticed that girls were missing from the room. "We fix computers in here," he finally said.

"That's not a good reason for no girls," I said.

"It sure is not," he said, and I took out my notebook to write that one down, which took a while. I knew Norman Winchell wanted to ask what I was writing, but he didn't, and finally he started typing again. For a little while, I pretended we were working together, and I wondered if he was pretending that, too.

When I was finished writing in my notebook, I looked around at all the computer stuff and asked, "Who breaks them all?"

Norman Winchell sighed like I should already know that answer. So, I said, "I am not trying to get Negative Attention, I just don't know who breaks all the computers. Do you?"

"Nobody really breaks them, they just . . . don't work sometimes."

"Is it because they are not Macs?" I asked, and I saw the corner of his mouth bend a little like a smile, before he stopped it. He thought I was smart now.

I waited for him to say more stuff I could write down, but nothing came, so I went to the door and said, *"I'll be back!"* in my best Arnold Schwarzenegger voice, which made Norman Winchell stop typing and make that almost-smile again.

It took me a few more visits to M-I-S to figure out why all the computer guys seemed a little grumpy. Computer guys are smart and have to know a lot of things about their job before they ever come to their first day of work and cannot learn as they work, like I do. Since they fix computers, I was thinking people might treat them like they are mechanics and not business people (like what happens to my dad at work, too) and maybe this makes them not want to talk much.

On my next visit, I handed Norman the mail I borrowed off the cart and Norman pretended to lift a top hat off his head, bowed and said in a P-B-S special Oliver Twist voice: "Why, ffffank you, kind sir. May I haff anotha?"

I answered with a bow that was a bit too low (luckily, I didn't fall) and did my best Oliver voice, too. "Sorry, I only have one mail for you, kind sir."

Norman pretended to put his imaginary hat back on and even adjusted it before he went back to his keyboard. When he realized I was staring at him, we fell into a game of staring without blinking. He had no idea how good I was at this, and that I always beat my sister. But when he smirked at me, I blinked, and he did a fake sounding *Ha-ha!* laugh before he started typing extra-loud on his cherry brown keys.

On my next visit, Norman Winchell surprised me by asking, "You're Liddy-Jean, right?"

"Yes."

"You work in Marketing. With Gina and Rose."

I nodded yes.

"I like Rose," he said, staring at me like I should get his secret message. And I did.

"Everyone does," I said, and I wanted to break the news that Rose could not be his girlfriend, but I didn't want to make him cry. I liked him.

Norman said in a quiet Oliver Twist voice, "You should tewl that Rose to wotch out for huh selwf."

I forgot to do my Englishman accent. "What is she watching out for?" I whispered.

But I knew.

He stopped typing again and folded his arms across his chest like Clark Kent in his thick glasses, and that made me wonder if he was hiding his handsome (Sometimes handsome sneaks up like that.) He whispered in a regular voice this time, "I'm not supposed to tell you this, but in this department, we can see everything. Every email. *Everything.*" He pointed at me. "All I am saying is, if a boss is worried a person might be better at their job than they are, that person could be in trouble. That's all I'm saying. Because I like Rose."

I stood there a while longer, afraid to ask, but finally I did.

"What can I do if somebody spills things on my desk on purpose to get me and Rose in trouble?"

"*You* can't do anything. But if it were happening to me, I could do something. And of course, the CEO can do something. He's the boss of all the bosses and he says hello to me every time he sees me."

"What can I do if somebody is mean to me?"

"You can do this," Norman said, surprising me when he stuck up his middle finger in front of his nose and slowly pushed his glasses closer to his face with the bad finger.

"That's a good trick," I said, even though when he did it, his eyes crossed a little. I pulled my glasses down to the end of my nose and stuck up my middle finger and slowly pushed the glasses back up.

He nodded his head, and I nodded back.

Then he said, "We both have to go back to work now . . . so . . . bye."

"Bye," I said, but I went to the door extra slow so I could hear some more tapping from Norman's retro keyboard. Before I left his door, I made sure nobody would see me leaving, before I went back to the Marketing Department.

Licking the Tabs

When Dad got his new job, he took Mom and my sister and me to McDonald's for dinner to celebrate. We always got McDonald's from the drive-thru and ate in the car or at home so Dad would not have to buy expensive drinks, even though it was one of my dreams to eat inside a McDonald's restaurant and sip on a real orange soda with the squeaky loud straw, instead of pretending with an old McDonald's cup and orange Kool-Aid from home.

Tonight Mom said we should "splurge" and she ordered a double cheeseburger and Dad ordered his usual Big Mac but added a large fries for him and Mom and two other fries so my sister and I could each have one and not have to share! When we drove up to the next drive-thru window to pick up the food, I was so excited to have my very own fries. Not splitting only happened on our birthdays.

Right when we were getting our bags of McDonald's, our cousins pulled up alongside our car, and I heard Mom groan a little before she rolled down her window. She really didn't like my Dad's sister Judy very much, but me and my sister loved our cousins, who were waving to us like crazy from the back seat, just like we were.

My sister begged, "Mom, can we go over? *Pleeeease?*"

"No, honey, don't you want to eat before it gets cold?" Mom said. Then she shouted over to Aunt Judy and Uncle Jeff, "We decided to take the kids out for a treat!"

My uncle just nodded, and Aunt Judy leaned across my uncle to shout over to Mom, "That's nice. Same with us, we're just grabbing a quick bite on the way to the airport."

"Oh?" Mom said, and her *Oh* was not happy.

Auntie Judy said, "We're going inside to eat, since we are taking the kids to Disney World for a week."

My sister Dawn and me were silent as Mom handed us our white bags, which looked too small to have extra fries inside. Dawn whined, "They're going to Disney World? Can I go with them? *PLEEEASE* Mom?!"

I wanted to pinch her to make her stop acting like she was not happy with the McDonald's, but instead, I opened the bag to give Dawn first grab at the bags of fries, which I never do, and that shut her right up.

Mom said, "Oh, that's great, Judy, I'm sure the kids will love it. We'll have to take the girls sometime . . . well, have fun kids!" Mom sounded in a rush, even though we were just going to eat in the parking lot.

Mom waved as she rolled up her window even though Auntie Judy was still talking. When they pulled away in their giant car, I heard Mom sigh softly. Even Dad watched as they parked and walked inside to go eat. Dad liked orange sodas, too, and when I get one on my birthday, I always give him a sip.

Dad quietly said to Mom, "You know I'll take the girls someday."

Mom answered back, "Jeff is a doctor, you can't expect to—"

"I know," Dad said quickly. "Let's just park and eat in the car. This shit gets cold so fast."

I reminded Dad, "You said S-H-I-T."

"Can I take mine inside to go eat with them?" Dawn asked.

I answered her, "I was going to share my fries with you so you can have extra, unless you don't want to stay here."

Dawn was quiet after that and I slowed down my chewing, to try to make it last. Dawn did too, but it was hard because we were both very hungry. Maybe if I ate extra slowly, I could make the fries last till my birthday, when I would get my very own pack again. I wondered if I could ever make enough money to buy the large size fries for my whole family, the ones that stood up all on their own in a shiny red cardboard holder with yellow stripes inside that looks like a circus tent.

The next day I was hard at work in the Marketing Department, forgetting all about fries and Disneyland, and I felt lucky again, just like I did before we saw my cousins. I was working at a great job, and going to be a famous writer, plus I got to work with Rose three extra days a week for a whole extra hour each day, and that was way better than McDonald's and a Disney World vacation.

Later, when I stopped by Rose's office to say hello, Rose warned me, "I might have to change some of your writing just a little bit to make it more professional. Is that okay?"

When I did not answer, Rose said, "Even if it's true that some bosses aren't nice to workers, we can't leave it exactly like you wrote it, or people won't think it's a serious business book."

"But I really did hear one of the bosses call a worker a dumb A-S-S, which is way worse than a smart A-S-S."

"I believe you, but we still have to change it, just a little bit."

I didn't like this idea, but I did not want Rose to think I was Just Impossible to work with, like some famous people.

"Ok," I said.

Rose didn't know I told Mom I wanted to stay at work longer for no extra pay since Rose said she would stay late to teach me new office skills. I told her we were starting with keyboard training since M-I-S Norman Winchell had left on my desk my very own retro keyboard with Cherry Brown keys! Since Mom liked Rose so much, she said yes without even talking to Dad first. "*Pleases* and *thank yous* all over the place to Rose, and to Norman."

"I will thank Rose, but Norman Winchell pretends he didn't give me the keyboard."

"Does Rose know this Norman Winchell?"

"Yes, she likes him very much." I do not like lying to Mom, except when it is for her own goodness.

Monday was our first day to stay after work and when Rose first started reading from my notebooks, I got scared she might think they were stupid since she kept giggling and shaking her head like she could not figure out (like my Auntie Theresa says) What on God's Green Earth she was reading. Finally, after she had read the first notebook (I write very big) she closed it and stared at me, and I could tell she was surprised.

"Am I in big trouble?" I asked in my most quiet voice, as I secretly crossed my fingers on both hands under the big metal desk between us.

"No, Liddy-Jean, not at all!" she finally said. "I think this will be a brilliant book! I hardly know what to say—some of your observa— some of your writing is . . . so . . ." She stopped, and I waited, feeling the edges of my eyes burning like I might cry, wondering if she changed her mind.

"I love the way you write, Liddy-Jean—you are so smart!"

I was holding my breath and finally took in some new air. "Do you promise I am smart?"

"Yes, and I promise you, I'll do everything I can to help you turn this into a real book. If that doesn't work, there are also publishers that will let you make a real book if we just pay to get it printed."

My heart hurt as I thought about Mom and Dad's nighttime discussions about how even though Dad got a new job, they were not sure how they could pay The Center this year. I could not ask for money. Besides, I wanted it to be a surprise. When I wiped one eye Rose said, "Don't worry about the cost, Liddy. I can take care of that if we have to." Then she stuck out her hand across the desk and we shook hands, as she said, "It will be my honor to help you make this a real book. You never know . . . maybe it will be so good, we'll find a real publisher to print it for us!"

"Can we do that now?"

"First we have to get these notebooks organized," she said. "That probably means we'll have to pull all these notebook pages out to make piles of all the different things you've written about. Is that okay?"

That was another idea I did not like one bit.

"It won't look like a book anymore," I said.

"It will later. And I will sit right here next to you the whole time while we tear out the pages," she said. I agreed, but it was only because I was already dizzy from her perfume.

I was glad I did agree, since she showed me how to use the three-hole punch that Gina said I could not touch because it was dangerous. Rose also gave me my very own Big Binder, not a kindergarten rainbow-colored one, a grown-up black one with thick shiny metal rings that could pinch my fingers and hold all the notebook paper.

Then Rose used special thick yellow pages to make book chapters and they each had colorful plastic flags Rose called *Tabs*. The Tabs looked just like flattened Jolly Rancher hard candy: lemon, lime, cherry, and grape, except the grape looked like a lollipop I once left in the bathtub too long and the color leaked out.

When Rose wasn't looking, I licked the red one just to make sure it did not taste like cherries. They didn't taste bad, but the plastic smell was nothing like cherry. Just to be sure, when Rose went to the bathroom, I gave a lick to all the other colors, too, but they all had one flavor: plastic.

I wrote on the bottom of one of my lists: "Employees would be happier if you could taste more of the office supplies," but then I realized this sounded like something a kid might wish for, so I scribbled it out. Besides, I didn't want Rose to be suspicious that I had been licking the Tabs. Now that I was going to be a famous writer, I had to stop doing kid things.

GOTCHA!

In my chapter about paychecks, I told the story how I earned six dollars shoveling snow and used the money to buy seven packs of tropical fruit Bubble Yum bubble gum, but I tried to eat it all at once so I would not have to share, and gagged until I threw up on the driveway. Mom made me leave it and I got in trouble when I sneaked back to pick it up with my mittens and ended up with mitten gum in my mouth.

Even though she was laughing like crazy, Rose suggested we had to "edit" this story out, and I told her it was Just Plain Silly to take out things that made her laugh, so she put it in the "Maybe" pile.

She smiled at me and gave the very top of my head a soft scratch so I would giggle. I loved when Rose did this, but she was the only one. Sometimes adults touch me like they are petting a dog, or a very little kid. But whenever Rose did that, I heard a Christmas song in my head: "Joy to the World."

"We have something to celebrate," Rose said.

"Like with cake?" I asked.

Rose told me she had a great idea about my book which could help it get published and we could talk about it more after work. "Liddy-Jean, I think this book is going to bring you lots more Egg McMuffins!"

I hoped this was true and since all I wanted to do was work on our project together, I said to Rose just like the Customer Service Ladies: "I cannot wait for the end of this workday!"

Finally five o'clock came and after everyone left, Rose could not wait to type the first two chapters with her pretty and super speedy fingers, but she stopped typing when I said, "Gina asked me what we are doing after work."

Even though Rose never has to look at the keyboard to type, she stopped typing when she looked at me. "What did you answer?"

I whispered even though nobody was there. "I told her you were teaching me extra work skills." I knew it was the right answer because Rose gave me a quick hug. I did not want Rose to worry about helping me, and I did not tell her the only thing I worried about was having a drink on my desk where Gina would spill it again.

The next day at work, I spotted on my desk a little round computer web camera, just like the ones I saw in the M-I-S department. It was pointed right where I always keep my soda. There was a tiny note folded and taped to it. Carefully, I took the note near the camera, and read it. It was just like the note Norman Winchell left me when he gave me a special keyboard at my desk, only this note said:

"Smile, kind sir, you're on Candid Camera!"

Later, I asked Rose what Candy Camera was, and she said, "Candid Camera? That is an old TV show where they use a secret camera to watch people do things." After hearing this, I went back to the little camera and gave a secret wave and tried not to look at it all day.

I made sure to put my drink where the camera was looking. I also made my drinks last the whole rest of the day, hoping my plan will work. When I came back from the bathroom, I saw my drink had spilled all over the folders on my desk that I was supposed to file, and Gina was in Rose's office asking who would be cleaning up the mess on my desk.

When Gina walked away, Rose said, "Sorry, Liddy-Jean, this is my fault—I thought the lid made it safe, but Gina says no more drinks at your desk, okay?"

"Sorry, Rose," I said, hiding my smile, because I was thinking: *Gotcha!*

Turtle Babies

I knew all about sex because a long time ago the counselors at The Center told Mom I had been asking a lot of questions about it, so Auntie Theresa told me I had to be Fast Tracked so I could learn stuff right away. Mom finally had that talk with me on my bed in the daytime. Since I was eighteen years old, Mom did not want me to hear this crazy news from anyone else but her.

I did not tell Mom, but I had already heard this news from the older kids at The Center. It turned out everything I had heard was true . . . except when David Burke said a turtle can come out of a girl if you have sex with a boy.

I guessed David was being stupid as usual, but since I want to know everything, he said, "When my mom was not watching TV with me, I saw a lady having a turtle baby on TV."

"A turtle popped out of the lady's vagina."

I ran to get Mom to tell her that a woman was having a turtle out of her vagina. But Mom said it was just a baby's head coming out, but I didn't believe her because she shut the TV off quick like she was lying about the turtle.

I would rather hear about sex from the other kids at The Center, since Mom is very uncomfortable talking about what a penis is for. (Turns out, it is not just for peeing.) When she told me this baby news, I asked a few questions while I had the chance.

"If I get stabbed with a penis, can I have a turtle instead of a baby?"

Mom answered, "Of course not, Liddy-Jean. And there is no stabbing," but I could tell she was hiding something.

Mom told me about sex that day and at first, I thought she was joking, except she looked scared to death to tell me about this penis business. She also said girls only could have a real baby, never a turtle, and I should remember that babies wake you up in the middle of the night. Mom knows how much I hate that, so this was the day I decided if a penis only made babies instead of turtles or puppies, I would stay far away from them.

I had chances to see a penis before Mom had warned me, and before that talk, I took every chance I could to sneak a peek. The boys at The Center were very interested in their penises and they spent a lot of time trying to get girls to be as interested too, but the girls never were.

Except me.

The first time I saw one it was from a younger boy named Dennis who said he had to pee but forgot to go to the bathroom first before he took it right out in the TV room at The Center when the counselors were busy getting the lunch table ready.

"My mom told me a long time ago that your privates are called private for a reason," I said, and the counselors walked him to the bathroom. The counselors acted like it was a very big deal and they even called his father to come pick him up and that was the last day I saw Dennis Burke.

"Can a girl make another girl have a baby?" I asked my mother during our talk.

Mom looked at me a long time before answering, "Yes, two women can have a baby, they can adopt, or get a man to . . . or if they use a . . .well, never mind the details. Do you remember what I told you about penises?"

"How could I forget?" I said, and I didn't want her to repeat the story, so I hit Mom with another question.

"If I don't want to have a baby that a penis makes, is it better to have a girlfriend instead of a boyfriend?"

Mom stared at me longer than when I had asked her about trading a baby for a turtle. Or maybe she was wondering why she did not think of having a girlfriend instead of a boyfriend before me.

Mom said, "Well you probably won't *want* to have a girlfriend instead of a boyfriend."

"Why not?" I asked, thinking of the tons of girls I liked better than boys.

Mom said, "Because girls *usually* would rather be with boys."

This wasn't true of any girl I knew, but I Let the Subject Drop as Mom tells me to do when I ask questions that give her a headache.

Today was a book working night, and Rose and I had been working a while before I went over to the table closest to Rose to work on my papers about bosses in the company and how they could behave better. Like the time I heard the Marketing Girls talk about a certain boss "rhymes with Tina" who goes through the trash to spy on the workers.

I forgot to pretend I was not listening, so I said, "I know how to rhyme, you mean Gina." They all stopped talking so I said, "Leave notes in the trash for them to read," and the girls laughed like it was the best idea ever.

Rose and I were working alone when she leaned over me to read my papers, and so my hand forgot how to write because she was leaning so close to me. When she was finished leaning over me, she did what she always does and gave my shoulder a good job pat. This made me think I liked girls better than boys. I didn't want to have another talk about it, so I decided tomorrow, when Steve is in the office, I could go visit his office to look at his muscles, just to make sure.

Rose said, "Sorry to distract you from your writing, Sweetie. But do you remember my suggestion about how we can make the book more fun to read?"

"No," I said.

"I told you when you were eating your Egg McMuffin, so maybe you didn't hear me. I suggested we might want to write the book as if we are teaching the employees how they can become bad bosses . . . how a Worker Bee can learn to become a Wand-Waver."

Her leaning so close had given me goose bumps which she might see on my arms. Just in case, I said, "You can't be my girlfriend."

"Why would you say that Liddy-Jean, of course we're girlfriends," she said.

"It would give my mom a headache, and you have a boyfriend," I said.

I did not mention the other reason, that I was pretty sure Rose might be closer to my mother's age than to mine, but I was not allowed to ask age questions anymore since Mom got mad at me for asking Mrs. Williams if she was seventy-five. (I was way off.)

Rose just smiled at me.

"Did I hurt your feelings?" I asked.

"Of course not," she said.

"It is not because of your old age. It is just because you already have a boyfriend named Gary," I said.

"Do the girls at work talk about him?" Rose asked.

I could not tell her that all the Marketing Girls thought he was a rotten boyfriend, and they said they were never, ever wrong about boyfriends.

"No," I lied and pretended to erase something in my notebook.

"What do you think of my suggestion, Liddy-Jean? It might be a funnier way to do the book. I tried it on the introduction, still using all your ideas, but making it more ironic—um, more like a joke, to teach people how to be the boss."

I felt lucky that Rose changed the subject.

I said, "But then the workers do less than they do now, since the bosses don't do much."

Rose smiled. "That is why it would be funny to read," she said, "and it would probably make it sell better in a bookstore."

She got me with that last one. I wanted it to sell more at a bookstore, so I agreed, even though I did not think it was a good idea at all to teach people how to do their jobs badly.

Rose figured out I was not happy about this idea and said, "It will be a 'How To' book to teach how to go from a Worker Bee to a Wand-Waver and at the same time we will be teaching people what not to do when they are a boss."

Then she smiled at me so sweetly that I imagined myself turning into melted candy on a cooking pan.

I decided to trust that Rose was making us a good book, so I told her I liked it very much even though I was too tired to read all those words. When we were done editing, she did what she always does and moved our book to a different place in her office and hid it under a stack of yellow envelopes.

"Why do you keep moving our book?"

"Just keeping it private," she said.

In my house the word "private" meant something that had nothing to do with books. I warned her, "Nobody should look at other people's privates."

"No, they shouldn't," Rose said.

PART 2
PLAY

Rose Likes to Say Her Name

I got some big bad news today.

Rose told me a new girl my age would be starting work in our department soon. She said she might be very shy, just like I was on my first day, so we had to help make her feel comfortable. I asked Rose if she was from The Center and she said no, but she does go to a place like The Center.

I do not like this idea at all, so I folded my arms and pinched my armpits to remind me to keep them folded. "Is she a Slow Learner like me?" I asked in my grumpy voice, and Rose looked surprised because I have never been fresh at work.

"She has some learning challenges, Liddy-Jean. We should never call anyone slow." She was right. Mom hates when anybody says that, mostly me. But I was angry.

I said, "One slow person for each department is plenty. Can we send her to work in the Shipping Department? That is all the way downstairs and slow people can move boxes. I have seen them."

Rose put her arm around me, like Mom sometimes does. Jackie noticed so she came rushing over. I have not seen Jackie since she said Gina decided her new job was to run all over Boston for Gina's dry cleaning and wine.

"What's the matter Liddy-Jean, don't you feel well?" Jackie asked.

I did not feel well, and I did not look up.

I stared at Rose's pretty shoes instead. She was wearing the sandals that looked like they had twisted red licorice strips for laces.

Rose said to Jackie, "I told her about the young woman coming to work with us, and Liddy-Jean isn't so sure it's a good idea."

"*Correction*," I said, putting my pointer finger up to the sky, like Mom sometimes does. "I am *very sure* it is not a good idea." I left my finger up for a while so they would know I meant business.

Jackie whispered to Rose, "Gina doesn't either."

I looked up and saw Jackie trying to hide a smile, but then I looked at Rose, who had a worried face on for me, and this is secretly one of my favorite faces. (Mom says it is because I get Full Attention.)

Jackie said, "We were hoping you would like to teach her all sorts of things you have learned about your job. You could be a good friend to her."

"No," I said, wanting to go home before I might cry at work. I squeezed my armpits harder so I would not make tears.

"I bet she'll be nice," Rose said, tightening her arm around my shoulder. Then Rose made me sit down at a table with her and Jackie. She kept her arm around me so I decided this might be a lucky table and I should eat my lunches on this table from now on.

Rose whispered, "You know you will always be our favorite, no matter who else comes to work here. You know that, don't you?" I liked the way Rose's arm felt around me, so I did not answer right away. This scheme worked because she hugged me even tighter to get my Full Attention and because of the hug, my chin accidentally was on her boob, which was very warm.

While I was wondering if boobs ever got fevers, Jackie said, "You know, Rose and I were thinking that you might be ready to train someone all on your own. If you promised to be nice and professional, we could start Kenzie off as your assistant."

They already had a name for her.

"Who's Kenzie?" I said, because I was not ready to stop being grumpy yet.

"That's the new young woman," Rose said. "You'll like her. I spoke with her mother on the phone, and she said Kenzie is looking forward to meeting you most of all, since she might not have as many friends as you do. I told Kenzie's mom how smart you are at your job and how quickly you learned to do everything around here. We all hope you will teach Kenzie everything you know about being a Marketing Girl."

She can buy my F-ing book, I thought only in my mind, because I would never say the real F-word, even in my imagination. But then I thought, I would like to teach someone to be a Marketing Girl. Maybe if Rose saw what a good teacher I was, she would like me even more than she does now.

When Jackie went back to her desk, Rose whispered so only I could hear: "Training a new person would make a great chapter for your book." And when she smiled, I smiled back.

The next day I was working at my new favorite table stuffing envelopes when the new girl came in with her mother. It made me remember my own first day and how scared I was to take a job, so I decided I should be Kenzie's friend as long as she wasn't a big jerk. If she was a big jerk, I would have my Plan B. I know about Plan B from Dad who says to always have one. My Plan B was to leave Rose for a whole day while I played sick at home watching game shows. Then maybe they would fire the new girl and beg me to come back to work.

As soon as she saw me, the girl named Kenzie walked away from her mother and came over to me. "Are you Liddy-Jean?" she asked. She didn't seem shy like they had promised.

"Yes," I said, noticing that her hair was almost the same color brown as Rose's hair, but her eyes were blue instead of brown. Her hair looked nothing like her mother's, and I wondered if Rose noticed too, since Rose was staring at Kenzie's mother's hair while they talked, because her mother's hair was long and gold, just like a queen's hair from a fairy tale.

"Can you teach me to do that?" Kenzie asked, pointing down to my table.

She was staring at my envelopes as if they were warm chocolate chip cookies and I remembered the first time I saw a stack of envelopes, dying to get my hands on them.

"Yes. I can teach you, easy-peasy!" I said, forgetting all about my plan to be mean because anyone who wanted to stuff an envelope that badly should be able to.

The first time I saw Jackie and Rose at a table stuffing envelopes, I watched their hands for a long time because they moved so fast! I wished that someday I could be able to stuff envelopes that fast. I hoped Kenzie will think that when she sees my skills.

Kenzie said, "My mom says I should help you with anything you ask because you're a good worker."

I liked this Kenzie-girl.

"O-K Kenzie-girl," I said, and I put my hand on her shoulder. "It will take you a long time to get good at your job like me, but that is O-K." I felt a little bad about being fresh, but she didn't seem to notice and was smiling at me. Kenzie had pretty, long hair (not the Standard Hair Cut like I had from The Center) and I worried the Marketing Girls might like her better than me . . . because I might like her better than me.

She walked over to my side of the table and stood right against my elbow. "My name is Kenzie," she said.

"I know," I said, and I made her wait a little while for the envelopes, since every time I saw somebody in training in the Marketing Department, they were always standing around waiting. "Excuse me please, I have to write that in my book."

"Write what?"

"Everyone has to wait for training. This is one of the things at work that should be better," I said. I knew Kenzie was watching as I wrote in my notebook, and I remembered to write in short sentences just like Rose is teaching me:

Wait too long for training.

Kenzie was bending down staring at my writing like I was already famous, and I guessed maybe she couldn't write as good as me. Across the room, I heard Kenzie's mother tell Rose that she swore she told the truth about how shy Kenzie was.

Rose laughed and said, "Everyone loves Liddy-Jean. Kenzie will have fun working here, Mrs. . . . ."

"Please, call me Jenny," Kenzie's mom said, putting her hand out to shake, "Mrs. is definitely not me."

"Same here," Rose said, and they both laughed, even though there was nothing funny going on. I hoped Rose wouldn't like Kenzie as much as she liked Kenzie's mother.

"That's my mom," Kenzie said to me, and I noticed she liked to point to whatever she was talking about, so I pointed at her mother, too.

"Where is your dad?" I asked.

"I only have one mom," she answered. "I used to have two moms, but now I just have one, like everybody does."

My stomach hurt when I thought of what it would be like to not have Dad, and it made me want to share my dad with her. I decided I would always be nice to Kenzie. I said, "My dad would like you because he likes blue eyes."

"I have green eyes, like my mom," and she pointed to her mom again. I grabbed her face and held her cheeks with both of my hands so I could check out the color of her eyes while she giggled.

They looked blue to me, but I shut up about it because of the missing dad thing, but I worried they sent us a girl who does not know her colors. It will be all up to me to make sure she uses the right Color Tabs. I could not wait to tell her not to lick them.

I showed Kenzie how to stuff the envelopes and how to sort them into small piles so they do not tip over. Before I could ask if she could count, I saw she was very good at counting to ten, and she kept looking up at my face to see if she was doing it right, and I liked that. *A lot.*

"That's good," I kept saying, and every time I did, she got so happy and smiled really big, so I said it a lot. I liked teaching someone that isn't my sister, especially since she was looking at my hands as if I was stuffing envelopes fast.

Rose talked with Kenzie's mom for a long time, and laughed more with her than she does in a whole day.

When her mom called her to get Kenzie to say goodbye, she shook her head no, because she wanted to keep stuffing envelopes so she could someday get as fast as me. I whispered, "Go hug your mom, or you will be sad when she leaves," and she did what I told her to do.

I liked being a boss.

When her mom finally stopped talking to Rose and left, Kenzie pretended not to notice and whispered: "Mothers treat you like babies, don't they?" I said yes, and I could not think of having two of them!

I showed Kenzie all the most important things, like the best place to put your lunch, and where all three candy and soda machines were, and of course the bathroom, where I knew she would love the squirt bottle of soap as much as I did. Lisa P. and Jackie told me I could show Kenzie around the building, and we were gone a long time.

When we got back, Lisa P. yelled, "Well, here they are! You look like best friends!" Jackie and even Rose looked so relieved about this, and I wondered if they thought I would punch her.

I would not have punched Kenzie even if she was mean, because she was smaller and wore extra girly clothes, not like me. She wore a pink shirt with a real skirt, not the kind that was secretly shorts, with sparkle leggings and dressy shoes like I had one time when I made my First Communion and refused to take a white Necco Wafer from a stranger, before I knew he was the priest.

Her shoes looked nice, but Kenzie said they hurt her feet a lot and she had begged her mother to buy them for her first day at work, so she had to wear them. She did this thing with her eyes whenever she talked about how much her mother babied her, where they rolled around in her head extra fast. I liked it, so I asked a lot of questions about her mother, so she would do it some more. When she looked down at the envelopes, I would secretly practice rolling my eyes too, until I started to feel dizzy.

Later, when Kenzie went off to the bathroom for the first time all by herself, Rose came by the table and said, "Hi there, stranger!"

I had forgotten about her all day because of Kenzie! The truth was, I forgot about her and the Wand-Wavers and Worker Bees book, too!

"Are we still working on the book after work?" Rose asked with such a pretty smile that I could not imagine how I could have forgotten about her. I told her yes, but as soon as work was over, it was Kenzie's idea for us both to go downstairs to the glass lobby to wait for her to be picked up while we pretended to be at a bus stop, so I had to ask Rose if it was O-K.

Kenzie had a lot of good ideas, but when we walked down the hallway, she said we should run, and I had to be a boss again and tell her we cannot run at work. So, instead she walked beside me holding my hand and swinging it back and forth as we laughed. I told her we were walking as fast as the salesmen did, only without the *whoosh-whoosh* sound of the shiny pants they wore, and she covered her mouth with her hand laughing her head off and saying "*Whoosh-whoosh!*"

We were both surprised when Kenzie's mom found us in the hallway before we got to the lobby. At first Kenzie was mad she had ruined our plans for playing the Bus Stop game by coming upstairs, but then I said, "You have to give your mom a hug," and after she did that, she forgot about being mad that her mom interrupted our game, and started telling her mom all about our day.

Kenzie's mom said, "Should I go let Rose know I'm taking you now?"

"I can tell her," I said, but I saw she didn't like the idea of not seeing Rose again and I did not blame her one bit.

Kenzie's mom said, "Maybe I should, since it's the first day."

I told her the bad news. "Rose is in a meeting with Gina who is having a very bad headache day."

Kenzie's mom looked disappointed about Gina's headache, but she smiled at me and said, "Okay Liddy-Jean. Thanks for being such a good friend to Kenzie on her first day. I owe you an ice cream. Rose, too." I jumped around and yelled *Yay* too loud when I heard this, since the idea of ice cream makes me forget I cannot yell at work. Kenzie copied me and we jumped together before hugging goodbye.

When I got back to the Marketing Department and told Rose that Kenzie's mom said goodbye and that she owes us ice cream, Rose walked fast to the doorway to see if she was still in the hallway.

"I told Kenzie's mom she couldn't come up to say goodbye to you since you had a meeting with You-Know-Who," I said, pointing to Gina's door, just like Kenzie would, and I rolled my eyes like her too.

"Jenny wanted to come say goodbye?" Rose asked, and I wondered why she looked sad.

"You bet she did," I said, and Rose smiled and smoothed her hair even though it was perfect.

Later, when the work day was over, Rose and I worked hard on the book, and I forgot all about Kenzie. It was strange how it worked like that. Rose said it was important for everyone to have friends our own age. Then she talked for a while about how nice Kenzie's mother was, and that her name was Jennifer, but she likes to be called Jenny.

"Can I call her that?" I asked, knowing I should not.

"We can ask next time she comes in," Rose said. "Did Kenzie tell you Jenny is an artist?"

"No. She told me that she treats Kenzie like a baby."

"She's just protecting her."

"Because she doesn't have a dad?" I asked.

"I—didn't know," Rose said.

"Kenzie used to have two moms but now she just has one, like me. She also wants me to pretend her eyes are not blue. She says they are green like her mom's," I said.

"Jenny's eyes are definitely green," Rose said, and she stared out the window, maybe to look at the blue sky, just to make sure.

After we were both writing for a long time, I heard Rose say to herself, "I can't imagine raising a child on my own," but I had no idea what she was talking about since I was writing a really smart part in the book with a lot of clever clues on how to spot a Wand-Waver.

"That must be hard for Jenny...Kenzie's mom," she said, but mostly to herself, as she ran her hand through her hair again. Then she looked at the ends of her hair like she was disappointed, and I was sure she was thinking about Kenzie's mother's perfect gold hair.

"Jenny's artwork is shown in galleries all over the country. Maybe next time she comes by, I'll ask her to show me the gallery in the city. Maybe this Saturday, unless she is busy painting . . ." Rose looked out the window again as she said so quietly, I could barely hear her, "I wonder how many hours a day a painter paints . . ."

"Six," I said, and for some reason, Rose laughed.

"If we go, would you want to come too, to keep Kenzie company?"

I tried to wink at Rose, but both my eyes closed. "Only if we can cash in on that ice cream . . . and if my mom says yes."

Any extra time with Rose was O-K by me, and I thought about how the Marketing Girls say Rose is always alone on the weekends and I was happy she was planning something fun with me and Kenzie, because I needed to find out if Kenzie wore her girly clothes on weekends, too.

I kept writing, but I noticed Rose was still pulling on the ends of her hair, maybe to make them grow, like I used to before Mom figured out that's why I was getting my mysterious headaches. "That doesn't work," I said.

"What doesn't work?"

"Pulling your hair will not make it grow like Kenzie's mom's hair and it gives you a headache."

Rose laughed at first, and then dropped her hand to her desk. I did not understand how anybody as pretty as Rose wanted to look like any other girl. But I understood later, since as soon as I got home, I asked Mom if I could borrow some of her Girl Clothes.

My first week with Kenzie went by fast and I knew she had a good time because when Friday afternoon came, she looked like she was going to cry because she would miss work. I wanted to tell her that crying at work would hurt her career, and if she cried, I would have to give her a Stern Warning.

I did not have to wait long.

When Kenzie's mom showed up early, she did cry, and her mother said, "Now Kenzie, I know I'm a little early, but don't worry, I'll wait for it to be five o'clock."

"But you've ruined the Bus Stop game," she said.

I butted in, "She wanted to wait for you in the glass lobby that looks like a bus stop."

"Oh, I see. I'll go back down in a minute. I want to say hello to someone first," she said, looking around the room like she lost a puppy.

"Okay but then go right downstairs, okay, Mom?" Kenzie said.

"Okay, honey, no worries." We watched her walk away, her hair moving like a waterfall as she turned to look in each of the offices.

"Rose is away in a meeting," I said.

"Oh," she said, "thank you, Liddy-Jean." Even though she smiled at me, she looked sad not to see Rose. "I guess I'll wait downstairs for Kenzie, then."

"Yes, Mom. Please!" Kenzie rolled her eyes to the back of her head. I think Kenzie wanted to look like a cool college girl when she did that, but she looked more like a zombie, so I made a note in my notebook to tell her to cool it on the eye-rolling.

We waited for a while stuffing more envelopes so her mom would have time to go all the way to her car, so we could wait like a real bus stop in the lobby.

Rose came back in the room in a hurry, just as Kenzie and I were leaving.

"Kenzie, is your mom here yet?" Rose asked.

"She was. She came early," Kenzie said, still pouting. "I told her to wait in the car."

"Oh," Rose said. "Then, I'll walk you down to her."

"No, thank you. Because Liddy-Jean is coming with me," Kenzie said, and when she went to put on her coat, I watched Rose looking sad that we were leaving. Kenzie did not notice and waved at Rose like she was on top of a float in the Macy's Thanksgiving Day parade. "Goodbye!!"

Rose waved back and then angrily looked down at her watch as if it was broken. She jumped when she saw me in her doorway.

"Kenzie's mom was looking for you," I said.

"Jenny did? How nice," she said as she got up from her chair. "Did she need to talk to me? Maybe I should go downstairs—"

"Yes, you should." I was telling a Small Lie, but it worked because Rose looked so happy again. "But you have to let Kenzie and me wait at the bus stop for a minute before you come outside."

"Yes, of course," Rose said, smiling.

Kenzie's mother waited before driving the car around to the pretend bus stop to pick Kenzie up at the door. Rose waited inside too, but not in the lobby with us so we could be alone at the bus stop. Even though Mom tells me I am one of the grown-ups now, luckily, Rose knew it would be no fun if a grown-up stood at the pretend bus stop with us.

Before Kenzie left, she turned to kiss my ear goodbye, and I laughed when we bonked heads. "Bye, bye, love!" she said in a voice that sounded a lot like her mom. As soon as Kenzie was out the door, Rose followed, and walked outside toward Jenny's car, tugging at the ends of her hair as she walked. I will remind her about that hair thing again.

Jenny spotted her and got out of the car to give her daughter a kiss hello and to shake Rose's hand like business people do and I watched them talk for a long time. Every time Jenny spoke, Rose would laugh and tug on her own hair again, and I wondered if Jenny was a comedian instead of an artist, since she must be very funny to make Rose laugh so much.

Kenzie was making faces in the window at me, and I guessed right that she was trying to act like a dog when she started panting and licking the inside of the car window. I was still laughing when the car pulled away and Rose came back inside the glass lobby. She was still looking at the car driving away, so she bumped into me.

"Oh! Liddy-Jean," she said, "what do you think about asking your mom to call me tonight to see if you can go to an art gallery with Jenny, Kenzie and me this Saturday?"

"Is a gallery just for grown-ups?" I asked, thinking the ice cream idea was much better.

"No, no. Anyone can go, and Jenny invited us both."

"You like to say her name," I said, and I saw Rose's face change color.

"What?" Rose said, laughing, but it was her fake laugh, the one she saves for Gina. As she walked away from me, she said, "You're so silly today . . . and what on earth were you and Kenzie laughing at when Jen—when they left?"

"Kenzie was pretending to be a dog in the car." I decided to keep the window-licking part out of it so Kenzie wouldn't get into trouble, since most adults are very picky about what you lick.

I watched Rose smoothing her hair as she went back up the steps to the offices, and I was excited to spend a Saturday with Kenzie. It wasn't until I was home asking Mom to call Rose, that I realized Rose and I forgot to say goodbye to each other.

ROSE

I am trying not to notice my hands are trembling, but how can I ignore this? I can barely write. If it's fear, it's a kind I haven't felt. This is more the rollercoaster variety . . . overwhelming fear, enveloped in excitement. But why? Because I met someone extraordinary, and she happens to be a she? I wish it were that simple. Or . . . do I? The truth is, I'm instantly addicted to the adrenaline rush of being rattled in just this way. If I am being honest, and I shouldn't, *I love it.*

"Please, call me J.," she said, and the name entered my veins—why do I want to say (and write) that name so badly? Why was I so desperate to get home, to escape and to lock the door behind me, to pull my notebook out from the bathroom closet? *WTF.*

From the closet.

Whatever this is—just take it, don't question it, don't squash it, like before. But this isn't like before. Feeling my heart, my blood moving, my breathing. For the first time. This would be laughable—*if it weren't so real.* At least from my view. It's as real as it can be, broadcasting live, and silent, from the bathroom closet.

Nothing has been real until now. *Not. One. Single. Thing.*

I know my hands are shaking because I might just do whatever it takes to *keep* feeling this way. Even though I know it's *impossible* that I'm not alone in how I feel. Of course, I am alone. There cannot be two people in the world that feel exactly this way.

Don't think about it.

It's done—you called LJ's mother, she asked what was wrong (she heard my voice tremble!), and the date is planned. Not a date, but whatever it is, it is mine at least for now, for a little while longer. Damn—the ridiculous *thrill* of texting J.— not breathing until the text pinged back, that crazy rush like I am fifteen again . . . what is wrong with me? I am not fifteen, I have wasted more than half of my lived life. My *not-lived life*.

That light color green. Even if I never see it again, if J. comes to her senses (why did I agree to meet this woman, I who am not free to meet anyone, I who am not free to write in a notebook in my own living room?) and if I come to my senses (what makes me think for a second this miraculous thing could be mine?) and even if I could stop moving forward, to never see what I saw today—I would still see that color everywhere, every day, every minute. There is a word for this. *Thunderstruck.* And it only happens once.

I have been writing for hours, I need a new notebook . . .

Maybe a green one.

JENNY

I couldn't help but notice Rose. Aren't Roses meant to be noticed?

I mean, so what that I noticed?

Easy now . . . third time I've told myself that today. *I can see what you're doing, and you need to slow the hell down.* True, I haven't felt alive in years. Not since the blackness of that first year, followed by the emptiness of the last few. Not since losing my whole life, Michelle, everything except our Kenzie, who kept me alive.

She is still what keeps me alive on my worst days. It certainly wasn't through any strength of my own. And it wasn't my painting, which I continued, but couldn't *feel* anymore. I painted to keep a roof over my head, to buy my daughter everything she needed or wanted, except the one thing I could not give back to her.

There was no joy, no passion for the work anymore . . . my art suffered along with me, even if I was the only one who noticed. As long as the paintings sold, the gallery was happy. Makes me wonder, what did anyone see in the paintings before, when I was alive, in love, and painting with a sane mind?

Anyone would notice a woman that beautiful. It might mean nothing more than that. Or . . . maybe I've still been living all this time, like a flower buried under last winter's snow. Had I been waiting for spring? Some sign that my life could return some day? More likely,

Rose is just a beautiful woman put in my path, and I am simply still human to notice her.

Since losing Michelle, I sleep motionless, as if I am the one trapped under a thick, frozen blanket. Afraid to move and slide to the empty space at my side, I lie on my back with my arms across my chest. So morbid, yet so comforting to imagine I could leave this Earth to be with her. But then I remember Kenzie and uncross my arms and feel the pain of staying.

As sleep would come, my thoughts of joining her would startle me awake, the greater fear of leaving my daughter kickstarting my heart back to life, reality gripping me until I lay blinking at the ceiling in the dark.

And now, who would have guessed I could crack through the frozen crust, roll to my left, and actually feel the cold side of my bed . . . I am still alive. Who knew?

I must have looked like an idiot when I came back upstairs looking for Rose. Kenzie didn't notice, but Liddy-Jean did. And when Rose wasn't there, I acknowledged feeling a tiny loss . . . such a strange feeling that loss was not connected to Michelle. Then, just as I was scolding myself for looking like a fool trying to find her, Rose showed up in the parking lot, and as she walked toward the car, I felt a distant tapping inside my crushed heart. What was that in there?

"Liddy-Jean said you were looking for me?" Rose said.

Yes, I sure was, and she caught me. *I suppose I* was *looking for you,* I thought as I wondered, why do you tug on your hair as if there is something about you not perfect? God has a sick sense of humor if a woman this beautiful doesn't know how ridiculously perfect she is. And why is it I actually *feel* her laugh?

So, what if I was looking for her? So, what if she came out to find me? So, what if I heard shyness in her voice when she asked about the gallery . . . was she fishing for an invitation? Before I had decided to, I told her I could show her the gallery if she had time this weekend, and her immediate answer made me catch my breath.

"I would love that," she said.

She would love that, a voice echoed inside me. *Did you hear that?*

And we made a date. An innocent date . . . after all, I know a straight woman when I see one. So, what's wrong with appreciating, or daring to notice, a rose? What's wrong with wanting to know her? And why was the whispering voice inside me (the one I always thought of as Michelle) now sounding playful and teasing, "This Rose could be your spring."

I whisper, "Go easy." Remember, when you are given a beautiful flower, it can bring you so much joy, right up until the moment it disappears.

One Sundae, Two Spoons

Mom waved to Rose from the door when she picked me up on Saturday because I asked her not to come to the car. Kenzie says that's what little kids' moms do when they are getting picked up, so she did not like it, so I did not like it either.

Rose looked so pretty that when I saw her, I accidentally told her a secret.

"I don't want to share you," and Rose gave my arm a soft squeeze. But I was wrong about that because as soon as we got to the gallery and I saw Kenzie outside spinning around a street lamp dressed in her pretty Girl Clothes, I begged Rose to let me jump out of the car.

"There she is," Rose said, but she was looking at Jenny sitting on a bench, sketching flowers that were the same yellow as her hair. Rose whispered, "Someone should be sketching her . . ."

I asked, "Please let me jump out? I want to surprise Kenzie before she sees me!"

Rose made me wait until she parked, but she did let me run ahead of her to sneak up on Kenzie as she was twirling around the lamp. She must have made herself dizzy since when I said "Boo!" she let go of the lamp, and fell backwards into the grass, right on her butt, laughing just like Mom did one night after a New Year's Eve party.

Kenzie's mom had most of her hair piled up fancy, except for the extra pieces that bounced around her face like wavy spaghetti, which made me think of lunch, and I thought maybe Rose thought so too. She was wearing a long skirt just like Rose, even though Rose never wore skirts in the office.

"Do you like spaghetti?" I asked Jenny.

"Hi Liddy-Jean, of course I do!"

"I think Rose likes it too," I said, watching her hair pieces bounce in the wind. Rose finally caught up to us and Jenny said, "You and Rose both look so pretty, but you didn't have to get dressed up."

"No?" Rose said as she looked at Jenny's pretty outfit with a big smile. "Well, I'm glad I did, or I would be feeling underdressed about now."

Rose asked where Jenny got her earrings from, and when Jenny said she made them, Rose reached out to touch one of them while Jenny stood frozen just like a statue.

"So beautiful," Rose said.

"Rose is cold, her hands are shaking," I said.

"Don't be silly," Rose laughed, turning back to Jenny with pink cheeks, "Liddy-Jean is so excited to be here."

"We are too," Jenny said, and Rose looked the happiest I have ever seen her.

Kenzie made fun of them by saying to me, "Where did you get those beautiful sneakers?" and when Kenzie bent down to touch one of them, I said, "Thank you darling, I got them at Wal-Mart. And where did you get that lovely butterfly shirt?" and Kenzie laughed and laughed.

"Very funny, you two," Jenny said. She had walked ahead to hold the gallery door open for all of us. Rose looked afraid to walk in, so I grabbed her hand and pulled her.

The gallery was big inside with lots of extra walls everywhere that looked like a white maze. Jenny's artwork was so pretty, but Kenzie showed me all the best things in five minutes, and we got tired of waiting for slowpokes Rose and Jenny. Luckily, the gallery had slippery wood floors which Kenzie and I took turns sliding on, until Rose told us we had to stop before we broke something, like ourselves. I thought this was unfair, since without the sliding game, the gallery was boring. I took Kenzie by the hand, and we hid around one of the walls. "Let's spy on them," I whispered, and Kenzie got excited at that so I covered her mouth, so she did not scream.

Rose called out, "Girls, don't go too far!"

Jenny said, "Kenzie knows her way around, and there is only one entrance in the front so they can't get too lost."

We took this as permission to keep hiding and Kenzie showed me how we could sneak around another wall until we were right behind them. We took turns peeking around the wall.

Seeing Jenny at the gallery with her artwork made Rose look at Jenny like she was a movie star. When she looked at Jenny's sculptures and paintings, she got extra quiet, and whenever Jenny wasn't looking, she stared at Jenny instead of the paintings, as if Jenny was magic for making them.

When Rose pointed to her favorite, Jenny said it was her favorite painting, too.

"I secretly hope it won't sell," Jenny said.

The painting was of a little baby gorilla, and Rose said something about how it reminded her of Kenzie. "There is something about the way the baby gorilla is sitting on the lap of the mother, with one foot under her, just the way Kenzie sits at work." Jenny nodded as Rose took a closer look, while we spied on them. "Why would you have it here to sell, if you love it so much?"

"I'm not as prolific as I used to be. I'm opposite of most artists, I paint when I'm happy," she said, and Jenny touched the baby gorilla's toe pad before walking us through the rest of the gallery. Before Rose left the room, I saw her touch the little toe, too. Kenzie and I snuck out from behind the wall and we each touched the little toe too and giggled before following them to the next room.

I heard Rose ask her, "So, does that mean you aren't happy?"

Jenny was careful to check if Kenzie was around before she answered, "Just not like I was . . . but . . . today I am."

I watched Rose after Jenny said that, and even though Rose still smiled and laughed, I could tell she was wishing she could find a way for Jenny to be happy again, and I wished that for Rose. I did not tell any of this to Kenzie.

It was Jenny's idea to get a bite to eat after the gallery. Kenzie and I tried our best to behave in the restaurant, but Rose said we were having an attack of the giggles. It started when we were playing with our big white napkins trying to make Halloween costumes. I made Kenzie laugh by putting my napkin around my ear and told her to guess who I was. I told her Vincent van Gogh, and she laughed her head off because everyone knows he cut off his ear. I told Kenzie not to worry. Even though her mom was a painter, I did not think she would ever do anything that stupid, because Rose said her mom has nice earrings, and what would she do with the extra?

Since we were being silly, Rose and Jenny thought we weren't listening to them, and probably Kenzie was not. But I was using my super skills of listening to people without looking at them, so even though I already knew Rose better than anyone at the table, I learned a lot more about her that day as she talked with Jenny.

She never said his name, but I knew Rose was talking about her boyfriend, Gary, when she whispered to Jenny. "He has addictions he's not willing to give up, the least of which is me."

I got worried about how serious Rose was, and when I snuck a peek at Jenny, I was sure she was worried, too. When I ducked under the table to get my napkin, and Kenzie ducked under to copy me, I heard Rose whisper, "I should explain that he didn't have a drug problem when I met him . . . or maybe he did, and he just cared enough to hide it from me. He doesn't now . . . I need to end things," Rose whispered, and Jenny nodded at her.

Jenny looked as happy about this idea as I was, but Rose kept checking her phone and Jenny noticed it too. Jenny touched her arm and asked if she needed to leave. Rose was quiet for a long time before she said Gary had called her four times.

I saw Jenny give Rose's arm a quick squeeze before she let go.

"At the risk of not minding my own business, nobody should have to put up with that," she said.

"You're right," Rose said, but she stopped talking about it because Kenzie was staring at her, and with her mouth slightly open. I reminded myself to teach Kenzie how to listen without looking at people.

Rose excused herself from the table and said, "Forgive me for being rude, but he'll just keep calling until I find out what he wants."

Jenny watched Rose as she went across the room and kept watching her as she made her phone call by the front door of the restaurant. Even when Kenzie was talking to her mother, Jenny kept watching Rose until she came back.

"Are you okay?" she asked.

"I'm fine," Rose said, but her smile was small. "I have to stop jumping when he says so, just to keep the peace."

Jenny nodded her head and said, "Good, then let's stop for ice cream on the way home."

Rose smiled at her, shaking her head as she said, "That is just what I need! You're a troublemaker, and I like that." And I could tell Rose really did.

Kenzie and I got matching flavors in our cones: half strawberry, half vanilla bean. Vanilla bean is just like vanilla except not all white. It has little specks of brown in it that look like dirt, but taste really good. Jenny said to Rose they should get one big sundae with two spoons.

They had to sit close together and eat out of the small cup, and I wished Kenzie and I did not get cones so we could do the same thing. Rose noticed me watching them and went and got Kenzie and me a big cup to plop our cones in upside down. She also gave us two plastic spoons. Now we were all sharing and the ice cream tasted so much better that way!

Jenny never asked Rose what it was that stupid Gary wanted, but I could tell she wanted to because she was so quiet while we ate. I knew Rose wanted to touch Jenny's hair, since she kept peeking at it, whenever Jenny wasn't looking.

"This is so sweet," Jenny said.

"Isn't it supposed to be?" Rose said.

Jenny nodded and stared back down to her ice cream and answered, "I forget sometimes that life is supposed to be sweet."

"Me too," Rose said.

Jenny stole a bite from Rose's side of the dish, so I did the same thing from Kenzie's side, and she hit my spoon like it was a sword fight. When I tried to hit her spoon back, a little pink ice cream spattered on Kenzie's dress.

"Now, now girls," Rose said like she was pretending to be a mother and Kenzie and I had another fit of giggles when she tried to lick it off her sleeve.

Jenny said, "After all this, I think I could paint all night."

Rose looked happy. "Good. Ice cream helps everything . . . but don't even *think* about stealing another bite from my side," she said, drawing a line down the middle of the sundae. That was what she said, but Rose looked at Jenny like she wanted her to steal all the bites she wanted.

Change of Plan

It was a Wednesday and Rose and I were working on the book. Rose was typing chapters four and five and I was working on the last of the ten clues on how to tell a Wand-Waver from a Worker Bee. Rose said I should make lists since I could get a lot of ideas down very fast also since Rose had to write most of my words over again and again.

I had lists of things I noticed about email, meetings, and all the things I learned at the office, and Rose read them all. "You're a great writer," she said.

"Then why do you write all my words over again?"

"Because you are more creative than other people, so I have to make sure people understand." I liked this. Then Rose spun her chair around to me and said, "Hey!" she said, "I have an idea!"

She said it as if she had just thought of it. I did this sometimes when I wanted something from Mom and Dad. I would think about it for a long time then say it like I had just thought of it, and not Plotting My Attack, like Mom says. Sometimes it even worked.

"You know what this book needs, Liddy-Jean?" Rose asked.

"A publisher?"

"Yes," she said, laughing, "but I was thinking, since this is going to be a short book, we could really use an artist to do some illustrations . . . little drawings to run throughout the book."

"Cartoons!" I said, liking that idea, but there was one problem I had to tell Rose. "I am great at drawing, except people. And that is all there is around here!"

Rose nodded, then she said, "Maybe Jenny can do it for us. What do you think, should we ask her? I mean, if she isn't too busy with her artwork . . ."

Before I could answer yes, Rose was already calling her. She also started smoothing her hair again and I giggled as I whispered, "*Pssst.* Jenny cannot see you."

Rose did not hear me because she was already explaining the cartoon idea to Jenny, and when she hung up, she had a giant smile on her face when she said Jenny could start working with us on this Friday! Jenny also said if we wanted to work more, she could work Saturday too. Rose had said yes, saying that Gary always disappeared on the weekends.

I would have been jealous about the time Jenny might take away from Rose and me, except, whenever Kenzie was around, I had so much fun I hardly noticed anyone else.

On Friday, Rose moved one of the small round tables into her office and put four chairs around it. She said it would be just like King Arthur's table, so we could share our ideas in a circle.

At the end of the work day, I was working with Kenzie in my cube when I saw Jenny come in, and I pretended not to notice her, so I could watch Rose. Rose didn't see her at first and Jenny stood in the doorway, watching Rose like Mom watches her favorite cooking show. Then I saw Jenny take one step, and then stop, like she forgot to wait for Simon Says.

I yelled over to her, "It's O-K, Jenny. Rose can see you now!"

Rose spun around to see Jenny, standing there, and said *"Oh!"* really loud.

"Hey there," Rose and Jenny both said at the same time, and they both laughed when Rose dropped one of the chairs on her own foot.

"You okay?" Jenny asked walking over to her.

Rose made a face from the pain. "I'm fine, just stupid. I'm so glad you decided to come."

Jenny answered, "There are no stupid people . . . only stupid chairs," and Rose laughed like it was the funniest joke she ever heard. Kenzie rolled her eyes at me and I rolled them back.

"Liddy-Jean insisted we work in here, so I'm afraid it's going to be a little cozy."

Jenny smiled. "Cozy's good," she said, and Rose nodded.

I looked around the Marketing Department, and everyone was getting ready to leave. Stephen and Jackie both poked their heads out of their offices to see us.

"It's just Rose's girlfriend, Jenny!" I yelled over, and both Jenny and Rose stared at me, so I checked to see if I had something spilled on my shirt, since usually, this is true.

I said, "Nope! Clean as a whistle!" just like Dad does.

When everyone finally left the office, Jenny opened her tracing paper book and showed us the cartoons she had worked on that she called Sloppy Sketches. They were a bunch of smiley Worker Bees holding their huge pencils over their shoulders with metal lunch boxes hanging off of them as they marched off to computers, just like a Worker Bee army! Jenny drew the Wand-Wavers as giant grizzly bears holding magic wands, who were so pudgy they would never pick up envelopes if they fell on the floor, and would never put roller skates on. Jenny could draw like magic, and Rose thought so, too.

I loved watching Jenny's hand draw the cartoons so fast. Rose watched Jenny when she was drawing too, but sometimes she forgot to watch her hand and stared at her face, which made me wonder if Rose would get much done with Kenzie's mom around.

Luckily, Jenny was good at taking my suggestions and she drew the Customer Service Bees heading into the restrooms two by two with their telephone headsets still strapped across their bee antlers. Best of all, the Worker Bees and Wand-Wavers all worked inside the "Corporate Hive" and it looked a lot like our building, with the bottom floor of the hive made of glass just like our lobby except it was shaped like a round bumblebee hive. Employee parking was in the tree branches, and the closest branches had signs: Reserved for Wand-Wavers!

After Jenny and Kenzie joined the team, writing the book started going much faster. The only problem was the stuff Kenzie wrote in her notebook. I told Rose in a secret whisper: "Not good."

Rose said, "But I bet you can find a way to teach her?"

I did not want to break the bad news to Rose: I have no idea how I write so good!

Mom let me work Saturday at Jenny's house and we did that whenever Rose's boyfriend had something to do to keep him busy so he would not be calling her to come home. One Saturday, very close to Christmastime, we worked at Rose's house. At first it was fun to see where Rose lived and I got to see her TV and look at her bedroom and I even got to borrow both of her toilets. At first Rose kept looking out the window and I thought she was afraid Gary might come home. But whenever her eyes were not on the window, they were on Jenny.

Finally, when Rose, Kenzie and me were all sitting on the floor and Jenny was standing up to show us her latest drawings just like an art teacher, Rose finally starting laughing like her happy self.

Then a man came in the front door without knocking, and stood right behind Jenny looking angry. Kenzie and I let out surprised yelps like my neighbor's Yorkshire terrier. The angry man looked at Rose, then back at Jenny, and then he looked down at the mess of all the cartoons on the floor, just like Mom does when I make a mess.

Since nobody wanted to talk, I said, "Mom says you are supposed to knock before coming into a house—," but I stopped when Rose squeezed my hand harder than a handshake and the man looked at me, then at Kenzie, then back to me.

Grasshopper. Missing a leg.

Jenny stood up and said, "You must be Gary," and the man didn't answer, did not take her handshake.

He said to Rose, "Nice to come home to a fucking mess."

"Gary," Rose said, so angry, and I could tell swearing was not allowed in Rose's house. Kenzie did not understand that Gary's bad language was nothing to giggle about, and Jenny put her hand on Kenzie's shoulder to shush her.

I had never heard anyone swear the very first day I ever met them, and now that the giggling had stopped Kenzie had on her surprised eyebrows and looked like she was catching flies with her mouth.

"I didn't realize it was so late," Rose said, as she bent to scoop some papers off the floor.

Jenny said, "It's okay, we should get going anyway," and she bent down to help, but Rose stopped her.

"No, I'll take care of this." Then I heard Rose whisper to Jenny, "Just please can you take the girls?"

Gary didn't move, or take off his coat, or even shut the door he had flung wide open, letting out all the heat. Mom would have been furious. I didn't plan to shake my head no at him about the door, but I did, because the room was getting cold.

Now Gary was staring at me again. I was afraid of him now, since most people try not to stare. But not him. Even from far away he smelled like Gina . . . maybe worse.

"Are you Gina's brother?" I asked.

"Girls, please go get your coats," Jenny said, and I hurried with Kenzie to get them from the kitchen, holding Kenzie's hand so she would not be afraid.

Kenzie let go of my hand to grab her coat and went out the kitchen door to wait on the steps. I stayed to button my coat because my mom made me promise since there was snow on the ground. I peeked into the living room.

Rose said, "You're not supposed to be here."

"I still live here, remember?" Then Gary pointed his finger at Jenny as he said, "Is this the woman you're talking to constantly?"

Rose said, "Gary, you're being rude."

Gary took one step closer to Rose and I wished I could pull her into the kitchen, but I was too scared, but I did not have to because Jenny stepped between Gary and Rose.

Gary was really mad now. "I come home to a bunch of ... strangers making a mess in my house, and I'm the one being rude?"

"Actually, it's my house," Rose said, but she didn't sound sure.

Jenny looked Gary right in the eye and said, "There's no need to speak that way in front of the kids. Rose, will you be okay if we leave?"

Rose nodded and Jenny came to the kitchen and took me outside where Kenzie was waiting, and we walked to the car. I could tell Jenny did not want to leave Rose with him. When we got in the car, she gave a small smile and told us to "Stay put." She locked the car doors and then she put up the I-Will-Only-Be-A-Minute-Finger.

Then she went right back in through the front door.

This was brave of her, especially because even with the car windows closed, I could hear Gary's yelling, and this time he was saying lots of really bad words . . . including a lot I had never heard before! I wished I had my notebook to write them down.

I pushed the button to unlock the car door and opened it just a little to hear Jenny say, "Rose, are you sure you're okay?"

Gary yelled, *"Get the f-u-c-k out, lady,"* so I closed and locked the car door again.

Kenzie moved closer to my side of the backseat and I put my arm around her and quickly kissed her ear with a head stab, which was a tradition by now. She giggled a little, but got scared all over again when we heard Gary calling Rose and Jenny bad names, even with the door closed.

"I know what that bad word means," Kenzie whispered.

"Which one?" I asked, since I did not know any of them.

"Queer," she said. "And I know what 'couple of Lezzies' means too."

"What does it mean?"

"He's calling my mother that because I had another mom. Her name was Michelle and she died from cancer the day after my birthday."

I could not even think about my mom dying. I asked, "Why does he call your mom names because she died?"

"It's because my moms were married."

"So?" I said. "Mom already told me about that during one of our Daytime Bed Talks."

Kenzie said, "Some people don't like two girls that get married. I miss Mom Michelle, and my mom does even worse than me . . ."

Kenzie started crying, so I sat even closer and kissed her ear again, which made her giggle a little and cry at the same time.

"Giggle or cry! Make up your mind! You can't do both!" I said, tickling her to make her laugh, and it worked. "Giggle or cry!" I kept saying until I did it too much and then it didn't make her laugh anymore and the tears came back.

Kenzie watched her mother finally leave the house and before she got in the car Kenzie whispered to me, "My mom never wanted ice cream after Mom Michelle died. Not even once . . ."

"But she ate ice cream with Rose," I said, and we both got quiet when her mom got in the car.

"Everything is going to be all right, girls," Jenny said. "Rose is okay."

I thought about Rose eating ice cream with Jenny while Kenzie's mom drove me home. I was sure Jenny hated leaving Rose alone with Gary, since she didn't talk at all and I saw her knuckles were getting white from grabbing the steering wheel, just like my dad's knuckles do when he uses his biggest wrench.

Jenny said, "We won't be able to work on Liddy-Jean's book at Rose's house anymore. That man needs help," she said, softly.

I said, "I think Rose needs the help," and Jenny looked at me like I was right.

We were all quiet the rest of the ride and I wondered if everybody was thinking of a plan to get Rose away from Gary.

Rose was so happy after meeting Jenny that I wondered if she had been sad in secret all this time so I never knew it. Now that Jenny was here, I was sure Rose thought Gary was like a cold, flat hamburger, while Jenny was a box of warm, salty French fries and a Disney World vacation, all in the same day.

On the way home, I watched Jenny drive with her window open a little bit and how that made small pieces of her long hair blow outside the window like yellow Xena whips and I knew Rose would like to see her hair do that. Jenny was so brave to go back in the house with that man yelling those bad words, and I decided I would never tell Mom anything about it since she might stop me from working on the book.

Kenzie was still holding my hand and now she was falling asleep on my shoulder and drooling a little on my jacket, but I liked it. I smiled and held Kenzie's hand tighter and she squeezed back in her sleep and I was happy that she was safe. Jenny looked in the car mirror at us and tried to smile.

"Do you think Rose feels safe to go to sleep?" I asked, but I was sorry I asked, because Jenny's smile disappeared. I wished Jenny could be holding Rose's hand while she drove, and maybe then Rose would know Jenny is the one she should love.

"We do not have to tell Mom about Gary."

"I do, Liddy-Jean, and Rose will also call her later."

Kenzie was sleeping on my shoulder and I watched in the car mirror how Jenny had the same worried line between her eyebrows my mom gets. I needed a plan to fix everything. I had to find a way to protect Rose from Gary, and from Gina, too, and maybe if my plan was good enough, my book could help lots of other people, too.

When I got home I did not ask Mom if I could stay up later like I always do and she asked if I was scared about what had happened today. "No way. It was just arguing like you and Dad do sometimes."

That was a Big Lie. I kissed Mom and Dad goodnight and snuck my flashlight under the covers so I could write down the list of all the people who needed my help the most: Rose, Jenny and Kenzie. I wondered if my book was famous could I help Mom and Dad and Steve and the Marketing Girls, and all my friends at The Center.

When I closed my notebook tight, I fell asleep thinking my notebook was like my mouth holding in one giant secret.

ROSE

He's sick and getting sicker. To see him so angry like that, and with the kids there . . . what the hell was he thinking? *Queer? Lezzies?* I've always seen him as weaker than me, so why was I paralyzed? I thought it was because of the kids, witnessing him like that—I realize it was as much from shame as it was fear. I had to tell Liddy-Jean's mother what happened, and thankfully she only asked that I not take Liddy-Jean to my house again. Humiliating. It felt like the time my neighbor called the police to check on me last year when G. was out of his mind. Since that day he had been more careful to not raise his voice. Until today, when I was sure he weould hit me again.

I also believed he would hurt himself as he threatens, every time I have asked him to leave. But now I realize it is his choice, not mine, and you can't force help on someone who refuses. But you can help yourself. He is not hanging onto me; he is hanging on to the life he chooses. I don't owe him anything—and he's already taken so much. Not money, strangely, I have no idea how he supports his habit. But he disappears a lot, and he does not have one loyal friend. I am it.

How do you handle a person who refuses help?

You leave them. You help yourself.

The girls at work have been saying that I have to see a therapist, and to let him fail. Fail at living. He's held me hostage for years with his idle threats, convincing me if I left him he would end his life.

While all these years, he's been ending mine.

I have been wondering, why now am I finally willing to risk what he might do to himself?

There is finally something I want.

I whispered this to myself to make sure I heard it. I want Jenny in my life, and I don't ever want the girls exposed to him ever again . . . I can't have them in my life as long as we are together.

The bigger question is why do I want this with her so damned much? The answer may not matter, it's already ruined now. Why would she want to see me ever again?

G. has been threatened by her from the first time I mentioned her name. Could he see I was completely in awe of this woman? Maybe he sees something more. Whatever it is, LJ sees it too. Her antenna is up whenever J. and I are together. Mine is up, too, from that first moment she walked into my life.

I'm aware of everything she does, the way she dresses, the way she walks, her voice, and her tenderness toward the girls. Toward me. Her puzzling *shyness* toward me, and mine toward her. What is that? I want to know everything about her, and while she's open to me about so many things, she's guarded, too. I haven't had the nerve to ask many questions. I spend too much time wondering about her past. She was with a woman, and they raised a daughter together . . .

G. saw I've never been so interested in anyone, least of all, him. I can't risk him scaring the girls like that again . . . I can't risk him scaring J. out of my life.

I dreamt of her.

I don't remember all of it, but we were at the gallery, alone. It was dark inside and I was following her like LJ used to follow me. Despite the darkness in the place, I could still see the shine in her hair as she moved from room to room . . . always just out of my reach, and that felt like a familiar pain. Was she nervous to show me her work? Her hands were shaking, just like mine. I took her hand and kissed it as her eyes locked on me and I woke up. I sure did wake up. I wanted to go back to that dream more than I have ever wanted anything in my entire life. *The memory of kissing her hand in a dream was more powerful than any contact in the sum of my entire life.*

There is finally something I want. Am I alone in what I feel? Does it matter?

I never had a plan with an end game with him. I see that it just bought him time—time he has stolen from my life.

Could I finally push him out? Could I do more than that if I had to?

KIM

I called Lisa P. from across the department from a phone that never gets used. I needed to keep an eye on Liddy-Jean to make sure she was not within earshot. I see Lisa P. pick up her phone.

"Lisa P., it's me, Kim."

"Kim? Where the hell are you? And you can call me Lisa when you call, I know which one I am!" she says, as she laughs at herself. "What the hell number are you calling on?"

"Look up," I say, and I give a wave from the farthest desk in the room and see Lisa P. give a big WTF with her hands.

"What's going on?"

"I needed to make sure Liddy-Jean wasn't near me, and this way, I will see her coming."

"Good thinking, Kim—she has caught us enough times. Why, what's going on?"

"Rose knows he needs to leave."

"No shit, Kim."

"I know . . . I know . . ." I said, "she's said it before, but this time might be different."

Lisa P. was quiet, then she said, "Finally. I think there's something Rose wants. A friendship with someone outside of work, or something more?"

I whispered into the phone, "Jenny. You see it, too?"

Lisa P. snorted into the phone, "How can you not? I think even Steve sees it."

"Poor guy," I say. "There was a time—"

"—I hoped that, too. We all did."

"But there is something happening with her and Jenny . . . it could be good for her," I say, but truthfully, I am thinking it could be great for her.

Lisa P. says, "Rose says Gary's very threatened by Jenny, and he had a freak-out in front of Jenny and the girls. I hope Rose didn't tell him anything."

I said, "She didn't have to. Everyone saw it. The crazy electricity in the air around Rose and her."

"Don't go all romance novel on me, Kim." But then she paused and said, "You know what I think? Kind of like she does with us, I think she just could not help talking about Jenny, even if it was to that asshole."

"She does mention her a lot," I agreed.

Lisa P. was quiet again. "Hey, are you wondering the same thing I'm wondering?"

I usually never know what Lisa P. is wondering, but this time I said, "Yes! Rose has a huge crush on her, and I'm all for it!"

"Especially if it gets her away from that loser-stain!" Lisa P. said giggling into the phone.

"Lisa, gotta go—Liddy-Jean just tracked me—I'm afraid she will come over!" I hung up on her, and I could hear Lisa P. laughing from across the room. I headed back to my desk, Liddy-Jean watching my every move. I saw her write something in the back of her notebook, her other hand curled around her pen to hide her writing.

"How is your day going, Liddy-Jean?" I asked.

Liddy closed her notebook fast, and was now wrapping a piece of tape across the notebook to hold it closed.

When she finally looked up at me, she said, "Why are you talking on the phone way over there so I cannot hear you?"

I love this girl. She doesn't miss a trick.

"No reason, Liddy-Jean, just needed to get something from that desk."

"You forgot it because your hands are empty. Lisa P. is going to laugh at you again."

FYIs, CEOs and PMS

I have learned that anything with the letters F-Y-I on it is a bad thing to get, so I decided to write a whole list about it in my book. F-Y-I means you're getting a warning, but, as my Auntie Theresa says, "When it's too f-ing late to do a damned thing about it." Jackie and Lisa P. say an F-Y-I is a very late C-Y-A (Cover Your A-S-S) from the person who should have started a project a long time ago.

Any messages from the C-E-O are usually like F-Y-Is because they always have hidden warnings. The C-E-O is like the principal at a school and important because they are the boss of the whole thing. (The Marketing Girls say the C-E-O is almost always a boy, which makes no sense since Mom makes all the decisions in my family except for on my dad's work bench in the garage, and my mom would not be good with the bad behavior I see around here.) I have many notes for my book about how when C-E-Os are around, all the Wand-Wavers act differently and if a Worker Bee wants to be successful, maybe they should do this, too:

1. If you are talking to an unimportant Worker Bee and the C-E-O comes into the room, you should stop talking right in the middle of a sentence and go talk to someone more important.

132

2. If a Boss's door is closed, you should never knock on it unless it is an emergency. Like if you are looking for Rose.

The second time I went to knock on Gina's closed door, Lisa P. tried calling out my name in a Whisper Yell, which is when you do all the things exactly like a yell, except for the yelling part. I didn't hear her Whisper-Yelling, so Lisa P. tried to stop me from knocking on Gina's door by catching my arm just before I knocked, but she scared me, so I did a regular type of yell.

Gina flung her door open with her usual red face but she had to control her temper because the C-E-O was with her and that's when I thought there might be a law against yelling at a person that is not as smart as you. Right now, this was a good law. Gina stared at us and said in a creepy witch voice just like the one that invited Hansel and Gretel in for a snack, before stuffing them in a bird cage, "Oh, hello Lisa, is everything okay with Liddy-Jean?"

But Gina's eyes were wide like she did not want the answer, and Lisa P. barely had a chance to say that I was just looking for Rose, before she closed the door again. Just before she did, I saw the C-E-O turn to look at me and I put my hand up to give him a salute, since he was like a famous person around here. The C-E-O smiled and did not get the chance to salute back before Gina closed the door. Later, I told Lisa P. that letting me knock might have been a better idea than scaring the crap out of me with the grabbing of the arm thing, and everyone agreed.

F-Y-I, Rose told me that marketing departments have a lot of P-M-S since mostly girls work there. This can create some very bad days for everyone, but not for me since I don't get P-M-S and I'm glad. I do get my "Monthly Visitor" as my mom says, and while I hate it, it makes me feel grown up, so I liked to tell people whenever I had it. All that changed when the counselors at The Center told me it's wrong to talk about things that are supposed to be private. I think they made up that rule because the first time I ever mentioned my period was at our bowling banquet when I accidentally got ketchup from my fries all over my pants. F-Y-I, the good news was, after that, nobody was that hungry, and I didn't have to share the ketchup.

I don't get P-M-S but once I cried when my period embarrassed me by showing up as a surprise (which is a very good reason to cry, if you ask me.) Crying at work is not allowed, but I have seen a lot of the Marketing Girls do it anyway. Sometimes they cry when Gina gives them an impossible Deadline. (The first time I was told a Deadline, I almost cried because I thought if you didn't finish your project in time, you get killed.)

Three times I almost cried at work:

1. When my Monthly Visitor came and Rose had to call my mom to bring me extra pants.

2. The first time Rose let me type on her computer and I thought I broke it (but I learned if you think too much without typing, a black screensaver comes on and that is not breaking it.)

3. The first time Rose went on vacation.

Some Marketing Girls (especially Jackie) have cried right in the middle of the room, or sometimes at their desks, but since you can see inside everyone's office because of the glass walls, the only good place to cry is the bathroom. And, bonus: no boys allowed. After I had been working at the company a while, I found out that the only people who get more upset than the Marketing Girls are the Decorator Boys.

The Decorator Boys are really called the "Visual Team," and they do all the pretty decorations in our big sales showroom. The decorations in the showroom are for taking pictures, and even though a lot of them are fake, they make the room and the stuff we sell look pretty. In the showroom there are cardboard boxes set up just like a real bed, with pillows and sheets and nobody told me until it was too late that you cannot flop on it like a real bed.

I heard The Marketing Girls say the Visual Team boys are gay, which means they like boys more than girls, but this seems the opposite, since they are always hanging around all the girls. This is another Mixed Message, if you ask me.

These boys are very funny and make a big show out of acting more like girls than the girls do. They giggle a lot, and they call each other "Mary" and talk about everybody. Usually talking about people is bad for business, but these boys make everyone laugh. They especially love to laugh about the clothes people wear to work. Even if I don't really get the jokes, it is always funny because of the way that they say it.

Some things I have heard the Decorator Boys say:

1. "Honey, was the electricity out when you picked out those shoes?"

2. "That bitch is so mean, her favorite plant is a face plant."

3. "I try to see things from your point of view, but I can't stick my head up my A-S-S."

4. "Hey, girl, I found your nose, it was in my business!"

5. "I'm not insulting you, I'm describing you."

5. "In loving memory of when I gave a S-H-I-T."

6. "Girl, the trash gets picked up tomorrow. Watch out."

7. "Mirrors don't lie, and lucky for her, they don't laugh."

I wondered if boys ever got P-M-S since they act so much like girls, and so I asked Jimmy, my favorite Decorator Boy. He waved his hand at me as if swatting an invisible fly and answered me as if he had been asked the question a hundred times. "Oh honey, every day is P-M-S day when you're tragically handsome, and gay."

Sometimes they say things that I do not understand, like, "Gay is the new black," or they look at a piece of fabric and say: "Oohh . . . *We* love that . . ." as if they are two people instead of one. When I asked Jimmy about that, he said "Honey, it's the Royal We," and everyone laughed, so I did too.

Gina never laughs.

Yesterday, I saw Gina looking for something in Rose's office while Rose was out at lunch. She looked through all of Rose's drawers, and I even saw her peek into the drawer where she keeps her bag. Mom says it is a no-no to look into a woman's bag, but bosses must be allowed. Because I spied on Gina doing this, before I left work, I put some fake notebooks out on top of a piece of paper on my desk, and did a trick Norman Winchell taught me. I traced around all the corners of the books with a pencil to make small L-shaped lines.

When I came in to work this morning I saw both my notebooks had been moved and put back, but not exactly in the same spot. I decided from now on, I would hide my real notebooks inside a big lunch bag in the refrigerator.

Rose called out for me, so I went to her office. She had stacks of thin catalogs set up on the table opposite her desk, with one of my favorite chairs pulled up to it.

"Why is that chair in here?" I asked.

"We have to do an emergency project today."

"With a Deadline?"

"Yes, with a deadline."

"When is the Deadline?"

136

"Yesterday," Rose said, and I knew what that meant: roller skates.

I looked at all the stacks of papers and guessed it might take two days for me to put them all in envelopes. "Don't worry, we're going to do this together. If we both work very hard, we might be able to finish by this afternoon."

"But the Deadline was yesterday," I said.

"Unfortunately, I was just told about this today."

I copied Lisa P. when I said: "Damned those F-Y-I's!" and Rose could not hide her smile.

When she showed me which envelopes to use, Rose had a serious face on, so I got to work without asking even one question, and even though I wanted to be happy I was in Rose's office doing a project with her, I was not, because Rose seemed scared. We worked quietly next to each other, me in my favorite chair and Rose standing up, stuffing four envelopes for each one I stuffed. I tried going faster and spilled a stack, so I had to slow down again.

When Rose bent to pick up the envelopes before I could get off my chair, I forgot to sneak a look down her shirt like I sometimes do. "You forgot one," I said, happy there was one more envelope under the table, but before she bent down to get it, Gina came in and closed Rose's door behind her.

Her hair looked especially bad and I guessed her eyes had a headache. "I need to speak with you," she said to Rose. The office seemed very small with the door closed, and Gina's voice was extra loud, and extra smelly, too. Rose said, "Liddy-Jean, maybe you should go take a break?"

"No," Gina said. "She should stay and work. I'll be brief, and this will be of a certain altitude to escape her notice."

I did not know what Gina was talking about, except my Auntie Theresa says nothing escapes my notice. I pretended not to listen by frowning extra hard at a stuck envelope.

Gina sat herself on the corner of Rose's desk. I knew by the way Gina was sitting that it was going to be a Daytime Bedroom Talk, only in an office. I was worried for Rose and also for me because I had to stuff envelopes extra slow so I would not drop another pile in front of Gina.

"We need to talk about this situation we're in."

"It's not a problem, I will have it all done by this afternoon," Rose said.

Gina was quiet for a minute and this was worse than when she was talking, and as the Decorator Boys would say: "She is so much smarter when her mouth is closed" but I did not say it. Finally, Gina said, "I want to know why this didn't get done as I asked you on Monday."

I stopped stuffing.

Rose answered, "Because you didn't ask me on Monday."

"Let's not go around about this again, Rose. I know what I asked you to do, and I want to know what I am supposed to say to Ronald about why it didn't get done."

"It will be done today," Rose said.

"That wasn't the question I asked you. Are you having trouble remembering what I asked you?"

I wanted to put my fingers in my ears, but I knew I would not be able to stuff envelopes that way, so I tried to whistle while I worked, like Snow White's dwarfs, until I got an envelope all spitty.

Rose answered, "I'm not having trouble remembering. The project will be done today. Can we leave it at that?"

"I am going to have to tell Ronald that somebody simply dropped the ball. If I can leave it at that, I will, but if he asks who is responsible, I won't lie."

"You won't?" Rose said.

The room was so quiet after Rose said that, that I had to look up. Gina's face was turning the color of a dirty brick.

"What are you implying?" she asked.

"If our team had been told about this project, we would have gotten it done, like we always do. Gina, you sent me that email at two-thirty in the morning. Last night."

I had been holding a paper for a long time, staring at it, forgetting to stuff it.

"Just get it done," Gina said.

I did not look up until she walked out. My heart was hurting for Rose. It was like at home, if I would hear my sister get a Daytime Talk from Mom, and how it was just the same as if it had happened to me. But Rose did not do a thing to deserve it.

Why I Hate White Chairs

"You don't have to be nervous, honey. Please sit," Gina said to me as she shut her door. When Gina said the name Honey, it sounds different, not like when Rose says it.

"I'm not nervous," I said. I was in my best Xena pose, hands grabbing my hips. "I just hate white chairs."

"Why do you hate white chairs?" she said with a funny look on her face.

"Because you cannot eat chocolate anywhere near them."

"I see," Gina said, moving closer to me. "Well, no worries then, I never eat sweets and I don't allow chocolate in here."

Just like my Auntie Theresa, I do not trust people who do not eat sweets, especially chocolate.

"Is it because of the chairs?" I asked.

"Is what because of the chairs?"

"That you don't like chocolate. Because, I would get rid of the chairs if I were you."

Gina's smile got bigger and scarier by the second and I wished Rose was with me.

"What if this lasts a whole hour? Then would you sit on a white chair?" she asked.

An hour was an awfully long time, and I was already getting a little tired standing, since she left me waiting while she was on a long phone call. Gina looked like she was waiting for an answer, so I said, "I don't know," even though Mom says that is not an answer. "But I will try to find out," I remembered to say.

Gina stopped smiling. She waited a long time to talk again, and I started to worry the meeting would last more than an hour.

Finally, she said, "When I was your age, I wouldn't have dreamed of not doing exactly what an adult told me to do. If my father told me to sit my bare ass down on a chair with tacks on it, I would do it."

I did not like the sound of Gina's father at all, and now I was feeling bad for her.

"Why?" I asked.

"Why what?" she asked back, and she sounded angry, as if I had already asked too many questions, but this was less questions than usual. But I guessed if I had a father that told me to sit on tacks, I would be angry all the time, too.

"Why did your father ask you to do that?"

"I didn't say he did. But not everyone is as kind to young people as I am," she said.

If Gina had any ideas about making me sit on tacks, I could just yell for Steve, since Gina called this meeting with me right after Rose left to go to her dentist. Gina would probably get into big trouble for the tack thing, and then Rose could take her job since all the Marketing Girls say she does her job anyway, and I knew Rose would never have an office with white chairs, especially with me around.

Now Gina's big lipstick smile looked like the Joker in Batman, so I looked away. She moved closer to me, making me look. "Liddy-Jean, since you came to work here, we haven't had a chance to chat."

Xena would look at Gina, and I tried but I ended up staring at one of those stupid white chairs instead. This made me step sideways to get away from it, but then I was too close to the other white chair, so I took a half step to the middle again and tried to stand exactly in the middle again, until I got it just perfect. By then, I had no idea what Gina had been saying to me, but at least my feet were exactly between the white chairs. When Gina got quiet for a minute, I realized Xena was right, again. I should have stayed looking at Gina.

"You see Liddy, even though I'm your boss, that doesn't mean we can't be friends. Just like you and Rose." But as she said this, she gave a little push to one of the chairs so it was just a little closer to me, and I had to move again.

I didn't think I could be friends with someone whose breath smelled that bad all the time, and I accidently made an icky face, even though I shouldn't have. Gina stared at me, then walked back around to her desk and sat down. I wondered if I would still be able to smell her all the way from over there, so I asked her a question to check. "Why do your hands shake like that?"

Gina looked surprised and put her hands under her desk. She said, "I'm just cold."

Yup, stinky breath.

"But it is warm in here," I said. "My mom would say you are catching a cold, so you shouldn't hand me anything." I put my hands behind my back, just in case.

"I won't," she said. Her big smile was back, like when a bad guy smiles on TV just before something bad happens. "Liddy-Jean, do you think a big boss can't be friends with one of her workers? The CEO and I are friends, and Ronald is the president of the entire company."

Xena would have put her hands back on her hips, so I did as I said, "Sometimes you don't say hello." She looked surprised, but I had been wanting to say that to her for a long time, since Mom says not saying hello to people is very rude.

"Okay. Well, I'm making time now. Hello Liddy-Jean. Why don't you tell me all about this project you're working on with Rose?"

I felt my mouth drop open, but I closed it, quick. "Envelopes," I answered, but I knew better.

Gina said, "Maybe I can help you, and it can be our little secret," she said, as she winked at me.

"That's O-K," I said. "Rose already asked Jenny to help us with

142

the book. That's Kenzie's mom."

"The book . . . oh, yes," she said, "Rose told me." Then she said, "You should always keep the book in one safe place, so you don't lose it."

"That's what I always tell Rose! Someday she will forget which pile of vanilla envelopes it is under, and we will lose it *FOREVER!*"

I had not meant to shout, but Gina stood up rubbing the side of her forehead like Mom does when I give her a headache. "Do you have a headache?" I asked, since I didn't want to talk about the book anymore. Just in case.

"No headache," she said. "Liddy-Jean, do you understand that I'm the only one who can make sure Rose doesn't lose her job over this book? None of us would want that . . . right?"

I was not sure if I should say yes or no, so I said both, just in case.

Gina walked around the desk again and pushed one of the chairs out of her way, and it was so close to me that I took a jump backwards just like in Simon Says. She smiled again when I did this, but this time her smile actually looked happy. She nudged the chair with her knee again and I moved to get my feet back in the middle. I learned when I was little if you moved your feet after you jumped, you lost Simon Says. Maybe if I told Gina she won the game we could stop.

Gina said, "Let's get back to the book—"

"We only work on the book after work time is over, never during work time." I was so glad that was the truth.

Gina got quiet for a minute, so I used the time to peek at the rest of her office. Very messy. Mom would say: shameful. There were papers everywhere and even a paper on the floor near her trash. I would never leave paper on the floor like that. If a Post-it note falls down from my desk, I pick it up, Pron-Toad.

"Liddy-Jean, why don't you ever call me Gin, or Ginny, like I've asked you to? You seem like a smart girl for someone with . . . for your age. I wonder why you can't seem to learn that?"

"I forget things if I don't write them down," I said, which was true.

When Gina walked past me, she sighed and her stinky breath

went directly up my nose, so, behind her back, I held my nose for just a second and it helped.

"Well, go write it down, then," she said. I heard her talk to Rose exactly like this, and I was glad Rose and I were being treated the same, because maybe this meant Gina was just mean to everyone and not just Rose.

Before I got out the door, she stopped me by grabbing my arm, harder than Mom did when I almost fell ice skating, and she hissed into my ear just like a snake, "This was a private conversation, okay Liddy-Jean?"

I slowly looked down just the way Xena would, with squinty eyes at Gina's hand, still holding my arm. That finally made her let go, but she still did not open the door wide enough for me to get out. "I am fatter than that," I said, pointing to the door like Kenzie would.

"A private conversation, Liddy . . . do you understand what that means?" she asked.

"Yes," I said. "No Privates talk at work. Vagina talk only happens at home."

This made her open the door wider for me. I learned a long time ago that people want to stop talking to you once you mention vagina.

Changing the Post-it Notes

"Hi Steve."

"Hey Liddy-Jean, what's shakin', bacon?"

I laughed like I always do when Steve says that. "I am not bacon," I said.

"So waz up, my girlfriend?"

"I am not your girlfriend!" I said, laughing at him.

Steve laughed too. "A guy is allowed to dream, can't he?"

"Dreams don't usually come true."

"I'm not sure about that, Liddy-Jean. I think you could make just about anything come true."

He might be right. I thought about how I usually did get whatever I worked hard enough for, and how folding laundry and clearing the dinner table for a whole year got me my bike.

"It is working that gets you things," I said, as I sat down in my favorite chair in his office. It was blue, exactly the color of Steve's eyes, and I figured he knew this since he wore blue shirts a lot.

"Why do you have a mirror by your desk?"

He looked in the mirror and said in his best mobster voice, "Hey, you talkin' to me? You talkin' to me?" I always laugh when he does this.

"I have it there because my dad always told me if you can't face the door, the next best thing is to have a mirror."

"Was your dad afraid of someone sneaking up on him?"

"He was a policeman."

I sat up extra straight in the blue chair. "A real one?" I asked.

"A real one."

"Where does he keep his police car? At your house?"

"No, Liddy-Jean. He died a few years ago."

"Oh," I said, trying not to cry for Steve, and also for Kenzie who lost one mom and never had a dad. My belly started a new stomachache just for Steve.

"What happened to his car?" I asked, hoping he would not cry at work about his daddy dying.

"They took it back to the police station."

"Was it raining?" I asked.

"Yes. Why did you ask that?"

"Because you are staring out the window, and it is raining," I said. "This is my favorite chair, you know why?"

Steve leaned over his desk and widened his eyes, huge, like a handsome monster. "Because it matches my gorgeous baby blues?" he said, blinking his eyelashes real fast so I would laugh.

"Yes," I said. Then I waited as long as I could before asking my question.

"Steve, if someone swears the first time you meet him and is doing drugs, can I get the police after him?" I asked.

Steve put his pen down and looked serious. "I'd have to know more before I could say for sure. Exactly who are we talking about?"

"It's a secret right now, but someday I might need your help, especially since your dad was a policeman," I said.

"Is something wrong? Because you need to tell me if there's anything wrong."

"Do you still love Rose?" I asked, knowing this would stop his questions.

"I never said—I—"

I whispered, "I don't blame you if you do."

Steve said, "Don't worry, she would never love me more than she loves you. Besides, Rose has a boyfriend."

I looked out the door and saw that Rose had come back from the dentist and was smiling at some of Jenny's cartoons she had on her wall. Jenny called them The Rejects.

"That is not the reason," I said. "Rose cannot be your girlfriend because she loves Jenny."

"Oh," he said, blinking, looking around to see if anyone else heard this news, but nobody was around. "Kenzie's mom?"

"Yep," I said. "So, I am going to change the yellow Post-it notes under my desk."

"Okay . . . um . . . do you need help with that?"

"Nope. Now they are now going to say: 'Liddy-Jean, Marketing Queen.' But I will still keep them hidden, because I like when they tickle my legs."

"Okay . . . so, Liddy-Jean . . . I still need to know why you might need a policeman."

"I cannot tell you right now. But if I do, I will call a meeting with you," I said.

Then I hopped off the blue-eye chair. "I have to go," I said, "but I can tell you two secrets."

"Tell me, Liddy."

"All the girls think you like looking at yourself." I point. "In that mirror."

"Oh," he said. "So . . . what's the other secret?"

I whispered this one, "You want to be a policeman, just like your dad."

I stared him down until he finally nodded his yes. "Bye Steve, smell you later," I said because he likes when we say this to each other. I walked out of his office and behind me, I heard him slide the mirror off his desk, right into his trash. I hoped it did not break because seven years is too long for a handsome guy to have bad luck.

First Date Plans

It was a long time before we were able to work on the book together on a Saturday and when we finally did, it was extra special because this time we were at Jenny's house, which was decorated with a million colored lights for Christmas. I loved them and Rose did, too.

Rose quietly said to Jenny, "Gary hates lights."

"What kind of person hates Christmas lights?" Jenny asked her.

I accidentally butted in and said, "Rose just told you."

They both looked at me and lowered their voices. I knew it was time to pretend not to listen, and I kept my mouth tightly closed while I unpacked my notebooks and snacks from my backpack. I even did a little humming, which worked.

"Your house is so beautiful," Rose said, but she was looking at Jenny, not her house.

"How have things been at home for you?"

"He says he's fishing all day, for what, I have no idea. Hard to catch fish from a bar stool."

Out of the corner of my eye, I saw Jenny nod her head. She had the same worried look I had seen before. I also saw the same look Rose has when Jenny is around. I was pretty sure if Kenzie and I were not there, they might hug.

Rose said to Jenny, "He said I'm supposed to be using the time today to think about our future."

"I'm guessing you've used up plenty of time on that," Jenny said, and she put her hand on Rose's shoulder.

"Plenty," Rose agreed, staring at her. "Not much else to think about there."

"You know you can call me anytime, if you want to talk," Jenny said, and she made Rose look her in the eyes. "I mean it, call me anytime, it's been too long since we got together . . . to do this."

Rose kept looking at her and Jenny finally took her hand off Rose's shoulder, to take out her drawing things from her bag.

It was hard for me to concentrate on the book after that because I never got to spend a lot of time with Kenzie except at work, and all she wanted to do was talk and play, and all she wanted to talk about lately was the dance I invited her to at The Center. She said yes right away, and I was happy she wanted to come, and then she asked if there would be real boys she could dance with, so I told her about Bobby.

After that, she kept saying Bobby's name, smiling really big and I could see a couple of her teeth had Oreos stuck in them. She would not smile so big if she knew Bobby like I did.

"You shouldn't smile that big," I warned her.

"Maybe he can be my boyfriend!" Kenzie said.

"Not with black Oreo teeth," I said.

"Let's go look," Kenzie said giggling all the way to the bathroom, and we both laughed at her black teeth. While she gargled with water, I was trying to decide if I was afraid she was going to steal Bobby, or if I was afraid Bobby would steal *her*. Either way, I wondered if I made a mistake to invite her. Kenzie shoved her open mouth into my face so I could check for more Oreos. All clear.

"Can I dance with Bobby?" she said.

"If he wants to, I guess," I answered, still a little angry, but things were looking a little better without the black Oreo teeth. "I have to get back to my notebooks." I didn't want to talk about this anymore, so I started reading over the latest list of boss complaints I got from the ladies' room stall. Rose had already edited my list using her own words, so I hardly recognized some of them. Editors!

"I have one pretty dress that makes me look so grown up, like a spelling teacher."

I liked teachers. "Wear that one," I said.

"Okay, you two . . . back to work!" Jenny said from across the room. I had not noticed she and Rose had moved over to the table. Kenzie got busy cutting out some strips of paper and rolling them. She said she was making magic wands and I pretended to work while I listened to Rose and Jenny again.

Jenny was laughing. "What am I going to do with her?"

"Liddy-Jean is the same way," Rose whispered back as if I was her daughter. I liked that.

"They both make no distinction between boys and girls and have crushes on both," Rose said.

"Some advantages to that," Jenny said, and Rose smiled before she looked back down at her work. Jenny said, "Think about it, didn't we all have crushes on both boys and girls when we were young? I think we learn not to, or, at least some of us do."

I peeked since they were both very quiet now and Rose said, "You're right. I haven't thought about this in years, but there was one girl in fifth grade I used to stare at. She was so pretty and at the time I thought I stared at her because I wanted to look like her. Her hair was long and blonde—"

Rose didn't finish her sentence, and looked like she was pretending she lost something, just like what I do when Mom asks me to do the dishes and I pretend I am too busy with homework. This never works, and, like Mom, it looked like Jenny did not believe her either.

"And what do you think of this theory of mine?" Jenny asked, leaning on her large sketchbook. She had been working on cartoons of a band of Worker Bees going to the hive with long stingers on their butts. They were using their stingers like Xena swords. I wished I could take a closer look, but I knew they would stop talking if I came over.

Rose said, "Now? Well, I still notice people's attractiveness regardless of their sex."

Jenny was not looking up at Rose, but her hand had stopped drawing the bees and I wondered if she was just pretending to study her drawing. I have pretended to study many times, especially after I break something.

Rose said, "Now that you mention it, I've noticed a change in the way I look at people, the older I get. I guess I am looking for something . . . different than I did back then. Or, more likely, I just didn't know what the hell I was looking for before."

Jenny put her pencil down on her pad, and finally looked at Rose for a moment before she looked away out the kitchen window. "I've been looking for the same thing for as long as I can remember," Jenny said. I saw Rose's eyes follow Jenny's hair down to where one golden curl touched her sketchbook like a spring.

Rose said, "Liddy-Jean invited me to be an extra chaperone at the dance at The Center, so why don't you stay for the dance instead of dropping off Kenzie? Don't feel obligated, but I'd love the company, and they can always use more chaperones."

Kenzie distracted me by hugging me hard around the head and I was afraid I would miss something since her arms had wrapped around both my ears which made me laugh at her. When I finally peeled her off, I heard Jenny say, "I'd love to go with you."

I peeked over at Rose and never saw her look so happy.

Jenny said, "Besides, with those two over there, they'll need more chaperones!"

Disco Balls and the Dress Named Jesus

All the students at The Center got to decorate the lunchroom for the dance, and we did such a good job that it didn't look anything like a lunchroom anymore. We twisted long lines of color streamers and Mr. Frankie, our janitor, hung them from the ceiling. We also covered the walls with shiny blue wax paper from the butcher shop.

One of the counselors hung a spinning mirrored disco ball up in the center of the room and we had spotlights in the corners of the floor pointed up to shine on it. The place started to look like a real dance club!

When the night finally came, Mom agreed to take me to the dance early, since I wanted to be there to see everyone come in and their faces when they saw the magical dance club we made out of an ordinary lunchroom. I was one of the first people there, but the music was already playing and it was all our favorite songs.

I was sad for every good song I heard without Kenzie, so I took out my notebook and sat on the floor and made a list of all the songs I would ask the D-J Mr. Frankie to play again, once Kenzie got there. The first one I wrote down was "Le Freak" by Chic and I drew three stars next to it so I would not forget to ask D-J Mr. Frankie to play that one first.

Bobby was the first to get there with his mother, and his mouth dropped open when he saw the room, and then me. He started jumping up and down and making sounds I had never heard before (and I have heard Bobby make a lot of sounds). He ran past me to stand right under the disco ball with his arms still up high and his mouth wide open in the happiest smile I have ever seen anyone have in my whole entire life, and I felt so happy tears might spill out.

"I promise I will keep an eye on him, it will not be hard," I said to Bobby's mom, and Mrs. Hanson got the joke since Bobby had not moved a single inch from that disco ball. His arms were probably tired because now they were down a little, but his smile was just as wide, staring up at the disco ball, the colored lights flashing across his teeth.

When Kenzie finally came, she was running in a few steps ahead of Jenny and squealing just like a baby pig at the lights and the music, and grabbed both my hands and pulled me out onto the dance floor to bounce-dance in a circle holding hands. More people were dancing and when I looked back at Jenny, she was now watching the door. She saw me looking at her and waved to me before peeking at the door again.

Jenny looked especially pretty and more dressed up than anyone in the room. Anyone, that is, until Rose walked in a few minutes later, right after we finally got Jenny to dance with us.

"Rose is here!" I shouted to Kenzie and Jenny over Cyndi Lauper singing "Girls Just Wanna Have Fun." Jenny turned around to see Rose walking in, and even over the loud music, I heard Jenny say, "Jesus" when she saw Rose's pretty dress.

Rose was wearing a white dress that looked fancy enough to wear to a wedding, except that it didn't have the long tail part that dragged on the floor, which was lucky, since that would be hard to dance in. She had not seen us yet, and I noticed she was smoothing her dress down with her hands the same as she does to her hair, but she looked as perfect as a model in a magazine. She was looking around the room for us, and finally saw Kenzie in the crowd. I looked back for Jenny, but she was standing where we had left her, looking like she was trying to copy Rose, smoothing out her clothes.

I shouted over the music, "Come on Jenny! It's just our Rose, she is just dressed extra pretty."

Jenny looked embarrassed and still did not move, so I dropped Kenzie's hand to run back and take Jenny's and then lead her over to Rose.

"Hi girls," Rose said, but she was only looking at Jenny, who was pulling my hand to make us walk more slowly. I held on and pulled back until we were finally all standing together.

"Hi . . . I'm sorry, I was running late," Rose said.

Kenzie said, "My mom made us late too. She changed clothes five times."

Jenny said, "It should have been six," to Rose, then turned to Kenzie and said, "When will you learn not to tell all my embarrassing secrets?"

"I had a clothes crisis myself," Rose said.

"This, right here . . . not a crisis," Jenny said. "You look amazing."

Rose shook her head, "No, you."

"Let's all dance together!" Kenzie said, taking my hand, which still held Jenny's and Kenzie grabbed Rose's hand with her other one. Although we did not plan it, Kenzie and I both pretended the loud music made us not hear Rose and Jenny saying no, and we dragged them out on the dance floor as "Greased Lightning" played. We all danced under the disco ball near Bobby, whose arms were now drooping down like a tired puppet. He was still smiling.

I said to Kenzie, "That's my friend Bobby."

"Oh," she said.

"Did that shatter all your dreams?" I asked, just like Auntie says.

"Does Bobby talk?"

"Not when he is near a disco ball," I said.

Rose and Jenny started doing a bunch of strange dances that nobody else knew, so a lot of the clients stopped dancing to watch them. Kenzie and I watched too, because they were spinning around like they had practiced all night, and then they started to do a funny dance where they bumped the sides of their butts together over and over again as they laughed. Rose called out over the music, "I haven't done The Bump in years! I'm not perfectly dressed for this!"

Jenny smiled at her and said, "Actually, you're dressed perfectly," and Rose had that shy and happy look again that I hoped would never go away.

I liked The Bum dance, and when Kenzie and I started doing it too, that is when everyone else copied Rose and Jenny, too. But it wasn't long before all The Bums had to stop because some of the boys were bumping each other too roughly and when a few kids fell down on the dance floor, others started copying the falling down part, too. They announced on the microphone that we all had to stop The Bum Dance.

Jenny yelled over the music, "Imagine if we two chaperones got kicked out of this dance for starting that?" Rose and Jenny could not stop laughing, and we all went back to regular dances. I told Rose her twirling dances were not as much fun to copy but they were less violent, and she and Jenny had to hold each other up from laughing so hard.

We were all having fun until the next song started, which was a very slow song called "Wishing on a Star." Kenzie knew how to slow dance, so she showed me how I should put both my hands on her waist, and we snuggled on the dance floor while Rose and Jenny wandered off.

I wondered if they did not know how to dance slow, and I was glad that Kenzie knew and could teach me. I had hugged Kenzie many times, but this was different since hugging her for a long time was much nicer. It was so warm dancing with her and I worried for a while that I might fall asleep since it was relaxing like when Mom rubbed my forehead at night. Good thing we kept stepping on each other's toes, which hurt enough to keep me awake and laughing.

"Ow, ow!" we both kept saying, but we laughed every time.

I looked for Jenny and Rose over Kenzie's shoulder. I saw them standing against a wall. It was dark over there, but I could still tell they were trying not to look at each other while they talked. Most of the time, Rose was looking at the floor in front of them, but she was smiling. Slow dancing felt very good, and I knew Jenny wanted to dance with Rose from the minute she had called Rose's dress "Jesus."

Kenzie said, "I was teasing Mom for changing her clothes so much. I kept singing, 'You're getting ready for your girrrlfriend!' and for the first time since Momma Michelle died, Mom laughed like crazy before she threw a pillow at me!"

This made Kenzie so happy, that I decided next time Mom was worried about grocery money, I might throw a pillow at her, too.

Luckily, I thought of a perfect plan and asked Kenzie to help. She went with me to talk to D-J Mr. Frankie, but since he was not our janitor tonight, I was a little afraid to talk to him now as a D-J. I told Kenzie I was scared, and she fixed this by shoving me closer to the D-J table, and that's how I knew Kenzie liked my plan, too.

D-J Mr. Frankie and The Plan

Mr. Frankie the D-J was happy to see us when we came over to his table. "Hellooo there girls," he said in his professional D-J voice. "Are you here to make a request?"

I didn't know what a request was, but I said yes with my head anyway.

"What would you like DJ Mr. Frankie to play for you?" he said, as if he was not D-J Mr. Frankie.

"I want to play a game to make sure everybody gets a chance to dance!"

"Well, that's a great idea!" he said. "What kind of a game do you want to play?"

"Since there are way more girls here than boys, I want to play a game that makes everyone dance both fast and slow with everyone, since Rose and Jenny are too shy to dance slow with each other." I pointed to them.

"Okaaaaay. Alright," D-J Mr. Frankie said, but he did not look too sure.

I imagined I was Xena, Warrior Princess when I said, "Excuse me, can I borrow your microphone?"

D-J Mr. Frankie was really not so sure about that idea, because he grabbed on to the microphone with both hands just like Bobby

157

does when he thinks I want his Batman doll. (I never want to play with his Batman doll, but I did want D-J Mr. Frankie's microphone pretty badly.)

D-J Mr. Frankie said, "Um, I guess so . . . but you can't say any naughty words."

This is how adults give younger people bad ideas, since I would *never* say bad words into a microphone! I reached for the microphone before he could change his mind and he helped take it off the stand for me. I told him, "The first song you play has to be fast. And then, the next song has to be very, very slow."

"Okay . . ." D-J Mr. Frankie looked like he was worried I might be stealing his job, and his eyes were searching for a counselor to rat me out.

D-J Mr. Frankie warned me once more, "Remember, no bad words, or I'll get into big trouble, okay?" He lowered the music, took the microphone back, and flipped the tiny switch on its side to turn it on and then handed it back to me.

I put my mouth near the microphone and said into it: "Let's play a game!" My voice was so loud that I scared myself and scared some people on the dance floor, too.

Now, most everybody was looking up at me, and only a few looked straight up, like the voice was yelling from the ceiling. I liked this microphone. I turned to D-J Mr. Frankie and said, "I feel like God," and he nodded his head a little sad like he was God before I took it from him. I wish I had not said that God part into the microphone.

"I want to play a game," I said again, and I waited until everybody was looking at me. "This is a game so everyone will get the chance to dance all songs, especially Rose and Jenny!" I saw them both looking at me from across the room, with their mouths wide open, catching flies.

"Everybody get your best friend and go out to the dance floor, right now!"

No one moved at first. People just looked at each other, and I saw Jenny and Rose look at each other, too.

I was God talking down from clouds, just like in the movies, as I explained the rules, "If you have a friend at the dance, then you have to play. It doesn't matter if your friend is a boy or a girl . . . just pick out your best friend right now and come on to the dance floor."

"We are going to dance two songs and you have to dance with your friend to both songs no matter how shy you are. *be brave!*" I might have yelled that last part a bit too loud, since lots of people plugged their ears.

Finally, people started slowly moving to the dance floor. Some started clapping and a few of the younger kids jumped in excitement, except for Bobby, who did not move from his spot, staring at the disco ball.

Kenzie said, "Heeey, I want to try the microphone!" but when she reached for it, I shook my head *no*, and she frowned at me. I don't usually say no to Kenzie, and she didn't like it one bit.

"Just trust me," I said, forgetting again that the microphone was on.

I said, extra loud, "Now everybody hold hands!"

Rose and Jenny were still not doing anything, and that is when Kenzie saw her chance at stardom and she grabbed the microphone from me before I could stop her.

She yelled into it, "Mommy, that means you, too! Everybody!!" More people covered their ears from her shouting and some cheered and laughed and started shouting along with Kenzie: "Everybody! Everybody!" The younger kids ran for their parents as if we had all planned this together, and pulled them out on the dance floor.

I saw Jenny and Rose shrug their shoulders at each other, and then Rose took Jenny's hand and they came onto the dance floor with the other chaperones and counselors.

It was working!

Everyone had found a dance partner, and Kenzie finally handed the microphone back to me with a proud look on her face. I warned everyone again: "Remember the rule, everybody has to dance *both* songs!"

Before I handed the microphone back to DJ Mr. Frankie, who was trying to get a song going, I reminded him: "One fast song, and one very slow song." He chose "Staying Alive" by the Bee Gees, and when we left D-J Mr. Frankie, Kenzie gave me a big hug on the dance floor, because my plan was a success! *Everybody* was dancing to the song and nobody was standing around the walls. I pulled Kenzie over to dance a little closer to Rose and Jenny, who were both doing John Travolta disco moves.

Finally, when the song was almost over, D-J Mr. Frankie changed the music over to a slow song called "Through the Fire," by Chaka Khan, and Jenny and Rose backed away from each other.

But I was ready for this.

"You have to dance both songs! Those are the rules!" I said.

Jenny said to Rose, laughing, "They don't realize they're breaking all the rules."

Rose said, "Right. *Life's* rules. Well, should we throw all the rules out the window and just dance?" she said, as she put her hands out to Jenny.

I was already dancing with Kenzie and I moved a little closer to them and heard Jenny say, "I wouldn't want to make you uncomfortable."

"Why are you so worried about me? You'll be dancing too," Rose said, laughing at her.

Jenny said back to Rose, "Hmm . . . well . . . how can I put this? I'm guessing I've danced with a few more women than you have."

That is when Rose said, "That's a relief, maybe *one* of us will be good at it!"

Jenny laughed and took Rose's hands. They looked uncomfortable at first, but soon they were laughing along with the other counselors dancing girl with girl and one couple of counselors was a man with a man, laughing like they were being so crazy to dance together. I wondered what the big deal was.

I secretly kept watching Rose and Jenny and by now they were hugging each other like good friends and not nervously talking any more as they rocked back and forth in a slow dance, just like I was doing with Kenzie, only they didn't step on each other's toes. Before long, I saw Rose was looking a little sleepy during the dance because her eyes weren't laughing anymore and were half closed. I wondered if she wanted to take a nap on Jenny's shoulder.

Jenny wasn't laughing anymore, either, but she looked wide awake. She also looked worried until she saw me staring and gave me a little wink. I wondered if she figured out my bigger scheme was working.

Rose and Jenny danced in a perfect little circle (Kenzie and I could only rock back and forth without tripping over each other) and their hug got closer, so I looked to see if maybe they were feeling the same way I felt when I was hugging Kenzie, and I think it was different. Jenny's eyes looked like she was not worried anymore and maybe she was getting sleepy too, like Rose, but then they stopped dancing, and stood apart.

I heard Jenny ask Rose if she was okay, but Rose was nodding her head as if nothing was wrong, which didn't seem true to me. I watched as they both walked off the dance floor. Jenny was following Rose, and she turned back to me and pointed to the corner of the room, "Girls, we'll be right over there, okay?"

I nodded, sad that my plan did not work.

I watched as they walked through the crowd to the end of the room. What made it extra sad was that Rose looked like she was wearing a wedding dress, and nobody in a wedding dress should ever stop dancing. They leaned against the wall, not looking at each other for a long time.

JENNY

I've done it now...no way out of this one . . . standing against a wall, pretending to watch a disco ball, desperately trying not to stare at her. Such a shot to the ego to realize I haven't evolved at all since high school. This woman. Rose. So damned beautiful—she clearly has no idea how she tortures me, and I have no idea how I'll get through this night without making a total fool of myself.

I shouldn't have danced with her; I should've stayed right here, a wallflower.

I'm glad she didn't see me at home before the dance, changing my clothes so many times while Kinzie stood there, alternating from teasing to whining about how I was making her late. "Getting ready for your girrrlfriend?" She deserved that pillow I threw at her. I smile thinking about it, and when I turn, Rose staring at me, smiling back. So beautiful that all I can do is look away.

I had told Kinzie to stop her teasing that I had a girlfriend, but her teasing felt good and she knew it. Did it mean someday she wouldn't think me a traitor to our Michelle? Would I still think it? Shoving that thought aside for another day . . .

I don't remember ever being so nervous getting ready to go anywhere. So nervous, I forgot Rose already had someone in her life...that disgusting man. How could that even be possible? Yet,

I had pushed this thought aside too while I changed outfits again. Skirt? Pants? Skirt?

She seemed to like the way I was dressed at the museum that Saturday, the day that started all of this. No, if I am being honest, it started before that. On that first day. She unnerved me with the way she looked at me, the way she stared at me, and, by contrast, how she wouldn't meet my eyes for every long. She was charming and funny and I walked away from her feeling a strange soreness at my ribs, at my cheeks; had it been that long since I used the muscles that make me laugh or smile?

Her obvious love of Liddy-Jean captured me on that first day, and her sweet kindness to Kinzie, and now, standing next to her at the dance, I am content to be a wallflower forever. Planted here, beside a Rose. I would love to paint her just as she looks tonight—never a fan of portrait painting, but I want to paint *her*.

Or, maybe I simply want to stare at her face for the time it would take to paint her. A voice inside reminds me: she's not yours to paint. Not yours for anything. But I can't stop thinking about how painting her would be so pleasurable and effortless, to stare at this woman for hours, for days. Would I remember to dip the brush?

ROSE

I wanted to tell Jenny, "I'm having a huge delayed reaction here—by about twenty years" . . . but I didn't. Instead, I leaned against a wall next to her at this silly dance, and didn't say a single thing. Finally, at this late stage in the game, I was feeling all the emotions I used to hear friends talk about in school but never understood.

Fear, nervousness . . . excitement . . . more fear . . . and a happiness which made me feel wine I had not drunk. All because of a dance with a *woman*? The excitement of being at a dance had always been lost on me, never much caring if a boy asked me to dance or not. I'd rather be with my friends. And while there was one girlfriend in particular that I had been devoted to, it never felt like this. But then again, I never had the courage to dance a slow dance with her.

Dancing with Jenny, hell, just standing next to her, I felt so . . . *alive*. It was then the thought struck me: maybe people had been feasting on this feeling all their lives, while I'd been settling for stale scraps. Why, in my mid-thirties, am I finally able to tap into the adrenaline rush those teenaged girls felt all through school, all through their lives? It was that rush that had sent me retreating, lightheaded, to lean against a wall, able to breathe again, except her nearness still made it hard to think . . . and now the silence between us had grown awkward.

"Our girls are having a ball," I managed, but saying it that way sounded intimate, and I felt Jenny turn to look at me. I could feel her eyes on me as I pretended to be watching the girls dance, waving to them. They weren't really dancing at all. It was more like hugging in a circle, but it was very sweet. Once again, I found myself envying Liddy-Jean. She wants to dance, she dances. She wants to hug, she hugs. She wants to feel love, she feels love.

I want to feel love.

Jenny said softly, "I wish you were having as good a time."

I made the mistake of looking at her, and my ability to speak completely ceased. I had never, ever, seen such a beautiful woman. Or person, for that matter. A ridiculous thought flashed through my mind: Maybe it could be enough just to look at her, if that was all I could have.

"What? No—I'm having a great time," and I attempted a smile, but my face seemed frozen so my mouth only twitched, as if I had told a lie. "Who knew holding up a wall could be so much fun?" I said.

Jenny's eyes bored into me. "Did I . . . say or do . . . something that made you uncomfortable?"

I had to look away again, hoping she didn't think I was turning away from her. I simply couldn't look at her. What the hell was wrong with me? Why am I so completely taken with her . . . and when had it become *so much more* than that?

I turned my head to the other side of the room to attempt to breathe air that was not laced with her scent. But it wasn't just her perfume that had gotten to me when we danced. Such softness . . . I felt a strange shiver pass through my body, as if I was cold in this stuffy cafeteria filled with people.

I let myself close my eyes now for just a second, telling myself to get a grip. When I opened my eyes again, Jenny had planted herself directly in front of my face.

"Rose, are you alright?"

"Yes, fine," I said. And I was. I took a deep breath, there was so much to say, but where to start—

"Excuse me for interrupting," a man's voice came from behind Jenny.

Jenny stepped aside and a tall, good-looking man stood before us, masterfully looking both sheepish and confident. He apologized again.

"I never, ever, do this . . . but I saw the two of you standing here, and I wondered if you were both alone?" His eyes were on me, and I found it ironic that while Jenny and I were standing so close together, he still considered us alone. I hadn't felt so *not* alone in my life!

He angled his body toward me to indicate more clearly which one of us he was interested in. I tried stepping back, but the brick wall was against my back.

He continued, "I'm taking a big chance here, and I'll be totally humiliated if you say no, since it was my son who told me to go ahead and ask the pretty woman in the white dress to dance. He claims I've been staring at you from the moment you walked in. Would you be kind enough to share one dance with me?"

He smiled a boyish grin, as I thought of a polite way to say no thank you.

I felt Jenny's eyes on me but couldn't turn back to look at her since I was foolishly sizing up the man for a fleeting second to see if he was a guy who could handle throwing Gary out of my house. I am disgusted at my weakness.

When I didn't answer he backed away and said, "I'm sorry, perhaps I shouldn't have—"

"Dance with him, Rose," Jenny said.

The firmness of Jenny's voice surprised me. I turned toward her, at a loss at how to signal that this was the last thing I wanted.

Jenny had a casual smile as she said, "Go along, Rose. I'll go find the girls and check on them."

Then she was gone.

Go along, Rose? Maybe she had been waiting for an opportunity to break from me. Her abrupt handing over of me to this man sliced through me and I felt a strange, burning sadness build in my gut. Maybe she couldn't get away from me fast enough, because she didn't once look back before I lost her in the crowd. Aside from that one shameless thought of using the man to toss Gary out of my life— Jenny wouldn't ever lose my attention in a million years. Nor would I use a man to get me away from another, no matter how much I wanted to.

Before I could sort it all out, the man sensed his opportunity was not lost, and he said, "I promise, just the one dance, then I'll be out of your way if you want, and I'll still be able to look my son in the eye. He is over there, watching us, but . . . no pressure." He gave a pleading smile as I looked over at his son, focused on us like all the pride he had for his father was riding on this single moment. Had this little boy lost his mom?

"Even your friend thinks you should dance with me," he said, and that I could not argue.

"Yes, she did," I said, trying to smile at him as my stomach burned.

He took the half smile as a yes and reached for my hand. I followed him, like a hesitant child conceding to take a bitter medicine. Hadn't I for so many years? As I walked, I searched for Jenny in the crowd and couldn't find her. Another slow song started as he stopped to dance and gently guided me closer to him. He gave a wave and thumbs-up to his son with the confidence of a hunter returning to camp with a deer. His son giggled with his friends as they watched us.

Why had I agreed to this?

I had not agreed. Jenny had agreed for me. Wake up, I told myself; whatever thoughts you have about that woman are ridiculous. Go along, Rose, she had said. And I went along. As I always do.

"I'm Derrick," he offered, as he guided us to a more open area on the floor. "My son attends The Center." Was he worried I would think he attended?

"I'm divorced," he offered, as a cherry on top. I was tempted to say, "I'm confused" but bit my tongue.

I thought about naming a different flower but couldn't come up

167

with one fast enough. "I'm Rose," I said, not even wanting to give him my name.

I imagined blurting out: *I'm a confused woman who's living with a man, while falling in love with a woman.* And that was the moment I realized I was falling in love with Jenny. I knew this now, as I felt the pit in my stomach from her leaving me with him.

Derrick encircled my waist now, but I held him away from my body and he politely did not further encroach. I didn't like the firmness of his hands, the hardness of his shoulder. Jenny had been so soft . . .

"Do you have a child attending The Center, Rose?"

"I have a young friend who attends. She invited me."

"Really? Awfully nice of you to come. I can't imagine being here if I didn't have to."

"I looked forward to it," I said, still scanning the room as we danced. More than that, it was all I had thought about for a week. I had been acting like a child, trying to get Liddy-Jean to talk about the dance every chance I got, once I knew Jenny would be going, with me. And now I had no idea where she was. I could see the girls dancing together out on the floor, and Liddy-Jean shot me a confused look. In that glance I could tell she wondered where Jenny was, and looked at me as if it was crazy to have traded a dance with Jenny for this man. It *was* crazy.

While I searched for her, I noticed Derrick gradually pulling me in closer, and by the time I realized it, it would have been awkward to pull away. So many times, I had been in that same position with men. Every time, in fact . . .

"Maybe I could give you a call sometime?" he said, as he adjusted his hand slightly tighter on my back.

I said, "I appreciate the dance, but I'm already . . . involved with someone."

Just then, the thought struck me that I had been thinking of Jenny, instead of Gary, and I nervously started to laugh.

"What's so funny?" he said.

"Just my life," I said.

"Well, you seem to be having a good time with me. Maybe you shouldn't be involved with that other guy," he said, joining me in a laugh.

"You know, you're right," I said, laughing harder. "I shouldn't be with that other guy."

"See?" he said, "Glad we agree. You need to dump him and go out with me."

Half right, I thought.

What I needed was this dance to end so I could find her. But then I thought, find her and tell her what? I had no frigging idea, but I knew one thing: I was so sick of staying in places where I didn't belong. I smiled again as I realized it took dancing with a man to make me realize I had fallen for a woman. I smiled again, and, thinking it was settled, he pulled me closer. He was right, it was settled.

Then, I saw Liddy-Jean point across the room, and I saw her.

At first I thought I had imagined seeing her, her figure shadowed in a darkened hallway leading into The Center, and then I lost her again as Derrick moved me in a frustrating circle, leaving me to crane my neck over his shoulder as I tried to find her. Had Jenny been watching me the whole time?

I found her again, in the opening of the same hallway.

In the moment my eyes found her, before she could rearrange her expression, I saw a crushed look on her face . . . it was a look that matched exactly what I felt when she handed me over to this man, *Go along Rose.*

Foolishly my heart pounded faster. *Go to her. Tell her. Tell her you think she belongs to you, although you have no right to claim her right now.* Yet, I did feel she belonged to me. Maybe because I belonged to her from the very beginning, maybe the first day we met, and after knowing her, I could never let myself belong to anyone else, except her.

When she saw I had spotted her, Jenny turned away and walked further down the darkness of the hallway, until I lost sight of her.

The overwhelming sense that I needed to follow her gripped me. *Go along, Rose!*

"Sorry, I have to go find the kids," I said, breaking from him, even though I knew Liddy-Jean and Kenzie were just a few feet away. As I turned away, he called out something I could not hear, because Liddy-Jean's shout of "Yaaay!" was so much louder.

Do Not Be Afraid of Permanent Ink

"What's the matter?" Kenzie said, and I realized I had forgotten to keep dancing with her so now I had to Spy-Dance so Kenzie would not Blow My Cover. I grabbed her hand and twirled her around saying "Shhh," in her ear so she would not laugh.

Jenny surprised me when she said, "Go along, Rose," and then walked away so that man could have a dance with Rose instead of her. Like my Auntie Theresa says, there is nothing worse than a clueless man, and this guy had no clue Rose wanted to follow Jenny.

I had to think of a plan . . .

I wanted to follow Rose, but Kenzie wanted me to dance another song, so I lied and said I had to use the bathroom first, which was luckily near that hallway. She didn't seem to mind since D-J Mr. Frankie was playing the Spice Girls again, so I asked her to do me a big favor, and watch Bobby for me.

Then, I pretended I was going into the bathroom but before the door closed behind me, I peeked out the crack to made sure no chaperones were looking, and ducked out of the bathroom to sneak down the same dark hallway Rose had just walked down trying to find Jenny.

It was scary to be in the hallway of The Center at night with no bright lights on, so I walked slowly and silently, just like a ninja.

171

I stopped near the end of the corridor when I heard Rose's voice around the corner.

"Why did you leave me there with him?"

I walked just a little farther down the hallway and stopped right at the end of the wall and peeked around the lockers. I felt my eyes stinging and wanting to cry because I had caused a fight between two best friends, since I was the one who tricked them both to slow dance together, and now Jenny didn't want Rose to dance with anyone else. I stayed still so I could hear, crossing my fingers on both hands for luck.

I heard Jenny say, "Why not? You were laughing and having a good time."

Rose answered, "I was laughing because I realized—"

Jenny put both her hands up, like she was a robber caught stealing, then she shook her head and said in a sad voice, "I'm sorry, Rose. You don't owe me any explanation. I'm the one that's standing in a dark hallway making a total fool of myself. I'm the one who was wrong."

"Wrong about what?" Rose asked.

Jenny said, "I have no right to say anything about who you want to spend time with."

"But I didn't want—"

"Please, don't." Jenny did not let Rose finish, and said, "It's my own fault. I've realized two things about myself tonight . . . and the first is that I've made a big mistake, and it's nothing you did. It's most definitely something I did."

"I don't understand . . . what did you do?" Rose asked.

"Can we just forget it? Please."

"No. Tell me," Rose said, moving closer to Jenny.

"I let myself look forward to this silly dance, okay?"

"I did too," Rose said.

Rose moved another step closer to Jenny, who was now leaning against a locker. Jenny put her hands back up again and shook her head in the dark. All I could see was two perfect black shadows of the two of them, and it would have looked like the perfect Valentine's Day card, except that Jenny looked like her hands were about to push

Rose away if she got one step closer.

Jenny was shaking her head now. "Never mind . . . it makes no difference. The ridiculous thing is, I knew all along I was doing it . . . and I did it anyway," she said as she tried to move past her, but Rose held her arm to stop her from walking away.

"What did you do?" Rose asked, sounding afraid to hear the answer, but Jenny shook her head again, and now Rose grabbed her by her other arm, and said, "Tell me, please."

Jenny shook her head again. "No. I don't want anything to change."

"What do you think you've done?"

Jenny raised her voice. "It's simple. I've spent too much time with you," she said, trying to pull away. "God, I hate making such a fool of myself! Please, can we just let it go? Rose, just *let me go*."

"Let you go? Let go of our friendship? I won't do that. You don't know how important you've become to me."

"No, Rose, *you* don't!" Jenny sounded angry now. "I've been keeping something from you, from the very beginning . . ."

Rose was not letting go of Jenny's arms, and I wanted to write in my notebook a reminder to tell Rose that grabbing people is wrong, and whenever I did that to my sister, my mother punished me, big time.

"Tell me," Rose said so quietly, and she must have thought Jenny could not hear her because she got even closer.

Jenny's shadow looked down at the floor instead of at Rose and said, "Of course you don't see it. You don't see that I want to be with you all the time. And I knew it was happening, right from the beginning . . . maybe the second we first met. But I let it happen anyway."

Rose said nothing back to her, but I could see that now her mouth had opened a little, like she was surprised. "What happened?" she asked in a tiny whisper.

Jenny laughed a little, but it was not a happy laugh. "This is going to sound pathetic . . . but . . . I just wanted to know if I could feel something again. Now, please stop asking questions. Or, I promise you, I'll make you even more uncomfortable—"

"Did you? Feel something again?" Rose whispered.

Jenny looked too tired to pull away from Rose's grip, and now her hands were on the locker she was leaning on.

Then Rose spoke so softly that I could barely hear. "Jenny, if I believed for a moment that I could be lucky enough to have you feel . . . something . . . for me, I would first tell you my life is such a mess that I can't bring you into the middle of it. Not you, and especially not Kenzie."

Jenny covered her face with her hands and I guessed by how quiet she got that she was crying, and Rose looked like she didn't know what to do next.

Just as I was wishing Rose could be strong like Xena, Rose said, "But if I could . . . I would want you in my life . . . every second of my life, in fact."

Then Rose took Jenny's hands away from hiding her face and she kissed one hand, and then the other, until Jenny leaned in closer to her and I wondered if they would slow dance right there in the hallway.

Rose said, "I won't give up my friendship with you, no matter what is happening in my life. But I have to know. Do you feel this too? Or am I just imagining—"

"That I might love you?" Jenny said.

Then Jenny slowly nodded her head yes and Rose hugged her, and Jenny lay her head on Rose's shoulder, just like I do when I would fall asleep watching TV and Dad carries me upstairs to my bed.

But this was different.

It was so quiet in the hallway, I could hear them both breathing. Then, over Rose's shoulder, I saw Jenny slowly lift her face toward the ceiling where a red light was now on her face like she was thanking God up in heaven, if God was hanging out in The Center. I could see tears on her cheeks sparkling, and I watched as she closed her eyes and held them shut like you should do when your most important

174

prayer might be answered like when I got a brand-new bike with absolutely no strawberry and banana taffy stuck on it.

Jenny whispered, "I've tried to keep this to myself . . . I didn't expect to feel this ever again, not after everything I lost."

"Kenzie's mother," Rose said, and Jenny nodded into her shoulder.

Rose whispered as she hugged her more tightly and said, "I have nothing like what you had to compare this to. I can only tell you, so much makes sense now . . . why I haven't been happy for so long, why so much was missing in my life. Long before Gary. I have no right to be thinking I could take care of you and Kenzie when my life is such a mess, but I'm thinking all the time how much I want to."

"Let me help you," Jenny whispered.

"No. I won't have you or Kenzie get mixed up in this, no matter how much I wish I could have you."

Rose hugged Jenny even closer, and I was so happy that I was going to let them know I was there with a big *Yaaay*, but before I could, Rose pulled away and took Jenny's face in her hands and gave her two kisses, one on each cheek. I hoped this would make it all better, since that always works when Mom kisses my cheeks.

Then the tiniest bit of light between their faces disappeared as Jenny kissed Rose right on the lips, just the way they do in the movies. I heard somebody whisper, "Yes," and maybe it was Rose, but it may have been me, and I covered my mouth just in case.

When the long kiss ended Rose said, "So that's what it's supposed to feel like . . . kissing somebody . . . because I never understood any of that before." I watched as Rose finally got to touch Jenny's hair the way I always knew she wanted to, moving it gently away from Jenny's face.

Rose asked, "You said you realized two things tonight . . . what else did you realize?"

Jenny answered, "It turns out I'm an insanely jealous person. When that guy—"

"What guy?" Rose laughed softly.

Jenny said, "I've felt this jealousy before, at your home . . ."

"I'm going to change my entire life," Rose said.

"Is that what you want?" Jenny asked, and now she was holding both of Rose's arms, maybe so she could not run away.

Rose leaned in to kiss her and I saw that the kiss was bigger than the last one and when Jenny held Rose's face to hers, Rose made a happy sound, and this time a giggle came out of my mouth before I could stop it, and when I bent over, a pen flew out of my pocket and made a big noise. I knew it was time for me to get the heck out of there and I ran down the hallway back to the dance.

A few minutes later, Rose and Jenny came to find me and Kenzie where we were dancing. I was guilty from spying and so tried not to look Rose in the eye.

"Liddy-Jean, can you come help me get some drinks for everybody?"

I nodded, and followed her to the vending machine, wondering if I was in big trouble for spying. Rose looked like she wanted to say something to me while two Cokes and two waters dropped into the bottom of the machine. She stayed quiet and weird as she reached for the sodas, so I helped her by talking first.

"I know all about what gay lesbians are," and Rose dropped a Coke, and the can spit out brown soda all over the floor. D-J Mr. Frankie ran over, magically turning into an expert Mr. Frankie janitor again.

When it was all cleaned up and we were alone at the soda machine with our drinks, Rose finally said to me, "Okay, Liddy-Jean, what does gay lesbians mean?"

I was surprised she didn't know. "I can tell you if this is not going to turn into a Daytime Coke Room Talk, because we are missing the dance." Rose looked confused, so I got right to my point.

I said, "Gay lesbians are girls who like girls, like boyfriends." Rose nodded but said nothing, so I said, "I know what bisexual is, too."

"Okay," she said.

Rose had a lot to learn, and if I had known this, I would have told her about all this stuff sooner. I helped Rose get one more

Coke out of the machine, as she said, "I suppose I do need a drink," laughing at herself as she popped open a Coke and took a long drink, as I explained, "Bi means two. Like a bicycle has two wheels. So, a bisexual is someone who does something twice, like kissing in a hallway, at least two times," I said, and Rose spewed her Coke right into the trash can.

I laughed at Rose, "Hey, can I try that?"

"Liddy-Jean, this is a grown-up thing . . ."

"Spitting in a trash can? Mom never does that," I said.

"No, Liddy. Is there something you want to talk with me about? Maybe about something you saw tonight?"

"I want to go back to Kenzie and Jenny so we all can dance again."

"We can do that, but I want you to tell me if something is bothering you," Rose said.

"Losing my favorite pen bothered me, not the kissing part . . . oops." In the spying world, this is called blowing my cover. "I lost my favorite pen."

Rose reached into her dress pocket and surprised me by handing me my pen.

I was so happy she found it and said, "It's O-K, Rose, you are supposed to kiss when you are in love," and I clicked the end of my pen to test if everything was still working perfect. It was.

Rose still looked worried as we walked out of the Coke room, but once Rose and I crossed the dance floor with the drinks, we both got distracted about how pretty Jenny was standing alone on the dance floor, waiting for us. Before we reached Jenny, Rose stopped me and said, "Liddy-Jean, you saw us in the hallway, didn't you?"

"I am not supposed to spy on people."

"It's not your fault. What you saw was inappropriate—I mean it was not good behavior at a dance, and I'm sorry you saw that. Private things shouldn't happen here."

"That is for sure," I said, "everyone knows that. Am I in trouble for spying?"

"No, Liddy-Jean. But I could be in trouble for kissing."

"You would be in bigger trouble if a penis goes into your vagina and makes you have a baby that looks like a turtle."

This must have been news to Rose, because she stopped talking. Then she took a deep breath, and put her hands on both my shoulders to stop me from walking to Kenzie. "I am not supposed to be kissing anybody at a dance."

"Because you are supposed to love Gary?"

"No. Because I am supposed to be a chaperone."

"I can keep a secret as long as someone tells me *exactly* what I am not supposed to say."

Rose smiled at me. "I don't want you to keep secrets, I just need some time to think."

"About kissing Jenny?" I asked, trying to wink.

She smiled at me. "Among other things," she said. "I'm sorry you have to keep such a grown-up-type secret for just a little while longer."

"I like to keep secrets. I have a lot of secrets I haven't even put in the book. Like, Jenny is so much prettier than Gary."

We both looked back at Jenny and started walking back to her again.

"Well, that's no secret," Rose said.

When the dance was over, on the way out I tugged on Rose's sleeve so she would bend down to let me whisper a secret into her ear.

"Even if you are scared, my Auntie Theresa says it is so much more exciting to just jump in and do a crossword in permanent ink."

Then I handed back my favorite pen to Rose. When she gave me a hug I said, "No kissing," to make her laugh, and it worked.

JENNY

Rose could be yours if you want her badly enough . . .

The Demon inside my head was speaking as usual, without any regard to reality.

I knew if I kissed her, I would be risking a world of pain if it went down as I suspected it would, but my judgment was so clouded after seeing her with that man. Jealousy made me play with fire. Jealousy this strong is something I don't ever want to feel again . . . I wanted to choke that guy with my bare hands. The way he wrapped his hands around her waist, the way he leaned into her, so entitled. Wow. I've got it bad . . .

There had been a connection between us right away, although at first Rose seemed unaware. Knowing she was unavailable, and straight, did nothing to stop this connection from waking me up at night, or sleepwalking through my days with ridiculous thoughts of how I wanted to build a life with her. How did I let this happen?

I deserved the lecture I gave my most impulsive friends. They all had done it at least once in their lives: falling for a straight woman, or married woman. Each time I gave them the "It could happen to anyone" thing, the truth was, I never thought it could ever happen to me. I would say, didn't they see it happening from a hundred miles away? Just as I did with Rose. And didn't they, at several points, choose to move forward to pursue the friendship anyway? As I did with Rose. I had judged them harshly, silently, and now I realized I had enjoyed the feeling of superiority when I turned out to be so damned right. I would be right this time, too. It would be a big mistake and not just for me.

I could blame it on losing my love to a terrible illness, leaving me alone with the beautiful child we adopted, whom I now dedicate my very life to, praying she will be all right with one (slightly damaged) mother, instead of two.

I never played games with straight girls. Even when I was young, careless and lonely. But that was before I lost Michelle; before I really knew what lonely was. What was it about Rose that had completely taken over me? How was I not the one calling the shots? Equal parts temptation and worry for her, keeping me up at night.

And now I was stupidly bargaining: *Maybe I could have just one more kiss.* Just one more time, then I could walk away . . . from the kiss, from the friendship, from the woman.

How ridiculous.

This was how The Demon inside me operated from the very beginning with her. At first The Demon only asked for little things: *Just invite her to the museum and then lunch. Maybe out for ice cream . . . what could it hurt? The kids are enjoying each other, and it's been so long since you could appreciate even looking at another person after Michelle. Why not join the book project? Even if it meant more time together, just do it to satisfy your hunger for a while, just until you get your head together.*

But my head hadn't been together since losing Michelle. And it was less together now. The Demon's advice only served to make me more starved, and I suspected this was its plan. Like eating pastry for breakfast. Having one sweet taste made you starve for it all day long. Like waking from a steamy dream that stays with you all day. It had been years since I had even thought of sex. And now, it was impossible not to. Rose had escalated every human need. I was starving all the time now. For sex, for food, for companionship of her.

And all this *before* we had kissed.

I realized too late that while I might have been able to walk away before, all I could do now was wait and hope, and if it fell apart, pray that what was left of me could survive another loss. At least when I lost Michelle, I had been strong at the start, for my daughter. I'm not strong now.

And now, Rose has happened.

There was no mistaking what Rose said after our moment in the hallway. She wouldn't let go of me, but she couldn't be with me. Even in the darkness, her face flushed with color, looking scared and guilty and all the other things you're supposed to be when you have just cheated on a person, even a person like Gary, by kissing another.

I would have coached any friend to abandon thoughts of being with Rose. I would have seen the stupidity of it from the very beginning, and now, I was completely in this woman's hands. Thankfully, she didn't seem to know it. If Rose knew I was a person with no strength or will to call my own, it would have been better if she shoved me away. But she didn't shove. She pulled me to her. And we kissed. The kiss lifted me out of darkness I didn't know I still walked through every day, and now, of all things, I wanted to live and I wanted a life with Rose.

My Demon whispered, *She clearly wants you. She may even love you. She definitely needs you. That Gary guy could be big trouble. And you don't back away from trouble when you love someone . . . do you?* The Demon was going for the soft sell this time. *You love her.*

I did love her. And maybe she did need me. As weak as I was, I knew I could love her beyond what she imagined love could be. *She does need me . . . even as a friend*, I reasoned, and now my voice sounded as convincing as The Demon's. Of course, it should, I thought, The Demon is Me.

Kenzie was two years old when we got her. We had so many wonderful years as a family. And now, I was heading toward my tenth year without Michelle. *Ten years.* I had not thought of the totality of it until right then.

My body was waking up from a deep hibernation. I was feeling parts of myself I assumed I had buried along with Michelle. It was springtime in Hornyville, for fuck's sake. And it started out as something so trivial, or that is what I told myself. Just fleeting thoughts of kissing the beautiful, kind woman with the picture-perfect name. It grew to an obsession so encompassing that it smothered any guilt about my loyalty to Michelle. That my body could desire a full life without her was shocking to me. To make matters worse, my body came to life with a vengeance as if making up for lost time. At the age of forty-three, in the span of a few short months, I had fallen for, and become obsessed with, a straight woman.

The awakening didn't come back to life gradually, either, but rather as an explosion in the middle of the night when I woke up in the throes of a full-blown orgasm, with dreams of making love to Rose. And now, every morning since, I was waking with desire for her. It was alarming how the sexual upsurge of my body happened so soon after meeting her. Just weeks after our museum trip, lunch, and then our stop for ice cream. Innocent enough, right? But that damned dish of ice cream was the moment I was catapulted into this insane love. I wanted to share every meal, every dessert with her. All the time that I had left on this Earth, and I can't even remember the flavor of the ice cream. Had I known I was in such a weakened state to be vulnerable to all of this simply from a museum and ice cream date with a beautiful woman, I would never have left the house. I would never have risked leaving my protective bubble of full-time mother and being the rare combination of a driven, yet passionless, artist. But now I had burst that bubble, and The Demon teamed up with my own body against me to make sure it would happen.

Worst of all, it was feeling incredibly wonderful to be alive. The kind of alive that you would do anything to keep. All my beautiful memories of Michelle could not stop me from falling in love with Rose. I wondered if Rose had any inkling of the starved soul she was dealing with, and the lengths I would go to have love again?

ROSE

It hits me at the oddest moments: I kissed a woman.

I tell myself stranger things have happened in the world. Maybe it meant nothing, and simply marked a moment in time. Why do I feel it means everything, and marks the beginning of time?

I only know after it happened, I couldn't take my eyes off her for a second, and really, how healthy is that? I would get nothing done but look at her. And who wouldn't? Stunning, interesting, creative, smart, and . . . so incredibly sensual. I couldn't ignore that any longer.

I wondered, how long have I been thinking about kissing her? Maybe, for a long time. But it was as if the thoughts had been taking place in a private corner of my brain. Private even from me. Secret conversations had taken place, and now I was hearing them all playing back loud and clear from a tiny stealth recorder, which had grown now into an enormous speaker, blaring in my ears from inside my head. I felt something for her from the first moment I met her—I had thought about how I could spend more time with her. Though my lack of experience struggled to imagine the details, I imagined touching her hair, or being touched by the hands of an artist. And now that I know what it is like to kiss her, how will I ever think of anything else?

How have I managed not to have these conversations with myself as it was unfolding? It's as if I knew the tiny seed was too fragile—too remarkable—for me to openly consider what it meant to fall in love with J. I was finally let in on the secret of what I felt, but only after my confession to her.

Stranger still, when I imagine what it would be like to be closer to her, it seems such a natural path to take, although natural is not the way I would describe that kiss. Supernatural, maybe. What would the rest of being with her be like? Have I waited for this all of my adult life? I never guessed the person I had been waiting for would come packaged as a beautiful woman. Or maybe I was keeping secrets from myself.

After last night, I can finally admit I have never wanted Gary, or any man before him, for that matter. Although, at one time, Gary seemed a kind man. His fall has been so gradual, I hadn't noticed until he was in too deep, and now he has evolved into someone I wouldn't speak to if we passed on the street. Except that now his failure has become mine as well.

At least my work life is on track. My career took a lucky turn right out of college, but after that, I worked hard to create a path for myself that brought me from marketing assistant to marketing manager and soon after, marketing director. When it became clear to most that I was qualified for Gina's position, and clear to a few I had been doing her job for years, this was a secret I had to keep if I wanted to keep the job I had.

It took a while for me to realize that Gary was anxious to secure my steadily increasing paycheck. I had bought myself a man in my life, and now, after kissing Jenny, it appears I bought entirely the wrong brand. Calvin Klein needs to be traded in for Vera Wang. DeNiro for Streep. Hercules for Xena. Now that I think about it, maybe I didn't enjoy Liddy-Jean's favorite show, Xena, for the Greek Gods. *Maybe it was the Amazons all along.*

The desire has obviously been within me. I may not have consciously chosen this, but when I kissed Jenny, my world flipped entirely on its axis: up was now down, right was now left, and man was now woman. And, though nothing would ever be as it was, I didn't care. I wanted to run to her, with my arms outstretched, and stow my baggage in a locker I kissed her against, in a dark hallway at a dance.

If Jenny knew Gary like I did, she would run, and not look back. It was my obligation to let her know how I am trapped, so she could make the decision if she wanted to keep a friendship with me . . . or more.

To top it all off, Liddy saw me in the hallway with Jenny. She didn't seem troubled, but she had seen us. I am left wondering why Jenny has not run from the baggage that is Gary—I had to push her away. I didn't have a chance to tell Jenny that confusion was not part of what I felt. I felt clarity for the first time in my life.

The Jealous Kitty

Sometimes after a really good weekend, I wonder if I will not want to be back at work, but I always want to see Rose, Kenzie, and Jenny. I try not to complain like other people I hear in the ladies' bathroom:

1. "Weren't we just here?"
2. "I can't believe it's only 2:30 . . ."
3. "Is it Friday yet?"
4. "Same S-H-I-T, different day."
5. "Another day, another dollar."
5. "You mean, 60 cents . . . men make the dollar."

I realized the difference between when I complain and the other Worker Bees do is that I never think these thoughts for very long. There are people at work who have been unhappy for years without stopping, and I am lucky, because I cannot do anything for that long!

After only a few minutes at work, I am very happy to be there again and always get sad when the end of the day is coming, especially if it is not a work-on-book night. If other people tried to be happy where they were, instead of where they are not, all Worker Bees would have a better life, but not better than the Wand-Wavers, of course. (Rose said we would put that part in the book, in my exact words.)

One of the suggestions I have in *Wand-Wavers and Worker Bees* is that once in a while the bosses should end those meetings with an announcement: "If this meeting has created a problem with any Deadlines, just let me know and I will help you." When I shared this suggestion with Rose and asked her to imagine how happy people would be if the boss offered to take the mail to the mailroom, or even stuff an envelope, she said I was very smart!

Kenzie is sometimes jealous when I talk to Jenny too much. This made me think about how the Worker Bees sometimes get jealous about the boss's attention. Many times after a company meeting the Worker Bees would complain that certain people always get called by name for everything good they did, while some names never got called. This makes the workers feel their jobs are not important.

It works this way: if one of the bosses gets their names called out for a successful project, they only mention Gina and "her team" and they would never say the names of the people that did all of the work. Sometimes they would not even mention the team at all!

The bosses never remember that while salesmen get compliments on the stuff they sold, the customer service ladies never got any attention making sure all that stuff gets to the customers. In the Product Development department, where the artist people are, they say they never get attention for inventing all the stuff the salesmen would sell.

Rose liked all of this and she added it to the book, though I heard her whisper to Jenny she was a little worried about her job if this book ever did get published. I was worried for her, too, and I decided not to tell her about my meeting with Gina. I wanted to fix that problem myself.

Rose and Jenny acted so differently toward each other since the night of the dance. I saw Rose look at Jenny many times, but she would only look when Jenny wasn't watching her. I wanted to hand them both a note to tell them it was silly and to stop.

When I wanted to look at Kenzie's pretty hair, I just looked at it. Sometimes, I would even tell her I was looking at her pretty hair.

But then I remembered about the girl in the Product Development Department who had the really big boobs and how I had made myself not look at them, even though I really wanted to. Probably Rose and Jenny wanted to look at each other *that* way, too.

Finally, I passed a note with a Handy List to Rose, just like I do with my book notes:

1. My mom says it is rude to stare at people.

2. If you do stare, you are supposed to try to keep looking into people's eyes, because it is bad to stare at someone if they have really big boobs, but Jenny does not have those, so it's ok for you to stare at her.

3. You should just tell Jenny you want to kiss her again.

After Rose read the note, she folded it up quickly and put it into her pocket, and I thought I was in trouble. But then she turned around in her seat to look at me and her face was red and she made funny wide-eyes that made me laugh out loud.

Kenzie said in her fake-teacher-bossy voice, "What's so funny, Liddy-Jean? You're supposed to be working."

I turned back around to my table but when I looked back a few seconds later, I saw not only Rose looking at Jenny, but now Jenny was looking at Rose, too. They stared for a long time at each other, and I felt like I was spying on them again, so I turned back to my own table.

Kenzie smiled and whispered in my ear.

"My mom loves Rose."

"No kidding," I said, and Kenzie got up and walked over to Rose and backed onto her lap to get a better look at what they were doing at the table. Jenny stopped drawing her cartoons to watch and Rose smiled at her over Kenzie's shoulder.

Kenzie told me she used to do this all the time with her other mother, Michelle, and she called her "My Little Lap Girl." Jenny might have been thinking this too, because she stopped drawing and was looking at the two of them as if she was watching a happy movie that makes your eyes cry anyway.

After a few minutes, Kenzie said, "Am I too heavy?" and Rose answered, "Nah. You're just right."

Even from across the living room I could see Jenny only wanted to be watching them and she kept tracing over the same lines on her cartoon again and again, until Kenzie told her mom to stop, and that it was time to draw a totally different picture.

I agreed, "Yes. Time to draw a totally different picture," and Rose smiled at me, like it was a secret message for her.

Things Go Wrong in a Bathroom

A lot of things can go wrong in a bathroom. Especially a bathroom at work.

There are too many fun things all in one room: paper on rolls, pop-up paper towels, pop-up paper Kleenex, blow dryers that feel good on the face, water, squirt soap, and *free* girl things for your "monthly visitor," as Mom and Auntie Theresa say. There are pads, like what I use, and also the same little cardboard tubes that Mom has in the bathroom closet that are just for her. The tubes look like tiny empty toilet paper rolls and stuffed inside with cotton just like one of Auntie Theresa's cannoli, but I am not supposed to say that at the dinner table.

I also have problems with squirt bottles of soap. Turns out they are really hard to stop squirting over and over and make the sink and floor pretty slimy. Since they do not last very long, I tried asking for more soap squirt bottles for Christmas but Mom took it off my list saying expensive bottles of squirt soap were only for public places, like work, and she switched back to bar soap.

I found out that this squirt-soap-only-in-public-places rule was not true, since Rose had a pretty big soap bottle with a squirt top in her bathroom. Turns out, squirt soap is a real time waster because Rose and Jenny kept knocking on the door to see if I was all right.

When I finally came out, I had to tell Rose she was out of soap. I love Rose because the bottle was full when I went in, but she knows it is impolite to talk about what people do in the bathroom.

Anyway, writing in bathrooms was getting me into trouble again. I knew some day this would happen since I can never keep a secret from Mom for very long, and with my sister, it made it especially hard. This morning I heard Mom and my sister talking, so I knew what was coming. I sat on my bed waiting and hoping Mom would not end up with a striped shirt again.

Mom came in trying to act casual before she asked me about the notebooks she found hiding behind the toilet.

Mom: "Liddy-Jean, I would like to hear more about this project you're working on with Rose."

Me: "What project?" But I knew.

Mom: "I saw your notebook in the bathroom, and the one in your backpack. Are you still getting extra training at work, or are you working on something different?"

Me: "Not the second one."

(I gave this a try, but I knew it would not work. That is when Mom patted my leg, but I was not fooled . . . this was a pat for more information.)

Mom: "Tell me what's going on, or I'll have to call Rose."

I started to cry. Sometimes this works, but in this case, it was a bad choice. It made my mother worried and that is the worst kind of face to see on a mother. This means *big* trouble because when Mom is worried, nothing will stop her from finding out what you are up to.

Mom: "I have to make sure nothing bad is happening, Liddy-Jean. Tell me right now what you've been up to."

I did not have to fake cry now, since her voice sounded angry.

Me: "But it's a secret."

And that's when Mom got up from the bed and I heard her pick up the phone in the kitchen. I tried to cry a little harder.

Mom: "Is Rose available, please?"

Me: "Mom, Boss Gina does not allow personal calls."

Mom did not answer me. There was nothing I could think of to do but listen to her talk to Rose and wait for her to find out all about the book.

Mom: "Hello Rose, it's Maggie Carpenter, Liddy-Jean's mom. I'm fine, thanks, and you? I'm calling about Liddy-Jean. She says she has a secret and I'm a little concerned that something's going on that I should know about. Can you please shed some light on this for—"

Mom got very quiet, except for saying uh-huh many times. I wondered if Mom would be mad that I was writing a book telling people the secrets of how to become a bad boss and this made me cry for real this time.

Mom: "You mean at the dance? Liddy didn't mention that . . . Uh-huh. I see."

What did the dance have to do with our book project?

Mom: "You mean Kenzie's mother? Um . . . Liddy-Jean didn't mention anything about that to me, and if she had, well, that's your personal business. I have talked with Liddy about certain . . . things . . . like that. Liddy is old enough to know that there are—uh, all kinds of—well, it's unfortunate she witnessed your private moment, Liddy-Jean has a spying habit that we're still working on."

Shoot! The spying! I smacked my hand to my forehead like they do on cartoons.

Mom walked into the living room still on the phone, making wide cartoon eyes at me that were not funny at all because the spying thing was not a new problem.

Mom: "I appreciate you telling me that, but no, that's not why I'm calling. But . . . well . . . good luck with that. I was calling to see how Liddy-Jean's extra training was going at work? She never tells me what you've been teaching her and I found a few notebooks . . ." Mom lowered her voice but I could still hear her. "At first, I thought she was keeping another bathroom journal, but there seemed to be a lot of notes about bees?"

Things got quiet again.

Mom: "A corporate what? No, she never mentioned that. She

said she was getting extra work training."

I was in big trouble. Mom hated Liddy-Jean-the-Liar worse than bathroom journals.

Mom walked down the hallway so I could not hear . . . but I followed her.

Mom: "Rose, it's sweet of you to be so encouraging, I just don't want her set up for a big disappointment . . . Oh. Really? Well, that's nice of you to say, and as I said, it's always good to encourage, but . . . It's just that people with challenges . . . well, they don't often become published authors, and I do worry about getting her hopes up—"

Mom stopped talking for a long time now and I hoped Rose was not in really big trouble too.

Mom: "Really? You must be helping her quite a bit if you think it might actually be—wow, that would be something. Thanks for filling me in. She enjoys working with you and the whole Marketing team. My husband and I both appreciate how great you have been with her. And . . . well, I hope things work out for you with . . . the other thing. Liddy likes Jenny very much, you've both been so good to her. You understand, I'll have to speak with Liddy about what she saw? All right, Rose, take care, and thank you again for all your extra time with her."

Mom was getting ready to hang up, so I scooted off to my room.

Mom: "I'm sure you heard most of that?"

Me: "I always try not to spy."

Mom: "Rose says you two are writing a book together and that you're doing a great job on it."

Me: "Yes."

I stayed quiet, which is sometimes best, so I don't accident-tell more secrets than I have to. I learned that from a detective show on TV where the detective would just be very quiet, and that trick would make the bad guy talk more. Mom stayed quiet too, and I wondered if Mom knew that trick.

Me: "Did Rose tell you Jenny is a great artist? Nobody can draw Worker Bees like that lady."

Mom: "I think it's wonderful you are writing a book, Liddy-Jean. I really do."

Me: "But it was supposed to be a surprise so that two great things could happen on the same day."

Mom: "What two great things?"

I didn't want to tell that part, since it was the only part of the book surprise I had left. So, I lied.

Me: "Two great things are having a Marketing Department job *and* writing a book."

Mom: "I see. You were going to surprise Dad and me with the book?"

Me: "But now I can't."

Mom: "Liddy, believe me, when the book is done it will still be a great surprise. Since it's nothing for Dad to be worried about, how about you can still keep it a secret from him, okay?"

Me: "And from Dawn, too?"

Mom nodded yes. But then she took my hand like she was going to give me some bad news, like it was time to go get another flu shot at the doctor's office, and so she was giving me Support.

Mom: "Liddy, Rose is being very, very nice to help you with the book."

Me: "And Jenny and Kenzie, too! Jenny drew a big beehive for the Worker Bees that looks just like our bus stop where Kenzie and I wait to be picked up after work. And the Wand-Wavers are these big, fat hungry bears who want to eat all the honey that the Worker Bees work so hard to make and—"

Mom: "Speaking of Jenny, I want to talk to you about Jenny and Rose in just a minute."

Uh, oh.

Mom: "But first, Liddy-Jean, I want you to understand that sometimes people say nice things because they want to encourage you to try new things. Like writing a book. Rose is a very good person, and she loves you very much, so she wants to encourage you to be a writer. I know you know what 'encourage' means."

Me: "It means when you are learning but you are not great yet. I don't *only* write in the bathroom anymore."

Mom: "I know, sweetheart."

Mom: "Honey," she said patting my hand, "I know Rose says she may have found a publisher, but I don't want you to be disappointed if your project doesn't become a real book."

Me: "It was already a real book a long time ago before Rose the Editor tore the pages out to organize me, but Rose told me it would be a real book again later, when we are done, and Rose never lies to me, not even once."

Mom: "I'm sure she's not lying to you, sweetheart. She just may be trying too hard to be a good friend to you. I just want you to remember, even if it doesn't become a real book, you're still having fun writing it, aren't you?"

Since I had never heard Mom be so wrong before, I wondered if the book project might be all for fun, just like she said. This was very bad news.

Mom: "Now, I want to talk to you about what happened at the dance."

Me: "Okay. Good luck," I said, because it was hard to concentrate after finding out my book project was not real.

Mom: "Rose says you saw her and Jenny kiss. I want to make sure you understand that Rose and Jenny are both adults and what they did is not wrong, except, maybe they shouldn't have done that at the dance."

I did not want Rose to be in trouble.

Me: "It is my fault because I tricked them into dancing together. I know how to fix things for Rose." Mom looked at me for a long time and didn't say anything.

Mom: "Are you worried about what you saw?"

Me: "I wasn't spying, I was just looking for them. As soon as they kissed like in a movie, I ran from the hallway so fast, but I dropped my pen and did not go back for it, so the jig was up."

I saw Mom smile a little so, as Mom would say, I worked that angle.

Me: "Rose and Jenny needed privacy more than I needed my pen."

Mom: "This isn't going to be a talk about your spying. I just want to make sure that it didn't bother you—what you saw, with Rose and Jenny."

Me: "I have seen lots of people kiss, in the movies and you and Dad, too, a long time ago."

Mom: "Your dad and I still kiss . . ."

Me: "Not on the couch watching TV anymore."

That made Mom quiet for a little bit.

Mom: "Liddy-Jean, since Rose and Jenny are both women, I know it's unusual—but I want to make sure you know that there's nothing wrong with it. Do you understand?"

Me: "Yes. Except for Gary."

Mom: "Who's Gary?"

Me: "Rose has a bad boyfriend. So, it is O-K she kissed Jenny instead of him. All the Marketing Girls say Gary does not like women, and we all agree that Jenny is prettier than Gary, and besides, if Rose marries Jenny, this will be very good because then Kenzie will have two moms again, just like she did before one of them died. Kenzie is nothing like me, because I think one mom is plenty."

Mom laughed at this, said her usual "Suppose So," and she gave me a quick hug and kissed me on the top of my head, and, like magic, I wasn't in trouble anymore.

I was happy until later, when I wrote down today's Mom Daytime Bed Talk. Rose only giving me encouragement, and the book project was not real, and I would not be a famous author. Worse than that, I would not be able to fix everything I planned . . . and there was so much to fix.

Lap Girl

Everything is different now. We all still worked on the book because I was afraid to tell Rose I did not want to work on a book that was not real. She kept asking me what was wrong, but I could not think of a nice way to tell her that friends do not lie to each other just to make Encouragement.

I did not tell this to anyone, not Mom, and not even Kenzie.

On Christmas, Kenzie called me to tell me a secret story on the phone. Rose had surprised Jenny with a secret Christmas present.

Kenzie whispered, "I wanted to spy on them, just like you do. But Mom went to meet Rose without me."

Now this was interesting! I took the phone and slid under my bed with it to make extra privacy.

"When Mom came home very early from meeting Rose, she had a present with her, and said it was a Christmas present from Rose. When I asked to see it, Mom carefully peeled off the wrapping, because it was so pretty. Under the wrapping I saw the exact same brown paper they use at Mom's gallery."

"What was it?" I asked, but I already knew.

"It was my mom's painting of the baby gorilla sitting on its mother. She sold it and I knew it made her sad since she left the empty space on the wall. It was Rose that bought it to give it back to my mom for a Christmas present! I could see my mom was trying not to cry happy tears."

"Wow!" I said, a bit louder than I should have.

Kenzie said, "Mom came upstairs to put the painting back on the wall just where it used to be—"

"And now your mom can touch the toe again every time she walks by it!" I said.

Now it was my turn to share a secret. I whispered into the phone, "The painting reminds your mom of you sitting on your mom Michelle's lap. Just like how you sit on Rose's lap now."

Kenzie liked that idea, and I liked it too. I especially liked that even though I found out the book was not real, some of my plans were still working.

JENNY

I'm guessing it's not a secret to Kenzie and Liddy-Jean, that I am the one that needs Rose the most. I tried and failed twice to tell Rose I couldn't continue working on the book project, and opted to just stare at her instead. I told myself I can't push her away because of Kenzie. Lies we tell ourselves.

The last time we worked together, Kenzie got between us, and I thought she was getting jealous, until she slid onto Rose's lap instead of mine for a look at the cartoons. Kenzie had done this a thousand times with Michelle, backed up into her lap and landed on her with no warning. Kenzie thought to ask if she could sit (after she sat) and Rose just laughed and hugged her while I melted watching them. I am not a public crier, even at funerals, but that was a close call. I couldn't draw a damn thing watching them sitting together like that, so I traced over the same lines twice until Kenzie told me to draw something different.

The corners of my eyes burned because I could hear Michelle saying, "My Little Lap Girl." How could I take Rose away from Kenzie after all she has already lost in her life? After all I'd lost, how could I take Rose from me?

It was late on a Friday afternoon when my phone rang. I had been getting ready to head out to meet her.

"It's me," Rose said, and I forgot to breathe at the sound of her voice.

"Yes?" Would this be the day she would tell me she couldn't see me anymore?

I had agreed to meet her in late afternoon, Christmas Eve, and arranged for a friend to come watch TV with Kenzie for an hour or two. My friend jumped at the chance to make me go out, hoping for the best, but too polite to ask questions. (Or did I still look too fragile?)

After a long hesitation, Rose said, "I just called to tell you—I mean—I *almost* was not able to get together tonight, but now . . . I can."

"All right," I said, gripping the phone so hard my knuckles ached.

"Oh Christ," she said softly.

"Rose . . . what is it?"

Rose said, "I can't stop myself from seeing you, alone . . . just this once."

I let myself breathe at last. She had canceled one week before, just like this.

"I'll see you soon," I said, hanging up before she changed her mind or I came to my senses.

No real danger of that.

We pulled up to the restaurant at exactly the same time, and parked with one empty space between us. The cars were getting dusted with a snowfall so light it flew in every direction except down. She signaled through the car window for me to get in her car, and I couldn't help but think how there was so much keeping us apart. Our two separate lives, our two separate cars, the parking space between us, the swirling snow, and ... *Gary.*

I heard a voice say in my head, *Go to her.* It sounded gentler than the usual voice, so I walked to Rose's car but hesitated at the door.

Now get in her car, silly, the voice insisted, but I didn't open the door right away.

Instead, I imagined I was peering through her house window instead of the car, watching the warm glow of the dashboard and the Christmas lights from the restaurant flickering against her face, like she was sitting by a fireplace. I remained where I had been for so long, frozen on the outside, looking in at the life I wanted. A life I used to have.

Rose leaned over and pushed the door open and I finally got inside; the car smelled like her, warm and sweet, the best air freshener ever, except it was just her. She had a beautifully wrapped present on her lap, and I thought how appropriate that it lay right there, only wickedly amused for a moment before the reality came back. She wasn't mine. I shouldn't be here. I won't survive getting hurt again. I shivered.

"You're cold," Rose said, and reached to hold both my hands.

"My car didn't have a chance to heat up," I said, knowing it was not the cold.

"You look beautiful," she said.

When I said nothing, she slid the present from her lap to mine, and the package felt warm underneath where it had been against her, and wicked thoughts seeped back. I had stopped myself from buying her so many things, and now I had no gift for her.

I wanted so badly to give Rose the freedom from guilt she needed to leave that man. *That is not yours to give,* the gentle voice said inside me. Was it Michelle? And just like that the voice went silent and I was alone with the only other woman I had ever loved.

I said, stupidly, "I didn't think I should get you a present."

"I didn't, either," she said. "Since I couldn't stop myself . . . Jenny, please open it."

Something in the way she spoke made me rage with wanting her, so I was grateful to have the tall present to hide my face as I carefully peeled back the wrapping. Under the gold foil paper, I recognized brown craft paper, and knew it was from the gallery even before I turned the painting over to look at it, but I never expected it would be mine.

It was the baby gorilla sitting on its mother. Years ago, when looking for my next painting subject, I had stumbled on a photo I took of a baby gorilla, long before Kenzie was born. Seeing it again, I was taken with the way it reminded me of how Kenzie sat on Michelle's lap, always with her one leg tucked under the other. (I never confessed to Michelle the painting I loved most had been the one where I turned the two loves of my life into apes!) Michelle had loved that painting, too, though she didn't know why. Someday I would tell her, I had thought, but I didn't get the chance.

She insisted on hanging it up in the hallway and I smiled at it every day when I passed it on the way to our bedroom. How many times had I winked at that baby gorilla as I passed, or touched the dab of dark paint on the pad of its tiniest toe? My little secret. The only one I had ever kept from Michelle, and then time ran out since I thought it would be cruel of me to tell her one more thing she would no longer have when she was gone.

I moved the painting away, protecting it from the tears rolling harmlessly down the front of my jacket to my lap. Rose was shaken by my tears. She said, "Jenny, I wanted to buy it for you so you could never sell it, because I don't think you would sell a gift I gave you."

Rose reached for my face to make me look at her and a pair of tears tumbled over the back of her hands. "You shouldn't have sold it. You said you loved it."

"I love you," I whispered, although I hadn't decided I would tell her that, and she kissed me before I could come to my senses and break from her. Our mouths parted, and I felt the searing heat in contrast to the cold around us. Her kiss was as desperate as mine; it was only our second, the first since the dance. I could feel myself drowning again and although it was the last thing on earth I wanted to do, I finally pulled her face away from mine.

"Please . . .," Rose said, and I was desperate to have her again.

This time I heard my inner voice, just barely there, *Protect yourself,* and I pulled away as far as I could.

"Rose, I'm not strong enough. I can't continue this if I can't have you."

Her eyes filled as she nodded, and I never saw anything more beautiful.

Before I left her, I closed the wrapping around the painting, and hugged it against my jacket as I went into the cold. I could have easily been persuaded to stay, but she was kind enough to let me go.

I watched in my rearview and Rose's car did not move. Even as I drove down to the end of the street, hers stayed still, surrounded by snowflakes. I wanted more than anything to turn back, but drove myself away, faster than I should have.

Later that night, I hung the painting back up in the hallway, where the nail had remained, waiting patiently. I touched the pad of the littlest toe to straighten the painting perfectly on the wall. It was back where it needed to be, where I could remind myself of the loss of my old life.

Much later, exhausted from the night, when I passed the painting in the hallway, I was surprised it had come back to me . . . and even more surprised it now reminded me of Rose holding Kenzie.

I stared at it and blinked, Scrooge-like, on Christmas Eve. It had not really changed, of course, but now the painting flipped back and forth from my old life to the life I could have had, with Rose. When Rose had pulled me to her, I couldn't get close enough, and weakly let her kiss me long and hard before I was able to pull away. It was all I could do to not crawl onto her. And so I had this thought too, when I looked at the painting: I wanted to be her lap girl, too.

The Office Game

I invented The Office Game and at first my sister liked it a lot. Dawn has never been to a real office before so I had to teach her everything from scratch. This was one of my favorite things about my job.

Office Game Rules:

1. I am the boss.

2. Dawn is the Worker Bee, so I am allowed to order her around and she has to do whatever I say and shecan never Question My Judgment.

3. The Boss gets the bigger desk.

We dragged in two boxes from the garage (I made sure hers was smaller) and I put a brand-new roll of tape on my desk and my plan was to make Dawn's first assignment to tape up the rules so she would not forget them. We each got three pencils, and I got all the long ones. (Even though the Worker Bees do all the actual work, it is important the Wand-Waver boss has the best office supplies. Auntie Theresa says: that is just the way the cookie crumbles.)

It took Dawn a long time to get the hang of the game, since she is only used to taking orders from Mom, Dad, and her teachers. I had to talk to her again and again about her Bad Morale and how it would be a Bad-In-Flu-Ants to the rest of her coworkers and could give them the flu, or ants, but she did not believe me.

"I don't have any coworkers," she said.

"Are you questioning my judgment?" I asked, in a surprised voice, exactly like I heard Gina talk to Rose.

"No," she finally said, after giving me a dirty look, and I told her to go back to her smaller box desk.

I waited for a while before I called her over to my big box desk to take some notes.

"You didn't bring a pencil and paper," I said and reminded her that since bosses don't ever write anything down, it was important that she should always have a pencil with her when she is called in to my office, since I might give her a To Do list.

"Bosses don't have to write things down?" Dawn asked.

"Nope."

"Ever?"

"Not ever." And I was sure of this. Writers are always Worker Bees.

Dawn went back to get her pencil, but I could tell her Morale was going bad again. I wondered how to keep employees working with Bad Morale?

When Dawn came back and sat in my guest chair, she said, "Hey, why do you have two nice chairs?"

I did not want my only Worker Bee to quit. "You get to sit in my guest chair, but only for now, and chocolate is not allowed."

"Why?" she asked with an angry face, but I left her angry face for just a minute since I got the idea to run to the bathroom to gargle with stinky strong mouthwash so I would smell like Gina. When I came back to my desk, I caught Dawn red-handed stealing one of my chairs.

"I'm trading it," she said, as she dragged it away. Dawn was shorter than me but pretty strong for an eleven-year-old.

I watched the legs make train tracks in the rug from my office to hers, and I got distracted by them, so before I knew it, she dragged her ugly chair over to my office, ruining the perfect train tracks.

Now I was mad. But I waited until she sat down to fire her.

"You are fired. You stole from the company."

"I made a trade!" Her Morale was really in a crappy toilet now, but this was O-K since she was no longer my Worker Bee.

"The Office Game is over: you lost. Now, excuse me, I have important work to get back to."

"That's unfair!" she yelled.

"Work is never fair," I answered back, not looking up from my big desk box. I have learned when a boss wants someone to think he is busy, you cannot look up from your desk, even if there is not much on it.

The game was played perfectly, until Dawn ran to go tell Mom and while she was gone, I wrote a note to put on her bed.

To: Dawn

I had to fire you because you were bad at work. A Worker Bee does not get mad at the Boss or you will not be successful. Good luck finding a new job.

From,
Liddy-Jean, Marketing Queen

Later, I heard something coming from Dawn's room and she was lying on her bed crying with her head buried under her pillow with my boss note sticking out from under there. I pretended I did not hear her because I was worried I might cry too.

At the dinner table, she would not talk to me, so I bragged to Mom and Dad what a great job Dawn did playing the Office Game.

I told them how proud I was that Dawn learned very quickly what it was like to work for a Bad Boss. Dawn got happy, and when I shared my dessert, she hugged me and I knew she did not think I was like Boss Gina anymore.

Now I had to do something about Bad Bosses who liked being that way.

What Are You Waiting For?

After Christmas vacation, I finally could go back to work. I hugged Rose because I had missed her so much, but when she mentioned working on the book, my bad attitude sneaked up on both of us.

I asked Rose if I could talk to her in private, just like the other Marketing Girls do, even though I did not want to talk about problems since Rose was so happy. Rose always looked different when she had not seen Jenny for a while, and since Mondays were book-working days, we would finally get to see Jenny and Kenzie later.

Rose took me into her office, and I asked the first question fast so I would not chicken out. "My book is just a nice game you play with me to make me feel good, and you don't have to pretend anymore, because I feel good most of the time."

Rose shook her head and said, "No, Liddy-Jean, that's not true." She put her hand on my knee, which felt even better than when Mom does it. "Why do you think that?"

"Because Mom says people say things that aren't true so they can be Encouragement."

"Your mom is right," Rose said, "sometimes some people do that. But I'm not one of those people. Liddy-Jean, you didn't tell your mom about the book until now . . . isn't that right?"

"Not to be sneaky," I said. "I did not want to ruin the surprise."

Rose said, "I wasn't going to tell you this yet, but I have news. I'm already talking to someone very important about publishing your book. I would not tell you that if the book was not real. Like I said a long time ago, it's my plan to help you make this a real published book."

I gave her a big hug even though I still was not sure if it was real, and Rose gave me a big hug right back.

Rose said, "I need to talk to you about something, else, too. I told your mom that we would give you a pen name to protect your identity."

"Why do I have to name our pens?"

"A pen name is when you take a pretend name, so nobody knows who you really are," she said.

"Like a spy," I said. I loved this idea.

"This is your book, and I wanted you to see your name on it, but it might be better to protect your privacy since some people might not understand this is all your work and I am only helping."

I thought of the lady that wrote Harry Potter and how she had two letters for her first name like me. I also thought about how much Rose helped me with the book.

"I have a name."

Rose was surprised. "What is it?"

"L. J. Rose," and I smiled huge because I knew it was a good one.

Rose smiled back and said, "*Wand-Wavers and Worker Bees*, by L. J. Rose. Really? You want my name on there?"

I liked the idea of having Rose's name with mine, especially since lately, Rose worked even harder on the book than I did, especially since Kenzie and Jenny joined our team. I find it hard to be a writer now because I am always laughing so hard at Kenzie's funny faces.

"You are my editor," I said.

"I suppose I do change some of what you write."

"You change all of it," I said, surprised she forgot.

"I only change the language, but it's all your ideas, so it's still your book, remember that . . . okay, Liddy-Jean?"

"L.J. Rose," I said.

We shook hands. This made me feel bad for how I had been thinking about Rose the Editor, but I solved this problem by hugging her one more time. I learned way back when I was little that people love it when I pass out the hugs.

I said to Rose, "It might be good to put the fake name on the book right now, just in case someone is already reading it."

Rose looked worried but right then, Kim came into her office, so I got the heck out of there before Rose could ask questions.

Later, when I was working with Rose out on the middle table, I saw her watch the door for Jenny (just like I used to do when I was first at work, waiting for Rose.) Today I was working with Rose on a huge envelope label project and we had a bad Deadline, so we didn't see Jenny come in until Lisa P. yelled hello to her.

That's when I got scared that maybe Rose had a throw-up stomachache because she made a sucking-in-air sound when she saw Jenny, and spilled envelopes after we had just made neat piles.

Her hands were shaking so I asked, "Are you sick or just cold?"

"I'm good," Rose said as Jenny came over to us with a big smile and Kenzie grabbed me in a tight hug.

By the way Jenny and Rose were acting, I guessed they did not kiss again since the dance. (They were not like Mom and Dad who could kiss whenever they wanted, but being worried about money is bad for kissing.) I think being worried about Gary was bad for kissing, too.

Jenny asked her, "Are you okay?" and now I had two worried people on my hands so, I asked Rose, "Can you go talk with Jenny in your office and keep her hands far away?"

Rose whispered to me, "Liddy-Jean, I would never touch anyone like that—I mean—we're—at work—"

"Keep your hands away from the envelopes, since you are making a big mess of things."

"Okay," Rose said.

They went into Rose's office, and I whispered to Kenzie, "You stay here and pretend to work without looking at Rose's office, and I will go spy and report back." Kenzie's eyes got huge, and I wished I had not told her my actual plan.

"You have surprised eyes," I whispered. "Pretend you are confused about making the envelopes into piles, and do not look up. I promise, I will tell you everything I get from spying." She agreed, but I had to make this quick since I was worried about her acting skills.

As I walked away, Kenzie shouted, "I am so confused about these piles!" and I gave her the sign to please shut up.

I snuck up to the side of Rose's office, and hid behind the copy machine, right near the door. From that spot, I could pretend to get more paper, and hear them perfectly through the crack.

"It's so good to lay my eyes on you," Jenny said really quiet, like it was a Big Secret. "Was your holiday week okay?"

"No," Rose said, "It was long. I was convinced today would never get here. My mind hasn't left Christmas Eve."

Jenny said in almost the same whisper, "It's been a long week for me, too."

I peeked through the crack of the door to see why they got so quiet. Rose looked serious. Jenny looked like she wanted to say something, but she opened her mouth and closed it again.

Finally, Rose said very quietly, "You should know . . . I can't stop thinking about you . . . not for a second."

Through the crack, I saw Jenny's hand reach out to touch Rose's arm, but she did not do it. "You need to do what's best for you," Jenny said.

Rose said, "I need to do what is best for both of us . . . I just need to find a way."

They stopped talking again, and, finally, Rose laughed, but it was a small, fake one. "I'm such a damned mess, I can't sleep, or eat, and I'm afraid I'm going to get fired, since Liddy-Jean is doing my job better than me these days."

Jenny said, "I thought I was the only one not sleeping."

"So much is happening to me, for the first time in my life, in fact

. . ." and then she said sadly, "But, Jenny, I still can't . . ."

Jenny interrupted, "I can't make you choose a different life, if it isn't who you are."

"That isn't it," Rose said, but while Jenny waited for more, Rose just kept her mouth shut, like I have to for a whole hour when Mom feels guilty and drags us all to church.

I hated to interrupt Rose and Jenny, but it didn't look like they were going to stop staring at each other anytime soon, and my leg was falling asleep against the copy machine. I got up with my leg still snoozing, which made me fall against the door to Rose's office, which sent Jenny flying right into Rose's arms with a yelp, sounding like a hungry puppy.

I didn't mean to do that, but it was a pretty smart move, because Rose had to catch Jenny, and when I came out from behind the door, they were still hugging.

"Whoopsie," I said.

Jackie came over to see what the noise was about.

Nobody would think anything weird was happening between Rose and Jenny, except that Rose was being so clumsy again, and couldn't get out of Jenny's arms, as my mom would say, "In A Timely Fashion," and the longer she stayed close to her, the redder her face got.

"Everything okay in here?" Jackie said right behind me, which made them both jump again.

Rose said, "Jenny . . . fell . . . the, the door pushed us together . . ."

Jackie said, "Something is pushing you together all right."

I saw Jackie try not to giggle, then she winked at me before heading right into Lisa P.'s office, probably to report there was illegal hugging going on. Even Steve popped his head out of his office, then walked over to Lisa P. and Jackie to get the full report, only he was not smiling like the girls were.

I went back to the envelope table and said, "Where's Kenzie?" even though I knew exactly where Kenzie was.

"I'm heeere!" Kenzie sang as she tumbled out from under the

table, and since she saw hugging that didn't include her, she ran over to Jenny and Rose and hugged them both together.

"Come on, Liddy!" Kenzie called out to me, with her head buried between Rose and Jenny's hug.

I knew it was not good office behavior, but the Marketing Girls and Steve were all leaving, and I could hear them laughing as they walked down the hallway. No harm now, I thought, and I joined the big family hug and smooshed my lips real close to Rose's ear and whispered what Auntie Theresa always says to my mom whenever she thinks Mom should do something:

"What are you waiting for? Your next life?"

Rose didn't seem to care that we were all at work now, since she squeezed Jenny tightly with me and Kenzie trapped in between, giggling.

On Friday, Rose surprised us all when she asked if we would like to work together again on Saturday and Jenny agreed, even though she looked worried. I wondered if she was thinking of Gary, just like I was.

PART 3
LOVE

A Great Day Can Change

On Saturday Rose picked me up at my house right on time and even surprised me with an Egg McMuffin sandwich. Two great things in one day!

I pointed up my finger and shouted, "Things are looking uuup!"

Rose laughed and I took the bag from her and remembered to say thanks, but I forgot to close the car door since I was too busy unwrapping. Mom followed me outside and closed the door for me, then walked around to lean against the car to talk to Rose.

"Thanks for picking her up, Rose," Mom said, "right, Liddy-Jean?"

I was supposed to say thank you again, but I already had a full mouth, so I nodded instead with a tail of bread sticking out of my mouth, and they both laughed at me.

"I love spending time with my friend, here," Rose said.

"She's looking forward to it. Liddy-Jean says the book project is going well. We're still keeping it a secret from Dad for now, since Liddy wants it to be a surprise."

When Rose said, "We've made some real progress—" I signaled to stop talking shaking my head. I didn't want her to tell Mom the news about the publisher just yet. Rose caught on and said, "I think we'll be finished in another week or so. Jenny is almost done with the illustrations."

"I hope things are going well for you both," Mom said, looking embarrassed like whenever she has to talk to me about a sex thing.

Rose answered, "Well, it's complicated, but thanks for asking."

"Most things that are worth it, are," Mom said. Then she gave Rose's arm a small pat and waved goodbye to me. "Have fun. Liddy, remember to say thank you to both Rose and Jenny, and share the snacks we packed with Kenzie."

I swallowed a big bite and said, "I know, I know: Pleases and Thank Yous All Over the Place."

Rose was talking to me while she drove, but I didn't hear a word until I was done with my last bite. Rose was supposed to be smarter than me, but she always had a bad plan to tell stories before I was done chewing.

I said, "Dad says, you never get a doggie's attention *after* giving him a bone."

Rose was happy while we drove. I wanted to tell her she looked just like I did on Christmas morning, like she might cry from being so happy about getting a new bicycle the exact pink of strawberry taffy. I was not jealous of Rose loving Jenny anymore and I did not want to hurt Rose's feelings that I didn't love her That Way anymore, because I had Kenzie and because Jenny could take care of Rose much better than I could. I still had not finished my plan on how to get rid of Gary . . . I only had the beginning of a plan.

I had Mom and Dad, Rose, Kenzie, the counselors at The Center, and even my sister. But Rose only had Jenny. I also had Steve who I loved, and not just because he had big dude muscles. Steve liked to come by my desk to talk with me, and sometimes even when there were no Marketing Girls around. He said he visited me because we were pals, but I think it was my question about maybe needing a policeman.

Steve said nobody in the world except me knew he really wanted to be a policeman. He said he didn't even tell his dad before his dad died, and it made me feel special he would tell me such an important secret. When he was a kid, he said he wanted to be the opposite of a policeman, which is a Mafia guy. I asked Auntie Theresa what that meant, and she said a Mafia guy is a very tough guy who also can cook lasagna, and I thought that might be a good plan for Steve, since even though Mom and Auntie Theresa laugh all the time, girls can always use a break in the kitchen.

When Rose and I pulled into Jenny's driveway, I could see Kenzie was watching for our car from her living room window as she ate cereal right out of the box, just like I do! She came running outside to the car with her arms out, just like in the movies when lovers have not seen each other in a very long time and then find each other on a mountain, or at the airport.

When she hugged me, she accidentally threw the entire box of cereal all over the ground and I yelled, "Oh no! You made bird food!"

I did not like this idea since I do not think birds will like the Lucky Charms color marshmallows as much as I did, so I could not stop staring at them sprinkled all over the ground. Jenny came out right after her, and she and Rose looked like they forgot how to say hello to each other again, even though it was just yesterday when they had seen each other. Rose also forgot how to talk, or even to get out of the car, until Jenny opened her door.

Kenzie and I left them in the driveway and ran into the house together.

"Mom says we can play for thirty minutes before we do book work!" Kenzie said. As a professional author, I should not have been so happy to hear this, but I was. We went right to Kenzie's favorite place, which was her giant toy closet and played for a long time with her new Christmas toys and games before I told her I had to go to the bathroom. Normally I would sneak off to check out the pump soap situation, but today I wanted to check on Rose.

Rose and Jenny were not at the kitchen table, but the book stuff was all spread out ready for work. I saw that Jenny had a bunch of new drawings and I was going to sneak a peek at them when I heard quiet talking. I tried hard not to spy on them again, but like Mom says about a plate of brownies: "I couldn't resist."

So, I went to the next room just like detectives do when they're sneaking up on bad guys, and sneaked myself down to the room down the hall. I could see from under the door that their shoes were standing very close to each other in the bedroom, with the door almost closed, maybe to keep out spies.

I ducked into the next bedroom and peeked through the side of the door until I could see them perfectly, and still hide.

I saw Jenny slowly reach up to touch Rose's face, just like I saw Laura Ingalls' sister Mary do when she got blinded and needed to touch people's cheeks so she could see what a person's looked like. Except Jenny could see perfectly fine, but she kept touching the side of Rose's cheek with her fingers and Rose closed her eyes like it was making her dreamy. I knew one thing for sure, Mary Ingalls only touched one person's face for that long, and that was the guy she wanted to marry.

"All I can think about is being with you," Rose said.

"Yes, we need to talk about that," Jenny said.

Rose said, "I haven't been with him for such a long time . . . it has never been right, but I need to explain why I can't leave right now . . . how I don't want you involved." She whispered, "Gary gets crazy sometimes."

"Has he threatened you?"

Rose said, "He's made serious threats about hurting himself whenever I've tried to end things . . . and I've tried many times. He knows I couldn't forgive myself if he . . ."

Jenny said, "He's holding you hostage."

"I know," Rose answered. "It's been years—"

"There's something you need to know," Jenny said as she stopped touching Rose's cheek. "Once we're finished with the book, I have to get some distance from this. From you."

Rose lowered her head and said so softly, "Please don't . . . I know I don't have any right to ask you—"

"I'm sorry," Jenny said. "I can't. If it was just me, I would wait forever, but I have to think of my daughter. I don't want her to have another loss."

Rose was deciding to wait for her next life and Jenny was not going to wait for her. I went back to Kenzie's room feeling so sad, and tears were burning my eyes. I thought about Kenzie, who was talking more and more about how much happier her mom was, just like when her other mom was alive, and she was happier too.

Last week Kenzie said she wanted two moms again, so this made me so sad for her, too. Luckily, Kenzie was keeping herself distracted talking away about an old pair of shoes she used to love that she was trying to jam her feet into. I could tell by listening to her that she had no idea what was happening between her mom and Rose. For Kenzie, even when secret things were going on, shoes can stay interesting for hours.

Rose finally called us to work on the book project, and when we came down, Rose and Jenny were trying hard to hide it, but they both looked miserable.

After a little while, Rose said, "I love our new system," like she always does, but I could tell she was also thinking this might be the last time we would all work together. Our system was that Jenny would show us new drawings, and I would give any new work notes to Kenzie, who would take a very long time to read each one out loud, and then Rose would do the editing. Kenzie loved that reading part because it was the only part she could do, since Kenzie did not get any better at making lists about work.

BANG, BANG!

We all jumped at the noise at the door.

I saw out the window it was Gary standing at Jenny's front door, banging on it again and looking very angry. He even had a stubbly beard, just like all the cartoon criminals have. Jenny put her hand on Rose's shoulder to stop her from getting up, and said, "Girls, time to take a break—you both go back and play in Kenzie's room again, okay? Shut the door and we will call you down when it's time to get back to work."

I grabbed Kenzie's hand and took her to the stairs. As we went up, I heard Jenny say, "Rose, don't move. I want you to stay inside with the girls, and lock this door behind me."

"I will not!" Rose said, but Jenny locked the doorknob herself and was out the door in a flash, slamming it behind her.

Upstairs, I kept Kenzie busy by telling her I wanted her to surprise me by getting out her six most favorite toys while I waited outside her door. It was a perfect plan, since I could close the door to Kenzie's room, and I knew she would get distracted by all her toys even more than her shoes. I went down the hallway fast, and peeked out the window down to the front yard.

Jenny was standing outside with Gary, blocking his way to the front steps and he was yelling so loudly I could hear him even with the window closed.

"I know she's here, tell her to get out here, now!" Gary growled like an angry dog and the whole time he rocked back and forth like a baby learning to walk who might fall down at any minute.

Gary yelled up at the house, "Rose, get the f— out here!"

Jenny said, "You're not welcome here, and you're in no condition to see anyone, especially the children—"

He ignored her. "Get me Rose, you dyke, or I'll bust in and get her myself. I will pull that f-ing door right off its hinges!"

Jenny said, "I already dialed 911. The police are on their way, so you'd better get lost."

I knew Jenny was lying because her cell phone was right here by her bed. That was when I remembered what Steve told me.

Next to Jenny's cell phone was a house phone and I dialed 911, just like Mom taught me to do if there was an emergency only. When someone picked up, I said, "I am Liddy-Jean Carpenter and I am at my friend Jenny's house so we can work on my book to be published. Jenny is drawing the cartoons and a bad man came here, and since Steve's father is dead, maybe you can send us a different policeman?"

The lady on the phone said, "Who is dead, miss? What's the address?"

Since I only know my address I was quiet, and she asked, "If you don't know your friend's address, what is her last name?" I was scared now, because I could not remember!

"Can you tell me what you saw when you went to your friend's house?"

"We are near a McDonald's where you can get an Egg McMuffin to take next door to the Drive-In Movies behind the pine trees."

The lady said to not worry, they would find the drive-in and she asked me nicely to please stay on the phone and not hang up. I did not hang up, but I put the phone down on the bed so I could run downstairs, just in time to see Rose go out the front door, even though Jenny told her not to.

I remembered what Steve told me his dad had taught him: "There are always two exits," so I ran to the back door, unlocked it, and remembered Steve also said, "If you are shorter than your enemy, it just means you need a bigger weapon."

I ran over to Jenny's shed in the backyard, where Kenzie said she keeps all her tools. I hoped I would find a Xena sword, and hoped I was smart enough to think of a great scheme if I did not. I grabbed the longest thing I could find and then I ran around the house to the front yard with a metal shovel raised way over my head. I would have twirled it like Xena, but it was too heavy, so I just did a Xena Warrior Princess yell right behind Gary, which scared him half to death. His eyes opened so wide and he raised both his hands up in front of his face like a big scaredy cat.

"Liddy-Jean, stop!" Rose yelled louder than me, and I slowly brought the shovel lower. When I did, Gary was not one bit afraid of me anymore, and Rose tried to grab the shovel from my hands without asking, but I was too fast.

"That's the retarded girl!" he said, spit flying out of his mouth.

I thought of how mad that word makes Mom and raised the shovel up again.

"Liddy-Jean!" Rose said. "Run back inside with Kenzie and lock the doors!"

Nope, I thought.

Rose had a look on her face that I never saw before and I wanted to see how using the "R" word worked out for Gary. Now Rose was the fast one, she grabbed the shovel from me and held it up, julst like I did.

Gary backed away from Rose and the shovel, but now he was up the steps close to Jenny, putting his finger right in her face, as he said, "Are you f-ing my wife?"

Jenny did not even blink when she said, "I don't *F* anyone, and she isn't your wife. Now get the hell out of here before the police arrive."

Gary raised his fist up like he was going to hit Jenny and Rose swung the shovel from behind him just like a baseball bat and smashed Gary on his head! He spinned around just like on cartoons, and fell off the stairs and face-planted in the Lucky Charms!

"Not very lucky charms for you, Gary!" I shouted, wondering if it was an ACME shovel, like on Bugs Bunny.

Gary did not move and I thought maybe Gary was dead, until he made some noises and rolled over holding his head, leaving some red in the snow that was brighter than school ketchup. This made my stomach hurt to look at, but looking at Gary was worse.

He yelled at Rose and Jenny, "I'll f-ing kill you both, don't you think I won't!" and that is when I wished I stayed inside the house like Rose told me to.

"I am scared," I said, and I could not believe my eyes when I saw Rose walk closer to him, like she was not afraid one bit. She put the end of the metal shovel right against his neck, and Gary's eyes got even wider than when he thought I was Xena.

Rose said in a calm voice, "Stop talking, or I'll start digging, starting . . . here." She pushed the shovel harder against his throat and until Gary made a choking sound and put his hands up in surrender. "Jenny, call the police!"

I said, "That is *all set!*" and right when I said it, we heard sirens getting louder, and two police cars came speeding down Jenny's street.

Because of my phone call, Rose had to convince the police that nobody was dead in the house, and they put handcuffs on Gary and put him in the police car. When the police went in the house to check everything out, Kenzie let out a loud scream when she saw them.

"Am I arrested?" Kenzie cried, and it took all three of us a long time to convince her she was not going to jail. She did not believe it until the policemen drove off with Gary in the police car, and I made Kenzie wave and yell, *"Good bye and good riddens!"* from her bedroom window as the police car drove away. She liked that.

After the last policeman left I heard Rose say to Jenny, "I'm so sorry . . . I know now you need to stay away from the mess that is my life." I could not hear the rest because Kenzie was making a confession to me that she took a small pink eraser from work and she thought the police had finally caught her.

"Can you take it?" Kenzie whispered to me, even though the cops were long gone. I nodded, taking the eraser from her sweaty hand and stuffing it into my pocket to bring back to work on Monday. One more secret between friends.

Rose was very quiet as we drove to my house, and before we got out of the car, she reached for my arm and said, "Liddy-Jean, do you know how brave you are?"

"Yes."

Rose said, "I never would have stood up for myself, if you didn't do it first."

"The shovel helped," I said.

"Yes, the shovel helped a lot. What made you think to do that?"

"I always thought I was not the sharpest tool in the shed, but turns out I was wrong." Rose got my joke, but she still looked sad.

I told her in my best Mom voice, "You shouldn't live with Gary anymore."

"I know. I promise he will never be anywhere near you again," she said.

"What about you?" She did not have an answer for that one. "You should live with Jenny so she can take care of you."

"I need to take care of myself," Rose said, when we pulled up to my house.

"You sure as H.E.-double-hockey-sticks took care of yourself today!" I said, and she gave me a big hug. "You also need to help Jenny take care of Kenzie. She definitely is a girl that needs two moms."

"Maybe . . . someday," she said, "but right now I need to go tell your mom what happened."

"No! Mom will worry, and I know how to keep secrets."

Then I took Rose's hand and gave it a squeeze, just like Mom does, and said, "Trust me, O-K?"

Rose shook her head, no. "I do trust you Liddy-Jean, but what happened today is too big a secret to not tell your parents."

"Please, Rose," I begged, "I will never ask another favor as long as I live. My mom and dad have too many worries already, and I need to get famous with my book so I can help them and maybe they will kiss on the couch again."

I gave my best scared look, and waited. The scared look was easy since last night I heard Mom and Dad talking about how they might have to sell our house.

"Liddy-Jean, I won't be able to see Jenny again until I know Gary is gone for good. Until then, we will only be able to work on the book at the office, after work. I'm sorry, but I can't see any of you outside of work until I know it's safe. You understand, right?"

I nodded my head, but I didn't understand.

"What about Kenzie?"

Rose said, "You'll still see Kenzie at work." Rose turned from me to knock on the door, but I grabbed Rose's hand to stop her. Rose did not understand there was no way I was going to let her, or Kenzie, or Jenny, go back to their old lives.

Just then, Mom opened the door, scaring us both. "Oh! I thought I heard a car, and I thought you'd be much later," Mom said.

"We had to quit early, I'm afraid," Rose said.

"Everything okay?" Mom asked.

226

I interrupted mom, "Rose is very underneath the weather."

"Come inside for some tea, then. Liddy-Jean's Dad and I have had a rough week too—"

"No, Mom, Rose is in a rush to go home and blow her nose, and she does not want to spread all her germs, thank you, Rose!" I said, hoping she would go.

Rose looked at me and at Mom, and I was sure Rose was going to tell Mom everything.

"See you on Monday!" I said, and I shut the door on Rose.

Mom was not happy. "Well, that was rude, Liddy-Jean, and with Rose not feeling well!"

Even though I tried not to think about it, all night long I kept seeing Gary's ugly face and hearing him say those terrible things, and the sound of the shovel as it whacked him on the head laying face down on the Lucky Charms.

ROSE

I convinced myself I could give J. the life she and her daughter deserved, if I could just get free of him. Long before I met J. he had convinced himself that I was having an affair with Stephen in our office, simply because I mentioned his name, once. It wasn't true, of course, I hadn't noticed Steve that way, or any man for that matter, and now I understood.

G. had finally guessed right I had fallen for someone, proving the theory that even a broken clock can be correct twice a day. My heart belonged to her. Right after I met her, I made the mistake of talking about her a few times, since it made me so happy to talk about her to anyone who would listen, even him, and he had bristled each time I mentioned her name ... and even when I didn't mention it.

Now, I am replaying the day again and again ... from the moment Liddy and Kenzie had gone off to play, I remembered how Liddy-Jean teased me once: *"What are you waiting for ... your next life?"*

This was the moment I decided I would reach for Jenny the next time we were alone, but Jenny didn't wait for me. When the girls had gone off to play, she reached for my hand and took it so gently I imagined I was floating from the chair as I followed behind her. It would have felt like a dream except my heart was pounding hard in my chest, reminding me how very real it was. She took me down the hallway to her bedroom, passing the painting I had bought back for her.

She had a pile of books by her nightstand, and I longed to read the titles of what kept her up at night, and one photograph of who I assumed was Michelle, tucked close to the side of her bed. Because the girls were just down the hall, Jenny closed the door, but not completely, just enough to shield us from view of the hallway.

Jenny whispered, "I know I shouldn't do this, but I want to be alone with you, just for a minute." Then she captured my face between her warm hands and kissed me like she possessed the very rights to my life, and, although she couldn't have known it, she did possess this. So this is it, I kept thinking . . . this is what life is supposed to be like. *I am supposed to feel like this when I am kissed . . . all this time, this was life's secret.*

It was only Jenny's strong will that kept us in check. I had leaned further into her but she stepped away and pulled my hands from her sides where I had gripped her soft hips, surprising myself with my boldness, my hunger for her. We both knew right then we shouldn't have stolen that moment.

A breaking levy came to mind, and there was nothing that would keep me from her, nothing that could make me understand the inappropriateness of what I wanted right then. I tried to free my hands to touch her again, but she held me back, firmly, and because she is stronger than me, it's Jenny who ends it.

"I need some distance from you, because I can't stop this from happening when we're together." She took a breath, and looked me in the eyes and said, "Rose, the book is nearly done now, we both know that. We both know we are just hanging on to see each other."

I had been dragging it out, mostly because I barely got through the weekends waiting for Monday. How would I be if there was no Monday with her to save me after a weekend away from her? And now this has happened. The stillness of my house without him in it is no comfort. Not when he could be released at any time. I still have to keep Jenny out of my life until I end it with Gary. My next step is to make sure she and the girls will be safe.

I would risk it all if it were just me, but I will not risk the people I love most in the world. I told Liddy-Jean I needed to take care of myself . . . and I will.

The Good Fella and the Lightning Bugs

Tuesday finally came and I brought the *The Last Unicorn* D-V-D back with a Post-it note stuck on it that said my mom allowed me to watch it. I got special permission to watch the movie alone in the back of the recreation room by telling the counselors that because of my babysister and her pouting, I never, ever, got to watch a movie all by myself, just like an adult.

I went off to the rec room alone. The movie was a little scary to watch in some places, but I watched almost all of it. As I watched, just like I hoped, I got ideas how to fix Rose's problem before she got more sad, and Jenny got more skinny.

Tomorrow I was going to have my very first meeting at work.

Rose stopped writing, and I thought it was going to be one of those times when she got quiet and sad again, but instead she surprised me by closing her laptop and saying, "L. J. Rose, I believe we've finished your book!" It was the first time I had seen Rose smile like that since Jenny stopped visiting us.

"Yaaay!" I said, as happy as I could, but I was wishing Jenny and Kenzie could be here to see this. I didn't say this to Rose, but since her smile disappeared as quickly as it came, I knew she was wishing it too.

Rose said, "I sent the edits for them to do a final proof and send it off to print." Then she put her arm around me and said, "The publisher is rushing this one because they have a good feeling about it. And even though you're using a pen name, we'll need to do some interviews for publicity." I liked this idea very much, since only famous people get interviewed!

It was time to update my Top Secret To Do List with my favorite thing, two big check marks!

1. Get a publisher. √
2. Make surprise plans with Rose's help. √
3. Have a Secret Meeting at work.
4. Use the movie to make Gary disappear.
5. Buy Bobby & Kenzie a present.
6. Buy Stephen a present.
7. Get famous person clothes.
8. Surprise Mom, Dad, and Dawn.
10. Matchmaking Scheme.

Rose helped me do all the planning we could without having to tell Mom and Dad, since some of the plans will cost a lot of money. Rose says I am an adult, but she would not agree to keep another secret from both Mom and Dad that I was getting a paycheck from a publisher. So, Rose said we would use her money until Mom and Dad knew about the publisher. She also said she had to tell Mom everything that happened with Gary.

I knew Mom might not let me work with Rose anymore if she found out about Gary, and I also knew Rose was not going to budge on this, so I had to move extra fast now.

I had to call my very first meeting at work.

I told Rose that I needed to call a meeting so she would not plan anything at that time. She looked surprised, but a little proud of me too, and she was very professional and did not even ask who

I was meeting with (which was a good thing, since I learned from watching the movie that I should not tell anyone any details when there is danger). I dropped a secret note on a desk to meet in the small lunchroom near the M-I-S department. I got a note back on my desk that two o'clock meeting time was good. Then I waited, and wished I picked an earlier time, but I wanted to make sure the small lunchroom was empty.

I got to the meeting a little early and sat in the back so I could see the whole room. At two, just when the meeting was supposed to happen, Steve walked into the lunchroom to get a cup of coffee.

"Hey Liddy-Jean," Stephen said in his usual cheerful voice, "are you waiting for a friend to join you?"

"Yes. Sort of," I said.

"Can I sit with you anyway?" he asked, and I nodded.

I got more nervous when he sat down and kept watching the kitchen door to see if anyone else was coming in. I forgot how handsome Stephen was, and for some reason, his muscles looked a lot bigger in the smaller lunchroom, and this I took as a lucky sign. Steve looked around the room and then whispered, "I followed your instructions and didn't tell anyone."

"Good," I said quietly, trying to sound like him. I slipped him the movie under the table but I accidentally got him right in the You-Know-What, and he made a "Moof!" sound.

"Sorry," I said.

"It's okay," he said in a really high voice, which he thought was funny, but I was too serious to laugh. He looked under the table.

He whispered, "Is this why you called the meeting? To give me back my movie?"

I whispered back, "I didn't want anyone to see."

"Because I let you borrow a PG-13 movie? This wasn't the R-rated version, or I never would've given it to you." He paused and said, "Uh-oh. I told you to make sure you asked your parents first. Did you get in trouble for watching this?"

"I didn't get in trouble."

He looked at the movie and made a funny face.

I said, "I put your movie inside *The Last Unicorn* case, so nobody knows."

Steve laughed, but I put my finger up to my lips and shook my head to shush him, just like my sixth grade teacher used to do. It worked. He said quietly, "Smart thinking."

He did his funny Goodfellas voice, and this time I understood his joke when he changed the words a little, like the movie. "Does my unicorn horn amuse you?" he kept saying, laughing at his own joke. It was funny, but it also made me wonder if Steve was ready to handle the job I needed him to do. I had doubts, but I had to just say it, since there was nobody else who could help.

I whispered, "I need you to be a Goodfella for me and make someone disappear."

Steve started to laugh again until he saw that I was not joking, and he stopped laughing, Pron-Toad.

"Liddy-Jean, what are you talking about?"

I took a deep breath before I said, "I need you to help Rose, and Kenzie's mom. Rose's boyfriend is bad and takes drugs, and he came to Jenny's house and yelled bad swear words that he did not spell, right on her front steps, and I bet you know how to make him go away since your dad was in the police."

Steve's face got very serious, which scared me a little, but luckily, he still looked handsome.

"Liddy-Jean, I'm gonna ask you a very important question. Has he hurt Rose or Kenzie's mom?"

"Not yet, but he said he would. Especially after Rose smashed his head with the shovel I gave her which made the shovel my favorite . . . no more drill."

Steve was quiet and he pulled his chair closer to me, and even though I thought he smelled good enough to marry, I stayed thinking about Gary, who smelled very bad. Steve said in a TV policeman voice, "I want you to tell me exactly what happened."

I decided to M-bellish a little since I could not hear everything

Gary said through Jenny's window. I took one more deep breath of Steve's good smell, for luck, and then, like Auntie Theresa says, I spilled out all my guts.

"Gary showed up making big trouble, so I called the police and Rose says she was only brave because of me, but I think it was the shovel, but now she can not be brave anymore and Rose will not see Jenny so she can keep Jenny protected, and Kenzie is worried about her mom because she is not eating suppers again like when her other mom died, and Kenzie does not know much except Gary called Rose and Jenny lezzies because they love each other, and Kenzie is very worried that her mom will not ever smile anymore, just like when her extra mom died, and I am worried Rose will not smile anymore without Jenny . . ."

I stopped there because I did not have time to tell him everything. And he looked like I told him too much. Steve leaned very close and said, "You don't have to worry about that guy anymore. Do you hear me? He's not going to hurt anybody, I promise you, I will make sure. Do you believe me?"

"Yes," I said, and I did. "I see your muscles grow ten times bigger today."

"Like the Grinch's heart," he said, and I nodded my head. Steve's face had changed to a red color and when he got up from the table and leaned down to me, he said, "Liddy, what does this have to do with the movie I let you borrow?"

"You said you wanted to be a policeman or a Goodfella like in the movie and police and Goodfellas always take care of the bad guys, so I thought maybe you could get the police to arrest him forever, or maybe just make him disappear," I said.

I even gave him a wink and pointed to my eye so he would not miss it. "But I don't want you to get in trouble for killing," I added, thinking I probably should have started with that part.

"I can't do what the Goodfellas do, that would be illegal, so I won't do that no matter how much that bastar—creep, deserves it, but if the police can't keep him in jail, I can at least scare the frigg—creep into never coming around again. Just don't you worry about it. Uh, sorry I almost swore, Liddy-Jean."

"Twice," I said.

He patted my shoulder like we had a deal and I jumped up and stole a kiss from his cheek. I surprised him and he laughed as he wiped his cheek because I got spit on him. He said, "I guess that kiss means you forgive me for almost swearing."

"Twice," we both said.

"I forgive you," I said, acting as if I was a Wand-Waver, twirling an imaginary wand over his head.

Before Steve got to the doorway, I called after him as quietly as I could, "Steve, please don't tell Rose or anyone that I asked you to make him disappear. I will have a lot of money very soon, and I'll buy you a big present."

Steve shook his head no.

"No presents for me Liddy-Jean. That would look like a payment and that would be against the law, okay?"

I did not understand but I said O-K anyway, because that meant I could write another checkmark on my Secret To Do List.

I never had any before, so I did not know this, but it turns out I am extra smart with money. Since Mom didn't know how much money I already had, I pretended I needed to borrow some from her to buy a present for Bobby. She said she could give me five dollars but I would have to use my allowance for the rest. I promised Mom that I would keep a list and I would be able to pay all the money back very soon.

Mom agreed to take me over to Bobby's house today so I could give him his perfect present. I wanted it to be a surprise, so I asked Bobby's mom if she could set the present up in his room while I kept him busy outside with some candy. I brought our favorite orange marshmallow Circus Peanuts. Bobby's mom says I could lead Bobby into the middle of traffic with a bag of those, so it was no problem getting him to follow me outside to the swing set.

I thought about how much older I felt since we used to play every day at The Center. I still loved Bobby, but I needed a more grown-up boyfriend, and I thought about how lucky it was that I finally picked Steve.

Bobby's mom called us inside, I saw she had followed my instructions perfectly. She had shut the blinds and turned off all the lights in Bobby's bedroom. I kept the empty Circus Peanuts bag in my hand so he would follow right behind me, because he always forgets we already ate them all.

I walked him into his dark bedroom and he saw the surprise mirror disco ball hanging from his ceiling, and when Bobby's mom turned it on, it filled the room with thousands of colored lightning bugs just like at the dance, and Bobby froze under it with his mouth open.

"You get to keep it," I whispered, because that would be my first question, and then he knocked me over onto his bed from hugging me so hard. Then we both rolled off the bed and fell on the floor together laughing, while the disco lightning bugs crawled all over us.

Wand-Wavers Arrive
and Somebody Disappears

Dear Mr. Roberts,

My name is Liddy-Jean Carpenter and I have been
going to The Center for a long time. I like it very
much even if they never let us have more than 2
Oreos at snack time. I am writing to you because I
will be rich soon and after I surprise Mom and Dad, I
will be giving The Center some things we need. My
list so far:

1. A BIG TV for adults, like me.
2. A BIG TV for little kids.
3. My Xena Warrior Princess Collection.
4. 10 cans of original Pringles and 10 bags of Oreos!
5. A real copy machine for the wintertime, and a real
   lemonade stand for the summer, so everyone can have
   practice jobs at The Center.
6. A copy of my book, *Wand-Wavers and Worker Bees* for
   each counselor, to make sure there are no Bad Bosses at
   The Center.

7. Brand-new glow-in-the-dark Halloween decorations (no scary ones).
8. Many squirt bottles of soap for the bathrooms and kitchen.
9. Giant squirt bottle soap refills.
10. BIG box of office supplies to play The Office Game.

As soon as Mom and Dad know the surprise that I am rich, I will go shopping and buy The Center all the stuff. Please keep it a secret until then. (It is O-K if Rose the Editor knows, because she types all my words for me.)

From,
Liddy-Jean Carpenter

When you have a To Do List at your job and you have to change it, this is called making an Update. I update my list a lot which looks like a bad thing, since the list gets messy. My To Do List was much smaller and now I only needed four check marks!

TO DO LIST:

1. Buy Kenzie a present.
2. Surprise Mom, Dad, and Dawn.
3. Use movie to make Gary disappear.
4. Matchmaking Scheme.

Rose asked me to sit down in her office after work and I can always tell when there is going to be bad news. I even looked around to see if the sun was going to make scary stripes on Rose's shirt through the window, but luckily, Rose's office is not near a window.

"Liddy-Jean, I have very good news, and some bad news about your book."

"Okay," I said.

"The good news is the publisher tested the book and all the tests came back saying that you will sell a lot of books. They already have lots of preorders!"

I let my air out in a "Whew!" and pretended to wipe sweat from my head like Steve does to make me laugh.

"The bad news is there has been a leak to the press. That means that your real name got out to the people that write stories for newspapers and magazines, and someone told them the author of the book works here."

I was secretly happy about this and tried not to smile!

"Does that mean I will be rich *and* famous?"

"Probably, Liddy," Rose said, "but now we have to let people know it's you that wrote it. The bad news is someone has been contacting the newspapers claiming to be the person who worked on your book, and now everyone in the Marketing Department has been getting calls."

"Somebody is stealing my book?" I asked and I could feel my tears coming, so I pinched myself so I would not cry at work.

Rose took my hand. "I will figure that part out, don't worry."

I already knew who was stealing it, but I did not tell Rose.

"There's more, too, but it's good news. They're giving you a very large advance, which means you'll get a lot of money even before it goes into stores, but this means you'll have to tell your parents a little sooner than we planned. This is the envelope with your check in it. It's very important you bring this home to your Mom and Dad and they can call me, okay?"

"But we were going to keep it a secret."

"Not from your parents, honey, it's time to tell them. After you do, give them this note, so they can call me."

"Like how to spend a million dollars?"

"It's not a million dollars, but it's a lot of money. The note inside explains I was trying to protect you, to keep you anonymous, but now it is important people know who the real writer is. You."

I knew Rose was trying to protect me. But what she did not know was that I had figured out a plan to protect her, too.

It was dinnertime and we were all listening to Dawn complain nonstop about too many peas on her plate. She claimed she got more than me so she would not be finishing the last twenty-six and a half (she said she accidentally squished one).

I loudly cleared my throat to get everyone's attention, but Dad thought I was choking and so he tapped me on the back and shouted in my ear, "Are you alright?"

"I was, until you yelled in my ear."

Then I said I had a Big Announcement.

Since Dad and Mom had never heard me say this before (Rose helped me practice that one) they both put down their forks to listen. Dawn put her fork down too, but I knew it was only because of the peas.

I stood up, took a deep breath, and put my hands on my hips. "My big announcement is I will be rich soon since my book will be in the stores and they did tests and the publisher thinks the book is going to sell *a lot*. But don't worry because if I need any new clothes for celebrity interviews, I can pay for them myself."

When nobody said a single word, I said, "I already have one big paycheck, and this is how I will pay back Mom for Bobby's disco ball, and now I can get Kenzie a big present, too, though I don't have any good ideas yet . . . and I have a note from Rose, too."

I took the wrinkled envelope from my pocket and placed it next to Mom, since Rose had written "Maggie" on the envelope.

"Rose says you can call her, and she will always be home since she never goes out anymore because all she wants to do is see Jenny and she can't."

I hadn't planned to say the last part about Jenny.

My parents did not have the smile you give a kid who says

something that is cute but is not true. Instead, they looked surprised and didn't say a single thing, so Dawn picked up the envelope, and pulled out the note from Rose and read it out loud.

"Dear Maggie, your daughter's book will be published by New Vision Publishing. Enclosed is a check for . . ." Dawn looked up and said, "I'm not good at reading long numbers. After the dollar sign is a ten, a five, and two zeros. Dad, how much money is that?"

Dad said the answer like a question, "Ten thousand, five hundred dollars?"

Dawn said, "Wow! Hey, Liddy-Jean, can I have ten dollars?"

"Sure," I said. "As long as you do not get greedy."

"Liddy-Jean . . ." Mom said, but then she stopped.

Dad said, "May I see that, Dawn?" And he took the note and read it. Rose trusted me, and I was so worried about losing the note and envelope with the check in it that I kept my hand in my pocket all the way home and even when I was watching TV until my wrist got a big red ring around it like the time I wore too many elastic bands to make a bracelet.

Dad said, "Liddy-Jean . . . wrote . . . a book?" Then he looked at Mom. "Did you know about this? Is this for real?"

"I guess it's for real now!" Mom said and she jumped up to give me a big hug.

"What is it about?"

He looked at Mom, but I answered, "It is a business book, and I am proud of myself!" I was proud of myself until I got distracted by mashed potatoes.

Mom said, "Liddy-Jean wrote a book, and her friend Rose helped her. She wanted it to be a surprise!"

"Well, it sure is! Liddy-Jean—this—is—fantastic!" Then he reached over and gave me a big hug that was so long that I had to dip my fork in the mashed potatoes behind his back. Mom got up to hug me too, and then she got up to go call Rose as Dawn said, "When do I get my ten dollars?"

Dad hugged me tighter and said, "You have no idea how proud

I am of you!"

I wondered if he would say that if he knew I got potatoes on the back of his sweater?

Mom and Dad were so weird after that, and it wasn't just because our phone was ringing off the hook with people who wanted to interview me about the book. I told them I wanted to pay for The Center from now on, and Dawn's flute lessons, too (even though her flute gives me headaches).

Mom kept apologizing to me for not believing all along that the book would be a real published book, but I told her not to worry, she was not the only one who thought that. Rose always said it would be published and I loved her for that . . . and I was pretty sure one other person believed it, and that was why I had to have my second Secret Meeting at work.

Bad News That Was Actually Good

Things were not just strange at home, but strange at work, and not just because everyone was hearing about the book. I heard Rose tell Kim P. that Steve got into a terrible fight and was hurt very bad. Then they started whispering so I couldn't hear any more.

I had not seen Steve since our Secret Meeting when I asked him to be my Goodfella, so I decided to keep my ears wide open around Rose today to see what I could learn without asking any questions.

At lunchtime, right around the time Rose usually went hiding somewhere because Jenny would be arriving to drop off Kenzie, I heard her take a phone call and she kept saying over and over again: "What? When? What?"

Since Rose's hearing is just fine, I was pretty sure she was getting bad news.

Or . . . maybe she was getting bad news that was actually good?

This can happen sometimes. Like when in third grade we found out our teacher Mrs. Donahue was going to have a baby and not come back for the rest of the year. We all thought it was bad news until we got a teacher that was twice as nice as Mrs. Donahue, and never gave homework on Fridays.

I sneaked over to Rose's door and used my trick of carrying a bunch of papers so it looked like I was reading, so I could stop at the copy machine near the doorway.

I heard Rose say, "Arrested? What happened?"

I hoped she was talking about Gary, but wondered if she was talking about Steve, and that maybe I got him arrested for being my Goodfella. Rose hung up the phone and opened the door to find me standing next to the pile of papers I had just dropped. She took me by my hand and brought me in her office.

"Your hand is sweaty," I said.

"Sorry, Liddy-Jean, I have to leave the office," Rose said. "You can work with Lisa P. today, so promise me you won't leave this room without letting her know."

"Are you taking Personal Time?" I asked, but all I could think of was Steve's muscles and what would happen to them if he was in jail. Would other guys draw ugly tattoos all over him? I had to try hard not to cry at work again.

"Who's in jail?" I asked, hiding my eyes since I might be crying.

"Liddy-Jean, honey, what did you hear?" Rose said.

"I heard you say he was arrested when I was reading some papers next to your door and dropped them, only not on purpose, like Gina did the coffee on my desk and I caught her with a secret camera."

"I . . . sweetheart, we need to talk about all this, but I can't talk about this right now because I need to go to the police station. But don't worry; it's not Steve. It's nobody you—" and then she stopped and said, "It's nobody you *like*."

"It wasn't Steve?"

"No, of course not, why would you think—"

"Gary got arrested by the cops again!" I was so happy that I could not control my yelling.

Rose stared at me, and her eyes got very wide. "How did you know that, and what makes you think this had to do with Steve?"

I answered, "Because you said it was nobody I liked, and I like everybody except Gary and Gina, and now, forever, anyone else with a name that starts with G."

Rose had me sit down in her office and pulled her chair close to me so that now I was looking right into her pretty eyes, which made me say more stuff I had not planned.

"Gina made me tell her a long time ago about our book, and I knew she was reading it, because I did my famous string trick to see if the vanilla envelopes were being moved after we left the office, and they were. Every single time. And I hardly ever spill things since I was twelve years old!"

Rose waited a long time before she said, softly, "We can talk more about that . . . Liddy-Jean, it was Gary that was arrested last night. And now I have to go take care of some things since he's going to be in jail for a very long time."

"Steve would like that news. Why is he not at work?"

Rose looked scared when she looked across the room at his office, lights still out. "I . . . don't know," she said, "but I will find out."

I pressed my lips closed to remind me not to say even one more thing.

Rose said, "I have to go now, Liddy. I'm sorry, but I have to leave, so how about you and me go tell Lisa P. that you'll help her today with any projects."

"Will you go find Steve?" I asked.

Rose nodded her head. "Yes, I will, but first I have to tell Gina I have to leave."

"Gina is not here. She left for another interview," I said. "When I accidently used the copy machine way over there, I heard her talking on the phone about my book again."

Rose blinked and said nothing, then she grabbed her keys from her desk, and took me over to Lisa P.'s office, before she ran out the Marketing Department door.

It was close to the time Kenzie and Jenny were supposed to get to work, and as soon as Lisa P. answered her phone, I snuck out to follow Rose down the hallway. Rose was almost running, so by the time I reached the top of the stairs, Rose had run into Jenny and Kenzie at the door. I bent down low so nobody could see me, hoping they didn't hear me make my bend-down groan Mom says I make

246

from eating too many snacks.

I stayed quiet and watched from the top of the stairs.

Kenzie gave Rose a quick hug before running to the elevator across the lobby. Kenzie yelled out, "I'm going up to work with Liddy-Jean, Mom! Bye!"

"You will wait for me at the elevator," Jenny yelled after Kenzie, and I could see she was very surprised to see Rose.

Kenzie pretended not to hear that last thing and jumped into the elevator doors, and up she went. She would be on this floor really soon, but she wouldn't see me at the top of the stairs, since I knew she would run right down the hallway to the Marketing Department and she would hide under my desk to surprise me.

I watched Jenny and Rose stand together for what seemed like a whole minute, and finally, Jenny spoke. "I've been so worried about you. I came here so many times just to make sure you were here at work. I've been calling you here, too—"

"I know. I couldn't . . ." Rose said, as Jenny stepped closer. "I'm sorry, but I have to go—there's been—something has happened, but I promise, we will talk later."

"Has he threatened you again?" Jenny asked and she sounded scared and angry.

"I may not have to worry anymore, but I have to go see for myself."

Jenny grabbed Rose by the arm as she said, "No. I don't want you anywhere near him!" and her voice sounded just like my mother's did when my sister almost walked into traffic when she was little.

"Jenny . . . Gary has been arrested. He was taken into custody after a fight last night. They're holding him, because he had drugs . . . and a gun."

"A gun—"

"I had no idea he even owned one," Rose said.

Jenny stared at her, letting all her breath out before Rose reached out to touch the side of her face really carefully, like she was afraid she'd hurt her. Only two fingers touched Jenny's cheek, but Jenny acted like it was more.

Rose said, "I just . . . I need to know he's really gone so you and the girls are safe. Forgive me for walking away from you right now. I hope it's the last time I ever have to."

Jenny nodded and Rose reached for her face with both hands this time and kissed her right on the mouth and held Jenny there before finally letting her go. Jenny would not have gone anywhere during that kiss, and now as Rose hurried out the door, Jenny looked like she wanted to run after her.

Usually watching a kiss makes me giggle, but it did not this time.

When Jenny was left standing alone, she walked over to one of the chairs we use for the Bus Stop game, and sat down. Then I saw her put her face in her hands and the sound of her voice went up the stairs right into my ears, "Please . . . please . . . I won't ask for another thing ever . . . not ever again."

When she finally took her hands off her face, they stayed pressed together, as tight as her eyes, just like Auntie Theresa does at church, when I know she is praying for love.

The Self-Steam Trick

Dear Rose,

I need to have a very important Secret Meeting
with you. Can we meet tonight after supper at the
7-Eleven near my house? Meeting time will be 7:00.
This is a very important meeting and has to do with
my plans for my next book, which I have already
started, and I even picked a title: "Building My Self-
Steam."

P.S. I need your help to find the perfect present for
Kenzie at the 7-Eleven. Please come because it is
important.

From,
Liddy-Jean, Marketing Queen

    I lied about the new book title because I figured the Self-Steam
word would remind her how important it was not to disappoint
people like me, so Rose would be there for sure.
    This is another Big Plus about not being like everyone else, since

when you ask to do something that grown-ups usually do, people do not want to discourage you. Even if they think the idea is not really important, they don't want to hurt your Self-Steam, so they will usually do whatever you say. The real trick is to act like it's the most important thing in the world.

Before I could meet Rose tonight, I had my important work meeting at one o'clock, so at 12:55 I told Jackie I had to go to the bathroom for an extra-long time. She laughed a little, but I am not sure why. Luckily, she didn't ask why I needed to take my backpack. I walked down a long hallway that I never get to go down, all the way to the last room at the end of the hall. I got a little scared when I looked up at the sign on the closed door:

Ronald Dodgeman, CEO

Everyone talked about how our C-E-O did not have an assistant, and that he did everything all by himself, but I wasn't happy about this, since I like assistants, and someday, I plan to have two of them: one to get my Egg McMuffin lunch in the wintertime, and one to make announcements on a speakerphone whenever I have a meeting to go to.

I moved my backpack to the other side of my back and put one hand on my hip, just like Xena, but before I knocked on the door, a woman came up from behind me and said, "Can I help you?"

"Nope, I need him to help me."

She looked at me with a sad face and said, "Are you lost?"

"Nope. I am here to see The Big Guy," I said, and knocked. Steve called our C-E-O The Big Guy, and anybody with a nickname like that was cool with me.

The woman left fast after my second knock, and I wondered if she was afraid she might get in trouble for not stopping me, like when I knocked on Gina's door to get Rose the heck on out of there.

"Come in," said a man's voice behind the door that sounded a little like Dad's, so I liked Ronald Dodgeman, C-E-O, before I even walked inside the office.

And I liked his office, too. It had huge windows and shiny, dark wood furniture, and there was not a white chair in sight, so I took my Xena hand off my hip. There was even a mini sized refrigerator!

Ronald Dodgeman, C-E-O, was sitting in a puffy brown leather chair, and I was happy it made him look smaller than I remembered the last time I saw him in Gina's office.

"Is that for Hobbits?" I asked, pointing to his refrigerator.

"Hobbits are certainly welcome to use it, and even though you are definitely not a Hobbit, you are welcome to use it, too."

I laughed. "That is for sure, I am taller than a lot of people at The Center."

"What Center?" he asked.

"The Center of Middle Earth," I said, and Ronald Dodgeman, C-E-O, got the joke right away and laughed, big time.

"You're Liddy-Jean . . . am I correct?"

"Correct about what?" I asked, and he smiled. I liked him.

"I have heard a lot about you."

"I am not even famous yet, but almost. What is in there?" I asked.

"In where?"

"Your Hobbit fridge," I said, imagining all my favorite cold treats and counting them on my fingers. When I got to my pinky finger, I said, "Pink lemonade?"

"No, but I wish I had some to offer you. So, what brings you here to see me, Liddy-Jean?"

"We had a meeting," I said nicely, trying hard not to make him feel dumb, since C-E-Os should remember when they have meetings.

"Yes, we did," he said. "I found your note under my door."

I pointed to the Hobbit refrigerator again, so he knew I was back to that. "You keep your lunch in there?"

"Sometimes. When my wife makes me go on a diet."

"I am a little fat like you, too," I said, patting my belly, and he smiled another real smile, just like all my friends do. "Mom says I like Oreos too much."

"My wife says that to me, too."

He had pictures on his shiny wood desk of his wife and children. Even though Mom tells me to be curious with my eyes, I picked up the photo of his wife for a closer look.

"She's pretty," I said, as I pointed to my eye I hoped was winking. "Congratulations on the great catch."

His smile got bigger, and it was still real. "Thanks for saying so . . . I'm very lucky."

"You sure are. And I don't lie," I said, being extra careful not to drop the picture as I put it back on his desk, hoping he did not see my fingerprints, and I laid it down flat so it would not fall.

"I've heard great things about all the work you do for the Marketing Department. You've been a great help to our company," he said.

"I know, and I have lots of money now, so if the company has any extra, it should go to the Customer Service ladies and my best friend, Rose."

"You like working for Rose?"

"Oh yes."

"And Gina?"

I decided not to answer and pressed my lips together tight, and I saw him nod his head a little.

"Tell me what I can help you out with, Liddy-Jean?"

Ronald Dodgeman, C-E-O, scooted his chair closer to his desk so he could fold his hands together on top of it, like it was his first day of school. I wanted to ask if his mother made him wear that tie, but I stayed professional.

"I'm not supposed to tell anyone, but Rose and I wrote a business book about Bad Bosses."

"You did? That is quite an accomplishment, Liddy-Jean."

"Oh, I know. My book will make better bosses in companies, even though Rose made me write it backwards to teach people how to be Bad Bosses, since she said it would be more fun to read that way. Rose is my editor, and you know how difficult editors can be."

I rolled my eyes.

"Well, I'm not a writer like you are, but I believe you," he said.

"Trust me, it can be a royal pain in the necklace."

I decided to take my backpack off and pull out the papers, which took a while. I said, "You wait very patiently, not like Gina, who thinks roller skates help you move faster. Trust me, they would not help me a bit."

"Me either," he said, "nobody wants to see that."

I placed the big pile of papers on his desk.

"Is that your book, right there?" he asked.

"Not the real book. I hope I do not get arrested for using the copy machine, but Rose would worry if the book was missing, since somebody has been secretly reading it."

"It's okay if I read it?" he asked.

"Did you read it already?"

"No, I haven't," he said as he stood up and walked around his desk to get a better look. "Why do you think somebody is secretly reading your book?"

"Wherever I hide it, I can tell from the string trick, but Rose thought it was me moving it on accident."

"But it wasn't you," he said.

I wondered if he ever used the string trick, since there sure were a lot of papers all over Ronald Dodgeman, C-E-O's desk. "Gina doesn't know the string trick," I said.

"I promise you, I would never go through anyone's private things. Nobody should be doing that." When he was standing up, he was tall and handsome. Not handsome like Steve, but like Dad.

"I would like to read your book, if that's okay with you. And if it's okay with Rose, of course."

I said, "We never, ever, never worked on the book during work time, not even once, so Rose should never get fired."

"Of course not. Rose is one of our best employees, and I've noticed how hard she works. Would you like to sit down, Liddy-Jean?" he said.

Ronald Dodgemen, C-E-O, walked over to the Hobbit fridge and took out a candy bar and gave it to me before he sat next to me on the other chair. "Thank you. I will eat it outside your door since a C-E-O should not see my chocolate face."

His man perfume smelled nice and I wondered if he ever got hot wearing a jacket every day, and luckily, I remembered that it was not polite to ask every question that pops into my head.

"Liddy-Jean, may I ask why you're worried about Rose getting fired?"

"Gina was worried about it. Sometimes I hear her on the phone when I do things near her copy machine, but I am not spying. She talks to people about my book just like the way bosses pretend they do all your work."

"Good bosses would never do that," he said, and he was not smiling now.

I patted the copy of the book before sliding it closer to him. "I have something else for you," I said, pulling out an envelope from my backpack.

"This is especially for you, Kind Sir," I said.

He gave a little bow back and smiled when he took the envelope. "Some secret information that I found on my desk one day. I do not know who left it on my desk, so we cannot talk about it, and you can open it later. There is a secret camera movie in there. Do you know how to use a U-S-B? My friend taught me—" I stopped before telling him Norman Winchell's name.

"I do," he said and he placed the envelope on top of my book and put everything right at the very front of his desk.

"Is that in first place?" I asked.

"Yes. That is my first-place spot for me to read today," he said. "I look forward to learning all about bad bosses."

"You have no idea what you are in for," I said, and he smiled. "You smile different than Gina," I said.

"Really?"

"You do not pretend."

"I don't ever pretend," he said, and I believed him.

"I try not to . . . but I am working on it!" I said.

"Thank you for coming to see me," he said.

"Bye," I said as I reached out to shake his hand, because that is how you tell a C-E-O that a meeting is over.

Being Rich Is Bad for Your Pants

After my meeting, I came back to the Marketing Department and noticed that Rose was still not back. Gina yelled to her assistant to shut her door so she could take a phone call. Just a few minutes later I saw her hurry quickly out of our department. She didn't take her coat or anything, and when she didn't come back for the whole rest of the day, all the Marketing Girls wondered where she was.

"She is probably in a meeting with Ronald Dodgeman, C-E-O," I said. "She might have some explaining to do." Everyone laughed like I had made the greatest joke, so I laughed too.

When Jenny showed up at the end of the workday to pick up Kenzie, she stayed an extra-long time asking Kenzie to show her things, but I knew she was waiting to see if Rose would show up. Rose did not. I finally had to go since I knew Mom was waiting in the parking lot.

Jenny took one more look at Rose's office as if she might magically appear at her desk. I used to do that back when I loved Rose. Before I left the Marketing Department, I told Jenny and Kenzie that I forgot something, and ran back to check one last time to make sure my secret note to Rose was still on her desk, right where I left it.

Since it was a Friday night and still light outside, I knew Mom would let me take a walk down to the 7-Eleven after dinner to buy everyone some treats. This was the very first time I ever felt rich since I didn't have to ask Mom or Dad for money and see the worried look if they did not have any extra.

I told Mom, "If I write a book about being rich, I will call it: *Being Rich Is Bad for Your Pants*, since now that I could afford to buy my own treats, my friend Norman Winchell from I-T would say, I needed an upgrade to a bigger size.

Just like I guessed she would, Dawn made a big fuss about going to 7-Eleven with me, but I told her I needed to go alone because how else could I bring her back a yummy surprise? This shut her up, which made me wonder if my next book should be called: *Secrets for Scheming Sisters*. But then I worried that most people would not understand the word "scheming." I only knew the word because for as long as I could remember, Mom would say, "Liddy-Jean you're always scheming," and she explained it meant "Inventing Secret Plans."

Mom did not know I was in the middle of a scheming plan right then.

It was just starting to get a little dark out, which always made me feel grown up, walking to the store when the streetlights were on. Before I even got to the end of my street, I could see Rose waiting outside the store for me with my note in her hands. Even from far away, I could see she was worried when she waved at me.

"Everything okay, Liddy-Jean?"

"Yes," I said, running the rest of the way down the street.

Rose gave me a big hug and asked, "So what's this secret meeting about?"

I looked around and saw the coast was clear. "I'll tell you after you help me pick out a treat for Dawn."

"All right," she said, "but I can't stay too long."

We walked inside the store and when I saw the rows of candy, I realized I had enough money that I could buy anything I wanted.

I said, "Being rich is good as long as I share . . . and being a little fat is not all that bad."

Rose said, "You're perfect, Liddy-Jean. Since this is the first time you've called an important meeting, why don't you tell me what else we need to meet about?"

"I had my *first* important meeting with Steve," I said. If I hadn't been so distracted by the Planters Peanut Bar, I would never have said that.

"Steve?" Rose said, turning away from the rows of candy. She looked at me and said in a very serious voice, "Why did you have an important meeting with Steve?"

Then I got lucky because the car pulled up right on time and parked in front of the store. Rose did not see Jenny get out of the car and walk to the large glass window, trying to see us better. I could see Kenzie in the back seat of the car, kneeling with her face pressed against the window and she was smiling very wide, waving wildly at me as if maybe I didn't see her there, acting crazy.

"We can start the meeting now," I said to Rose, trying not to laugh at Kenzie who Rose also did not see whack her hand on the car window from waving so hard at me.

"Liddy-Jean, Steve is okay and he is getting better, but he got hurt, so can you tell me what you and Steve had an important meeting about?"

"Hey, look who's here!" I said in my best surprised voice and pointed to the window.

Jenny was standing outside her car, looking so pretty even though she was too thin. Rose turned and spotted Jenny as she stepped closer to the store window and then turned back to me and gently took me by the chin to look at her,. "Is this our meeting?" she asked, her eyes watering.

"You're supposed to go outside now," I said to Rose, since I

258

could see that Jenny was looking like she was not going to move. I wondered, how long I would have to keep telling everyone what to do? I gave Rose a gentle push and said, "What are you waiting for, your next life?"

Rose whispered, "I think I'm only beginning to understand all you've done for me. How can I thank you, Liddy-Jean?" But she figured that out quick and kissed me on top of my head before leaving the store. She thanked me so perfectly I wondered if I should dump Steve . . . but then I remembered his muscles, and that I needed to let Rose be with Jenny. Plus, this was the gift I planned to give Kenzie, so I could make one more checkmark on my list and she would get all that Extra Mom business she wanted.

Get Big Present for Kenzie—Done!

I stayed inside watching from the candy aisle as Rose walked to where Jenny was waiting. She was shivering in the cold until Rose came over to her and gave her the most beautiful hug I ever saw, even better than in the movies. I saw Jenny's eyes close at first, then look up to heaven, and I knew she was saying thank you to God, just like I do when everything finally goes right at the end of the day. Rose pulled away from the hug to hold Jenny's face in her hands. She kissed her once on each cheek and Jenny closed her eyes again and I knew she was not cold anymore.

Kenzie's face was in the car window, bouncing and smiling as wide as a clown. I knew she was proud of herself because she had remembered to give her mom the other Secret Meeting note after they got home from work, just as I asked her to. Kenzie started bouncing on her knees on the back seat, with two thumbs-up, and she bounced so high she bumped her head on the car ceiling and tipped over backwards in the seat. I started laughing at her as I wondered if maybe someday Kenzie could steal my heart away from Steve?

Poor Steve. He had no idea how hard it was to keep me as his girlfriend when I liked so many different people all in one day. One thing I knew for sure, I could update my To Do List with one more checkmark:

Matchmaking Scheme—Done!

The next day at work, I was feeling proud of myself as I watched Rose looking so happy in her office. She only looked worried once and that was when I asked why Steve was out sick for another day. When Jenny and Kenzie finally came, I watched Rose follow Jenny into the hallway, not wanting to let her go.

Kenzie was giving me a big squeeze hello when I jumped because a door slammed when Gina came out of her office.

"Where is Rose?" she said, way too loud for my ears, so I blocked them in case she yelled again. Gina looked in Rose's office and headed to the hallway, so I had to do something to slow her down.

"Maybe she's in the bathroom," I said, because it could always be true, even though I knew it was not.

Gina stopped walking and turned around slowly to stare right at me. I closed my eyes tight, and I could hear Gina walking over to my desk. When it got totally quiet again, I dared to open my eyes.

Gina had bent over and her face was so close to mine that I let out a yelp like a puppy.

"Why are you covering your ears?"

"They hurt," I said, which was true, but not right now.

"Take your hands off your ears," she said, and when she said it she talked through her bottom teeth. She stood over me until I slowly took my hands down.

"I'd like you to stop playing and tell Rose I had to go to a meeting with Ronald."

"Dodgeman, C-E-O," I said, and Gina looked disgusted at me like my sister looks at a plate of peas. She finally started walking away, until I let something slip out.

"I know him. He has a Hobbit fridge with Cadbury chocolate that you can eat on his chairs." This all slipped out and Gina slowly turned back and came over to me again, just like in a horror movie.

Across the room, I saw Jackie sneak into the hallway to get Rose.

"Liddy-Jean . . . how do you know him?" Gina asked, and I saw her lip move like when a dog is about to growl or bite.

"We had a meeting once."

"Have you been telling lies, Liddy-Jean?"

"Nope. Except Rose is not in the bathroom, she is right behind you."

Gina spun around and snapped at Rose, "From now on, I want you to keep that . . . that . . ."

"Girl?" I said

"Out of my face!" she yelled.

When she stomped away, Rose come over to comfort me, but I did not need that. "Do not worry one bit, Rose. From now on, she will only see my face on books."

STEVE

A lot of people say they would do anything to help someone in trouble, but very few guys actually would. My dad was a policeman and he always expected me to be one of those guys, even though he warned me it would not be the easiest life. He thought the best man in the world never turned away from a friend in trouble. Especially, if that friend happened to be a lady.

I told him at his bedside I wanted to become a cop like him and luckily he didn't live long enough to see things hadn't worked out because I quit the training after he died. I still told myself I would be a hero to someone if they needed it, but I guess you never know until that moment happens.

I was thinking this as I walked into the bar, with my plan to scare the guy. I was also thinking with a guy like this, things could get ugly, fast and I better watch my back.

It was easy to track Gary from Rose's house to his local bar. I used the tricks Dad taught me after he retired from the force. When I got to the bar, I could hear Dad's voice in my head, warning me that even scumbags could have buddies, but when I laid eyes on him, I was relieved to size him up as a guy who had few friends. He looked like a guy who staggers into a bar already drunk, and one that other guys pretend not to notice.

I got right behind his barstool without him seeing me. "We need to have a talk about a mutual friend," I said.

"Fuck off," he answered, without turning around, and I was relieved his words were slurring and weak. I can take this guy, if things go south. I thought about Rose and wrenched his arm behind his back and dragged him out of the bar before I could change my mind. I guessed right that any dude who could have stopped me, pretended not to notice. Once we were outside, I spun him around, and hoped he couldn't feel my hands shaking. This was way different in real life than the movies. I was scared shitless.

Even outside the guy reeked of booze, and he could barely stand without swaying. Maybe this would be a piece of cake?

I thought this as his punch cracked me hard under my jaw and when I landed on both knees, I spit blood in the alley as he laughed. I thought I swallowed a piece of glass until I realized it was one, maybe two, of my teeth. I only coughed up one.

He laughed again like he was surprised he'd landed the punch, and then he turned to run, but his drunk ass misjudged the wall, and smacked his shoulder against the brick corner trying to get out of the alley. The bastard fell right into a row of trash cans, then rolled into a spill of garbage as he struggled to get up, his clothes tie-dyed in the wet filth.

At that moment, he looked so pathetic I wondered if I could have the wrong guy. I couldn't imagine Rose being with somebody like this, but I had tailed him, and knew it was him.

I stepped over him, barely able to speak with my jaw throbbing and maybe unhinged. "I am here for Rose."

"That fucking bitch—she sent you here? You're that fucker Steve, aren't you? From her office!"

I was surprised he knew my name, and it threw me off my game as I wiped my mouth on my arm, leaving a dark streak of blood.

"I thought she was fucking that dyke," he seethed.

Something snapped in me, and I came very close to kicking the shit out of him, but I learned from Dad you never kick a guy when he's down, even a low-life like this. But he rolled up and lunged at me, and I reeled back, dodging the surprise attack. Now I felt justified in knocking him back down with a boot to his crotch.

With him rolling back in the garbage heap I was able to step back to gulp some air . . . *a hero doesn't puke. Goodfellas don't puke* . . .

When my head cleared of the rancid smell, I leaned over him and pulled his head off the ground by his hair and spat at him through my bloody mouth, every word like a knife to my jaw, "If you go near either of those women or kids again, I will hunt you down. Do you understand me?"

The guy didn't know it, but I hadn't hunted anything down in my life, hadn't fought anyone past the age of seven, and that was over a plastic baseball glove. As Liddy-Jean would say, even heroes have to *M-bellish* sometimes.

"Hunt me down?" Gary spewed up at me. "I'll show you who the hunter is, you cocksucker! I'll kill those two dykes first then the two retards, then I'll come for you, saving the dumbest motherfucker for last!"

He wrenched his arm behind the back of his pants and when I saw the flash of a gun, without thinking I kicked it from his hand and put my full weight on his arm, hearing a crunch. Instinctively, as I had imagined my father doing a hundred times, I kicked the gun out of his reach while he screamed over his broken arm.

My heart was pounding. I could have been shot. I felt lightheaded, and fearing I might faint, I had to disable him first. I pulled his head up higher, gave an undercut punch to the jaw, a mirror image to the punch he landed on me, only the bastard's head hit the alley pavement. He was out cold, and I rolled down right next to him, my head spinning, jaw pounding, wondering if I also busted my wrist.

With my other hand I fished my phone out of my pocket and tried to speak when the 911 operator answered, but nothing understandable came out of my swollen face. Gary came to, gasping for air, and tried grabbing me again, but I flipped him over by his broken arm as he screamed on his stomach, and wrenched his unbroken arm behind his back. The adrenaline popped me up and in a second, I had planted my foot on his bent arm against his back with all my weight.

All in one move. Dad taught me that one.

The bartender appeared at the front of the alley, and he stared blankly, like what he was seeing was exactly what he expected, and I spit another stream of blood on the pavement so I could talk. "Call the police," I mumbled through a mouth that felt like a thick sponge.

"You sure, buddy?' The bartender said. "You look like you've kicked his ass pretty good. They could take you in for that."

I said, "He had a gun."

That wasn't all he would have when I got through with him.

While I had him down, I checked for more weapons and found his pockets filled wih drugs. He had enough junk to set him up for a year or two in a no-rent, twelve-by-twelve cement apartment. Prison.

Later, when a pair of cops showed up, the older cop said to me, "Thanks, kid. We've been watching this one."

The older cop rifled through his coat and pulled out a bag. "Hmm. A gun and narcotics. You're making this way too easy, pal."

Gary protested weakly when he saw the bag they pulled out of his pocket.

The younger cop said to me, "We were hoping to catch him making a delivery. But the gun is a nice surprise."

Yeah, nice surprise. My legs went weak, so I moved to lean against the brick wall. Somehow, I found my voice. "He also threatened to kill two lady friends of mine, and two young women," I mumbled, wondering if a hero was supposed to feel faint during his big moment with the cops. "So, I walked him out of the bar to have a talk with him, and he took a swing at me."

"Looks like he landed that swing," the older cop said, staring at the side of my face. "We already called for an ambulance, we'll make it a double."

The bartender spoke up, "Actually, officers, this guy here might be a little confused. It was Gary who asked *him* to step outside."

The cop lowered his voice a little and said to me, "Why don't

265

you stick with that story, son. I think the bartender is in much better shape to remember how it all went down. You don't look like the sort of guy who comes into a bar looking for trouble."

I understood and nodded my head. After cuffing Gary and laying him back down, the younger officer went back to the police cruiser.

Free of him, the older cop put his heavy hand on my shoulder. He was a strong man with kind eyes, like my dad's.

"It might have happened that way," I said, "before he sucker-punched me." I spoke with a tongue that had grown heavy and dumb and the whole side of my head felt like it was swelling with each heartbeat.

"You'll need to get that jaw looked at," he said, as he pulled a notebook from his shirt pocket. "I'll need your friend's name . . . the woman."

I didn't want to answer, for Rose's sake. The cop waited patiently.

I mumbled, "This guy's name is Gary, he was my friend's boyfriend."

"We need her name. Take your time, son."

For just a second, with the help of my pounding head and fuzzy vision, I thought he was my dad.

He broke the spell when he said, "We know this guy's a dealer, but I still need all the information." I finally gave him Rose's name, and he took all my information as well, and when the two rescues arrived, I failed at my attempt to convince him my jaw was not broken because the talking option had closed along with my jaw.

Because my scuffle was with a known drug dealer, the cops simply asked me not to leave town on the off chance they needed me for more questioning, but I was free to go, and take care of my injury. They didn't call again, though I had hoped they would. After my head cleared a bit the next day, I wanted to see if the older cop really resembled my dad, so I could ignore for just a minute that my dad had been dead for three years.

Later I learned Gary's gun had been unregistered, and this, coupled with the narcotics possession, meant he wouldn't be seeing

266

the light of day for quite a while. But I still didn't feel like a hero. I felt like a guy with a missing tooth, two black eyes, a sprained wrist and a balloon jaw. Clearly, I could never be a cop or a Goodfella. Or, at least that's what I thought until I opened my mail later that week.

It was an envelope sent from the office with something wrapped up inside and a note written on three yellow Post-its. The Post-its were stuck together in a row, and taped in the back, just in case. I winced when I tried to smile.

Dear Steve,

Thank you for saving our lives. You are my hero and a Goodfella but now you need to be a policeman, since you should do better things than be a Wand-Waver. I know because Ronald Dodgeman, CEO, is a good friend of mine and being a Wand-Waver is not as much fun as it looks.

Love (your muscles ha ha ha)
Liddy-Jean Marketing Queen

I unwrapped the package inside, which was rolled in bubble wrap and I also noticed (because, like my dad, I notice everything) Liddy-Jean couldn't resist squeezing a few rows of the bubbles until they popped flat. She had sent me a hand mirror about the size of the one I used to keep at my desk in the office. This one was blue, and on the back, she had decorated it with star-shaped stickers that said "Sheriff." She had attached another Post-it note to the front of the mirror that read: "So bad guys will not sneak up on you."

So, after making my first citizen's arrest, I decided as soon as I was well enough and they had room in the next class, I would return to complete my police training. I reminded myself that I had been called on to help, and now at last *I knew* I was one of those guys that can and will act when called.

Liddy-Jean knew I should be a cop before I did.

When Rose came to visit me at home, I told her: "I got into a fight with a drunk over a couple of girls," and she kissed me on my good cheek and gave me homemade soup.

I've loved Rose for a long time now, but I think I fell a little more in love with her. There was always a distance about her, long before she loved Jenny, and I had guessed it had nothing to do with Gary. She was unavailable, and so of course, I wanted her. But Rose loved me like a brother, and she had told me so when I started spending too much time in her office trying to get her to notice me. This was long before Liddy-Jean came to work for us, and long before Rose met Jenny and would never notice anyone else again.

Ever since I decided to go back to the police academy, I felt sure that wherever my dad was, he was proud of me. He would have been proud that I was smart enough to take the Post-it advice of Liddy-Jean, Marketing Queen, and give my notice at work.

Why I Love Cardboard Boxes

Steve came back to work with a big fat face, purple bruises, and a giant bandage on top of his nose. "My God, Steve! Look at you!" Jackie P. said, and I watched from my desk as Jackie met him at the door. She gave him a careful hug since his arm was sleeping in a white hammock tied around his neck and resting against his belly. It was all my fault that Steve was not as handsome now, and I wondered if all the Marketing Girls would hate me.

Steve talked a little funny when he said, "I'm fine, no worries. Just a little crack in my jaw. I'll be back to normal in a few weeks. Where's Rose?"

Steve looked around, so I ducked behind my cube wall, trying to think of what to say, since I never talked to a person that looked that bad before . . . especially one I might get blamed for.

"Rose has been in a meeting all morning," I heard Jackie say, "and I haven't seen Gina. She left for a meeting yesterday, and didn't come back."

When they were talking, I saw two ladies and a man I had never seen before come into the Marketing Department, each carrying some cardboard boxes. They had the big ones that I loved the most because they are not too heavy, and I can almost fit inside. Steve and Jackie must like those boxes too, because when those people walked across the department toward Gina's office Steve and Jackie stared at those boxes like it was Christmas. When the other Marketing Girls came over to Steve and Jackie, I finally had to come out of my cube. Nobody noticed me walking over because everyone was staring at those boxes.

Jackie said, "I can't believe what I'm seeing!"

Steve said through his tight mouth, "This. Is. So. Epic!"

Everyone in the Marketing Department was staring at the people and boxes going into Gina's office. Finally, they shut the door so we could not see the cardboard boxes any more.

"Holy shit!" Kim said, and I giggled because she never uses a four-letter word. "Do you think this means—"

Right then, Rose came back in the office, and behind her was Ronald Dodgeman, C-E-O. I waved at both of them, but I was worried for Rose because she looked nervous.

Ronald Dodgeman, C-E-O, winked at me and gave me a wave back before he said, "Quick announcement, everyone. Gina has decided to leave the company and pursue other ventures. However, I am here because I have wonderful news to share . . . let's give a big congratulations to Rose, who has been promoted, effective immediately, to Vice President of Marketing!"

I did not mean to scream "*Yaaay!*" but after I did, everyone started clapping, and I wondered if some of the clapping was for me, since *My Plan Worked!* When Rose looked at me, I pushed past Ronald Dodgeman, C-E-O (I remembered to say excuse me) so I could give Rose a big hug.

Then, everyone copied me.

"Rose is finally in charge!" I heard Jackie P. say, and Steve hugged her, and then when he could get close enough, he hugged Rose, too.

I stayed close so I could hear them. Rose said, "There's a rumor going around that you had something to do with Gary. Following in your dad's footsteps?"

Steve looked like it was hard for him to smile, but he said through his tight lips, "That's just a rumor."

270

I could tell by the way he looked down at the floor instead of at Rose that this was a Little Lie, because Mom says I look at the floor, too.

"Steve . . ." Rose said, "how did you get mixed up with Gary?"

"Just helping a friend," he said.

"You're a mess," Rose said, "a beautiful mess!" and Rose hugged him again. Steve was still in love with Rose, but he looked different now. He knew Rose loved Jenny.

Rose hugged him tighter until he made a funny groan and Rose realized she had been squeezing his arm in the hammock in between the hug. "You're killing me," he said with a little smile.

"You could have been killed," Rose whispered to him before the Marketing Girls interrupted her with more hugs.

If Steve had been killed it would have been all my fault, and I was worried I might cry at work.

"How does it feel to be a hero?" Jackie asked Steve.

"Sore," he said, and when I peeked at him, he was closer and Steve looked like he had a big wad of bubble gum hiding inside his purple cheek. Jackie hugged him again.

"Ouch," he said, making her laugh.

I was still afraid, but it was time for me to stop hiding.

"Hi Steve," I said sounding like when my sister knows I am mad at her.

"Liddy-Jean! What's shakin' bacon?"

"You look bad . . . and do you have any extra gum?" I asked.

"No, sorry," Steve said, walking closer to me. "I don't think I will be chewing gum for a long time." I had to pretend Steve had movie makeup on his face, so I would not cry.

"Hey, Liddy-Jean, you want to help me get some of my things so I can work from home this week? I only have one good arm so maybe you can help me pack a box?"

"No, thank you," I said to Steve because I did not want to cry right in front of him.

I looked at his taped fingers poking out of the white hammock.

They were fat and purple, like sausages . . . like his cheek. I made sure Jackie had gone back in her office before I whispered, "Are you mad at me for getting you beat up?"

Steve tried to smile. "What? I'm not beat up! You call this beat up? You should see the other guy!" Then he lifted his one good arm and flexed his muscle to remind me he was still strong. I laughed and I felt better, but when he walked to his office, I got sad because he walked like my grandpa. It took a while before Steve turned back to give me a wave and a thumbs-up with his good hand.

Gabby, Xena, and Auntie Theresa

I was under Auntie Theresa's couch, and I noticed since the last time I had been here, it was harder to get my butt stuffed in to crawl under it. I had a book with me, but I had forgotten my flashlight, and the book was trapped under my belly anyway, so all I could do was lie there and listen to Auntie Theresa and Mom.

Auntie Theresa asked, "Sometimes I think growing up in our Italian family gave me a warped view of things."

"You think?" Mom said, in that way that she does when she wants to say to her sister: Of course, you dummy.

Auntie Theresa said, "While you're over there, pass me some more herbs. Do you know, I was seventeen before I realized duct tape was not for removing a woman's mustache?"

"I was eighteen," Mom said, and they laughed at weird things like they always do.

We were cooking at Auntie Theresa's house, which was what we did now that Auntie Theresa made Uncle William move out. He never liked Auntie Theresa to have company on the weekends, or on weekdays, either, even though Mom would say we were not company. Now we could come over every weekend and Mom and Auntie Theresa were so happy.

I wished I could see better where I was, because in Auntie

Theresa's kitchen there was a row of spongy herbs planted in tiny color pots and she would let me pat the tops of them like they were her pets.

"Rose and Jenny are finally together," Mom said.

"Who the F are Rose and Jerry?" Auntie Theresa said, and I covered my mouth to trap my giggle.

"Rose and *Jenny*," Mom said.

"Right," Auntie Theresa said. "Rose called you about Harvard Business School wanting *Wand-Wavers and Worker Bees*."

"Yup. What do you suppose will happen when Harvard finds out it was Liddy-Jean who wrote one of the most popular business books of the year?"

I was so happy I was hiding in my best spot, because this was turning out to be a good one.

Mom said, "I have put off telling Liddy-Jean that William moved out, in case the split didn't stick."

Auntie Theresa said, "No need to tell Liddy-Jean. She told me to ditch him and asked, what was I waiting for, my next life?"

Liddy-Jean, Interview Queen

Keeping the secret that it was me that wrote the book was getting harder to keep, once tons of books started piling up in the window of the bookstore near my house, and they were stacked up in giant pyramid shapes in the book section of the grocery store, too. There were even posters begging people to buy the book. There were so many books in the windows of stores that I was hoping nobody at work would guess my pen name was L.J. Rose. It was especially hard at work when I heard one of the secretaries calling their bosses "a bunch of Wand-Wavers!"

I was worried that since there were so many copies of my book laying around, maybe it was because nobody wanted it. On lunch tables, and on desks at work, and I even saw one on the bus! I was upset about this until Rose explained that the books were everywhere because it was selling like crazy, and that is why I had lots of money!

After Gina got fired, and Rose got her job, Rose started getting calls from TV and radio people who said they knew I was the real writer. Then they started calling my house too, and Dad guessed they found out by tracking who was getting paid, because I sure was getting paid!

There was so much money that Mom and Dad had to hire somebody to put it in the bank for me, and I even asked them to give Dawn her own bank account so I could fill it with one hundred dollars, so she would stop asking me for ten dollars every single minute of my life.

Dad and Mom also had to have somebody take all my phone calls, since it made no sense to lie about the book anymore. The tricky part was the news people waiting outside our house to take pictures and try to get interviews. Me and Kenzie had to stop playing the Bus Stop game at work since it is hard to pretend you were waiting for a bus when people are taking pictures of you though the glass doors.

People have no idea how hard it is to do a celebrity interview, since it looks so easy when you watch them on TV. Well, it is not easy. Today's interview starts with me taking a very long plane ride yesterday with Rose and Mom, all the way to California. There were fussy children crying on the plane and Mom says this is because children are so spoiled these days. I think she is right because I never hear other parents tell their kids that if they do not knock it off, they will give them something to *really* cry about, like my mom used to say, and this always worked.

Just when the plane ride finally got quiet and I started to get sleepy, Mom and Rose decided they are going to talk and get all excited about my book and Mom's dream of me someday getting to talk to Oprah.

I faked like I was sleeping and pretty soon Mom and Rose were talking about something I knew they would never talk about in front of me. They both sounded serious and their voices were so quiet I had to listen extra hard. I knew right away they were talking about Gary. I rolled over and pulled my blanket over my head, just in case they peeked at me.

I heard Mom whisper to Rose, "There wasn't anyone to help you get away from him?"

"I felt too guilty and embarrassed to ask for help."

"Why would you feel guilty?" Mom asked.

"When he was drinking, I knew Gary wouldn't want to be physical, so . . . I served him drinks even though I knew he had a problem. Especially after I had fallen in love with someone else."

"You know who claims total credit she got the two of you together."

"Well, actually, she did," Rose said.

"With all that going on in your personal life, you helped my daughter write a business book. That is pretty remarkable."

"Actually," Rose said, "working with her fixed a lot of things in my life. I wish I had the confidence she has as a young person, I could have used a set of parents like the ones Liddy-Jean has."

Mom said, "Nope. It's all her, not me."

"You must have done just the right things to build her confidence, especially after she heard what her doctor said, all he thought she would never be able to do . . ."

It was very quiet and I thought maybe I was falling asleep until Mom said, "I didn't know she heard that . . . and if she heard that, she heard so much more . . ."

I was tired of pretend sleeping, and when I peeked out from under the blanket, both Rose and Mom were looking down at me.

"I didn't know," Mom said again, but this time, to me.

I saw her eyes were watery and I thought of the dropped ice-cream cone again and I whispered, "I am sorry I eat my ice cream so fast," and Mom patted my cheek and I patted Mom's hand. "Don't cry Mom. It is just like you said, he was a stupid f-ing doctor."

Rose laughed and Mom bent down and hugged me. "Yes honey, he sure f-ing was."

Once we were in California, I was interviewed just like a real celebrity.

Interviewer: "Can you tell us any other books you have planned?"

Me: "Definitely no more bathroom books, right Rose?"

The audience surprised me by laughing.

Rose: "Right, but we covered that in another interview,

remember?"

Me: "I love Rose even though she is my editor." (I whispered to the Interviewer: *She is trying to edit me right now.*")

The audience loved that part.

Me: "Rose knew I was going to be a great writer before Jenny and Kenzie."

Interviewer: "Are Jenny and Kenzie your sisters?"

I could not stop laughing at this part.

Me: "No! Jenny is the woman Rose fell in love with, right before she hit her mean boyfriend with a shovel—"

Rose: "I don't think anyone needs to hear my—"

Me: "And Gary got sent to jail because he had a gun. Ladies and gentlemen, guns are *bad news!*"

The audience is clapping now and so I keep talking louder while they laugh.

Me: "Jenny is Kenzie's mom, and my best friend Kenzie is another one, just like me."

Interviewer: "Another one?"

Me: "And my next book will be how I secretly helped to get Rose and Jenny to make some love together even though they are both girls! The title is: *Liddy-Jean and the Matchmaker Scheme.* It will be a series of books, like Harry Potter, a little bit less magic, and lots more lesbians."

The audience laughed like crazy at that one.

Two Great Things All in One Day

Dear Mom and Dad,

I have a secret planned. Rose helped me because I
had to use the phone and I am only good at talking
to Grandma and Steve on the phone, even though
when I do this it is just a crying shame I cannot
see Steve's muscles. For this secret, Dad will need
to drive the car, and we must NOT go out in our
pajamas.

Love,
Liddy-Jean, Marketing Queen

It was early in the morning on Saturday when I made the
announcement: "Everyone, it is time to get in the car for your
surprise!" I said it just like I was a boss in the army.

Ever since I got lots of money, I could say things to people and
they would do them because they knew I could pay for it, and so we
all piled into the car.

Dad started driving just like I told him and when I told Dad to
turn into the drive-thru, Dawn let out a happy scream, "I knew it!

We're going to McDonald's for breakfast!" (She yelled it at me, even though I was the one who planned the whole thing.)

I had a good plan but I hoped I wouldn't be too distracted once that Egg McMuffin got in the car with us. Dad ordered all the food I wrote on a notebook page, and I surprised Mom and Dad when I took out the money to pay for everything. Then I asked Dad to pull into a parking space for us to eat in the car since Dawn had not followed instructions about changing out of her stupid pajamas. I waited until everyone took a first bite so I could tell the secret right at the moment when everyone thought the day could not get any better.

I couldn't wait anymore, and before I took a giant bite of my Egg McMuffin, I said, "Rose helped me make the plans, and I am taking us all to Disney World for a whole week!"

Dawn screeched right into my earholes, sending a piece of pancake flying out of her mouth and sticking to my hair. Mom didn't notice because she was too busy asking questions and it was hard for me to pay attention since the Egg McMuffin tasted especially good, not just because the smell was trapped in the car, but because I had bought it all by myself.

Mom said, "But Liddy-Jean, how on earth—"

Then she must have remembered I was rich. She was always forgetting this, just like I do. "Honey, that's awfully sweet of you but your dad and I—"

Then Dad said, "Now, Maggie, I think we can take some time off from work . . ."

"Because you have a rich daughter now!" I yelled with my mouth full, knowing I would not get in trouble, and besides, I had to yell this over Dawn's screams about meeting Pluto, her favorite Disney character (and my worst, since he never says a G-damned thing).

Mom turned around in the front seat to look at me and I could tell she was going to cry, but not because she dropped ice cream. It was a I-just-got-what-I-wanted-for-Christmas kind of cry. I got embarrassed since I don't understand why adults cry when they are happy, so I stared back into my Egg McMuffin, so I could not see

Mom crying anymore. Dad took a wild animal bite of his hash browns to make me laugh and then gave me one of my favorite things, his I-Am-So-Proud-Of-You wink.

I tried to stop Mom's happy tears by saying, "When we get to Disney World, you do not ever have to worry if you drop your ice cream, because now I can always buy you a new one." But this just made Mom cry harder, and so Dad had to give up his napkin even though he had lots of ketchup on his mouth.

I wondered if all those times Mom and Dad told me I could do anything I wanted in my life, if they believed it? I know they believe it now. Dawn must have known I was feeling proud since she threw the other half of her pancake at me, but she missed, and it hit the window and stuck there from the syrup glue. She could not stop laughing so I crunched my Egg McMuffin wrapper into a ball and threw it right at her boobs, laughing just like Mom and Auntie Theresa do, and it made me glad me and my sister were becoming grown-ups, just like them.

Liddy-Jean, Marketing Queen

Dear Oprah Winfrey,

I bet you get at least 10 letters a day, and I got help writing this letter from Rose but I did write a book and if you ask me, not everybody can do that. If you ever get bored reading letters, you should read my book, because you are a Boss and there are things you need to know.

I am writing to you because Mom loves you and thinks you should be President of the United States. She also thinks I should be on your TV show even though it is just on cable. This is very important to Mom, so we should do it. Do not worry, I know you have a talk show and luckily, I have plenty of things to talk about, like my business book *Wand-Wavers and Worker Bees.* I am sending you this one for free!

Rose said I need to tell you this is a real book that you can buy in bookstores, and I also want to tell you it is nothing at all like a Bathroom Journal. Rose does all my typing and corrects my spelling, so this is why this letter and my book seem like I am telling a Big

Lie. (I do not lie, but my sister Dawn does. A lot. But that is another story, and I will write that book too so I can come on your show 2 times.)

Please call my mom to tell her when I should be on your show, but do not call our house before 9:00 in the morning or Mom will think you are rude and have Bad Breeding. (I do not know what Bad Breeding is but I think it has to do with my grandmother's kittens that were born in her garage in a cardboard box, instead of a nice cat bed from HomeGoods.) You probably know what Bad Breeding is, since Mom says you know everything. One more thing: You should not hold the phone close to your ear when you call Mom, because Mom will scream in your ear if she believes you are Oprah.

Sincerely,
Liddy-Jean Carpenter

P.S. My doctors say I have IDD, which means sometimes I can have slow learning. All my agents tell me I should say that a lot (even if me, Mom, Dad, Rose, Jenny, Kenzie, and Steve do not believe it). I think it is very good for the book business, even though it should not matter to anyone.

P.P.S. Did you know when people with disabilities make too much money in their bank account, the people in Washington DC take things away that Mom says I need? If anyone can fix this, Oprah can!

I had to take a long time off from work, since my book tour went on for weeks, with lots of fun, new places to visit each day. Auntie Theresa stayed with Dawn so Mom and sometimes even Dad could go with me. Sometimes they looked like they were pretending they were on a romantic honeymoon at all the nice hotels we stayed in. Since mostly the interviewer wanted to talk with just me, Rose was happy to go back home to her new family with Jenny and Kenzie, who she was missing something awful.

When I finally got back to work in the Marketing Department, going to work felt like my first day all over again, except that all the people I loved in the Marketing Department surrounded me as soon as I walked in, and they all started clapping and cheering even though I did not even do any work yet!

"Surprise!" Rose yelled out, and everyone clapped harder, and I dropped my bag lunch, worried my apple crushed my potato chips (which I just learned I could eat any kind I wanted). Lisa P. and Jackie rushed over to help chase my rolling apple. It turns out they really did not need to get it since I spotted a giant cake waiting for me, so I yelled out, "Do not worry, ladies! I will not be getting to that apple anytime soon!"

Mom and Dad did not really drop me off at work like usual and snuck back in to surprise me right there in the Marketing Department to see me get my cake! When I hugged them, everybody was clapping so much that I turned around to see if maybe Oprah had followed me home from my interview with her in California, and maybe everyone was clapping for her. Mom would have fainted seeing her twice in one week.

It turns out even though Oprah called me her good friend, Oprah was not here today. All that clapping was just for me, and it may have been a good thing, since Oprah told me she does not eat cake like she used to.

"Is that giant cake for me to share?" I asked, hoping I was wrong.

A deep voice said behind me "Unless you plan to eat it all by yourself, young lady." I got scared that I was in trouble with the police for wanting the cake all to myself, but then I realized, the policeman standing in the doorway was Steve! His muscles looked extra big in his police uniform, so I ran over to give him a big hug, and that's when I saw Jenny and Kenzie were there too, even though it was not a Kenzie work day! I ran over to them to hug them both.

"We are here to see your big surprise!" Kenzie said.

"Thank you for my surprise cake!" I remembered to say, and this was a good thing, since there is nothing more important to Mom than hearing me say thank yous all over the place. Boss Rose walked over to me, and gave me a giant hug, which made me wonder why I always notice when her boobs hug me, since my mother hugged me all the time and I never notice hers. Maybe you only notice boobs that do not live in your house every day? I stopped thinking this when Rose gave Jenny a kiss and a hug too.

"There's an even bigger surprise," Rose said to everyone. "Since you are a famous writer now, the whole department thought you deserved this." Rose walked over to her old office.

Inside, there was a brand-new desk and behind it was Steve's pretty blue chair that matched his eyes! The office was decorated with streamers and the aluminum foil balloons that never make a loud noise if they pop. There was a pack of every single color Post-it Notes on my desk, with a big pile of notebooks and even my own Hobbit-sized refrigerator with a Post-it note that read: *Enjoy, Liddy-Jean! From your friend, Ronald Dodgeman.* He forgot the C-E-O part, and next time I see him, I will remind him to fix it.

"I get to sit in here?" I asked. "Right next to that bag of orange marshmallow circus peanuts and a giant squirt bottle of Handi-sizer?"

"Of course, Liddy-Jean, who else would be sitting in *your* office?"

"You?" I said.

Then Rose pointed to the door which had a professional sign made of brown wood and white carved-in letters, just like the executives get:

LIDDY-JEAN
MARKETING QUEEN

This would not be the first time I broke a rule at work . . . I had hugged people at work, I had spied on people at work, I used secret cameras, had Secret Meetings, and made secret friends. I even told Little Lies at work.

But this was the first time I *Happy Cried* at work.

About the Author

Mari SanGiovanni is the Goldie-winning author of *Greetings from Jamaica Wish You Were Queer, Camptown Ladies,* and *80% Done with Straight Girls,* all published by Bywater Books. An alumnus of Rhode Island School of Design, Mari is also an artist, screenplay writer, and filmmaker and owner of the film production company, Love Is Love Productions. Her award-winning LGBTQ short film, *The Sibling Rule,* won Best LGBTQ film at the Sydney World Fest, Best LGBTQ film and Best Women Short from the LA Independent Shorts Awards, and was the winner of Best LGBTQ short film at the Liverpool Indie Awards.

Twitter | @MariSanGiovanni
Instagram | sangiovannimari
Facebook | facebook.com//mari.sangiovanni/
Website | https://marisangiovanni.com/

Bywater Books believes that all people have the right to read or not read what they want—and that we are all entitled to make those choices ourselves. But to ensure these freedoms, books and information must remain accessible. Any effort to eliminate or restrict these rights stands in opposition to freedom of choice.

Please join with us by opposing book bans and censorship of the LGBTQ+ and BIPOC communities.

At Bywater Books, we are all stories.

For more information about Bywater Books, our authors, and our titles, please visit our website.

https://bywaterbooks.com